HIDDEN TREASURE
SECRETS OF CLEOPATRA'S GOLD

THE RISKY BUSINESS CHRONICLES BOOK 5

A COLTEN X. BURNETT NOVEL

HEP ALDRIDGE

Copyright © 2023 Hep Aldridge

Published by Hep Aldridge LLC.

All rights reserved

No part of this book may be reproduced, scanned or distributed In any printed or electronic form without permission from the author.

This is a work of fiction. Any resemblance of characters to actual persons, living or dead is purely coincidental. The Author holds exclusive rights to this work. Unauthorized duplication is prohibited.

Cover Design by H. Aldridge & A. Ferguson

Special thanks to my editor Janell Parque
http://janelparque.blogspot.com

To be the first to hear about news, new book releases and bargains from Hep Aldridge

GO HERE TO SIGN UP TO BE ON THE VIP LIST
http//mailchi.mp/b0c291dd854f/hep-aldridge

Learn more about Hep and his background on his webpage
http//hepaldridge.com

You can write directly to Hep and connect with him online.
EMAIL: cxburnett@gmail.com
FACEBOOK: https//www.facebook.com/hep.aldridge7
X: https//x.com/AldridgeHep
INSTAGRAM: https://www.instagram.com/hepaldridge/

PROLOGUE

The Ask

It was the last day of our vacation in Paris; Tess and I were spending the afternoon at a small street café off the Boulevard du Montparnasse, enjoying a bottle of wine, some cheese, and freshly baked bread. The sun was shining, and for the first time in a long while, I was totally relaxed, soaking in the Parisian ambiance and basking in the glow of the lovely woman sitting across from me.

We had spent the afternoon visiting the Musee du Quai Branly at the foot of the Eiffel Tower and strolling along the Avenue des Champs-Elysees, stopping at the park there, enjoying the beauty of the city around us and being together again. We finally wound up at this quaint little sidewalk bistro, sharing the waning moments of this magical day; we lightly touched each other's fingers as we quietly watched the sun setting. Ahh, Paris… truly the city of romance.

Tess smiled sweetly, and no kidding, my heart fluttered as she said, "Colt, I have a favor to ask."

I could refuse this woman nothing and said, "Of course, what is it?" as I sipped my wine.

"I hesitate even to bring it up; it's kind of a big deal," she replied.

"Please, ask away, Tess; I'll be happy to help."

"All right, well... there's a man in Damascus who has seven stolen golden statues, and I would like you to get them for me." It all came out in a rush... along with the mouthful of wine I was about to enjoy.

"What!" I exclaimed as I reached for my napkin.

"Well, you're an international treasure hunter, and I just thought you would be the perfect person to ask for help," she said with a wry smile.

I stared at her in disbelief and said, "What on earth are you talking about?"

She looked at me quizzically and, as if speaking to a non-comprehending student, slowly said, "There's a man in Damascus that has seven stolen...."

I stopped her and said, "Tess, I got that part. I mean, what the hell are you talking about?"

"Oh, you mean the details?"

"No, I mean, you're kidding, right? This is a joke."

Now, she looked a little petulant, and Tess never looked petulant as she said, "No, Colt, this is no joke. I really need your help."

As I stared at her and the look on her face, it hit me that this beautiful, intelligent lady was serious. I slowly refilled my glass, took a sip, and had one last look at our peaceful surroundings before I said, "Okay, Tess, one more time from the beginning; what are you talking about...? I want details."

...and so, our peaceful evening ended as another adventure began.

CHAPTER ONE

The Risky Business team's recent excursion to New Mexico had been an eventful one. It was a success, somewhat, but a positive outcome nonetheless. We all eased back into our study, research, and relaxation routines. It had been a grueling but rewarding three and a half months. Doc was up to his ears continuing his research on Montezuma's treasure, going over Winchester's journals as they had come to be known. I was back in touch with Nils, Gus, and the crew of the Falcon as they continued to work the wreck site around Amelia Island. Joe returned to his lab and continued to study the drilling device we had been given by our "otherworldly" friend "Jeannie" in Ecuador, which had been very useful in our recent discovery in New Mexico. Joe had astutely realized after our last venture that there was a lot he needed to learn about its use and functions.

Dimitri and Reggie were undergoing basic helicopter flight training under the tutelage of O'Reilly, who felt they should at least be able to start up, take off, and land the aircraft in case of emergencies, which, in my opinion, was a good idea. Actually, their flying was still being debated. I was busy putting the finishing touches on my much-needed vacation with Tess. We were planning on leaving for Paris next week.

She would be flying in from Cairo, where she was finishing up some meetings with the head of the Department of Antiquities. We were both looking forward to the much-needed extended vacation and seeing each other. All went as planned until she dropped the bomb—apparently, to her, a reasonable request on our last night in Paris. This is really where this story begins. Her request that my team help recover stolen golden statues from a black-market art/arms dealer in Syria floored me. I couldn't quite believe what she was asking until she filled me in on the details.

She had been working under contract as a consultant with the Cairo Museum when they were notified of a major discovery near Sakkara. The entrance to an unlooted burial chamber had been discovered, and from the cartouche on its seal and initial inspection of hieroglyphs, it was the burial site of a high priest. The museum team packed up, with Tess in tow, and headed to the site. It did indeed turn out to be a high priest's burial, and when opened, the importance of this personage became even more apparent.

His funerary collection was amazing, but the crowning discovery was seven golden statues approximately the size of the Hollywood Oscars. Under a resinous coating on the base of each one, there seemed to be hieroglyphic writings that mentioned Cleopatra, whose tomb has never been discovered. The unexpected treasures were immediately whisked away to the museum for further investigation. Portions of the statues had been covered with a patina or resin of some sort, covering or hiding most of the inscriptions.

Tess, a world-renowned expert in hieroglyphic writing, had initially deciphered Cleopatra's name in one of the inscriptions while still in the tomb. Once back at the museum, it became evident that a special lab in Cairo would have to remove the coating. Arrangements were made over the next two days to transport the seven golden statues. Tess believed that the inscriptions were part of a narrative, and together, they might provide information on the location of Cleopatra's tomb.

This hypothesis created quite a stir within the Egyptian archaeological community since it was impossible to keep a discovery of this magnitude a secret, much to Tess's dismay. A frenzy was building as the items began their journey to the lab.

They never arrived....

While *en route*, the transporter was ambushed, guards were killed, and the statues were stolen. That was five years ago.

Fast forward to our vacation in Paris.

CHAPTER TWO

As I mentioned, Tess was a world-renowned expert in hieroglyphic decipherment, but that was only one of her many areas of expertise. She was also an art historian, archaeologist, linguistic expert, and social anthropologist, to name a few of her talents. She was always in demand worldwide for her skills and knowledge, one of the reasons we didn't get to see much of one another... but I digress.

She came by her vocation honestly; her father had been an internationally-known archaeologist, making discoveries that caused history books to be re-written and creating quite the name for himself. Her mother, an art historian and professor of Art History, cultivated her daughter's love of art. Over the years, Tess had created a name for herself in the world of black-market antiquities. However, her fame was based on her success in repatriating stolen artifacts, much to the chagrin of those profiting from the illegal trade.

Now, to Paris.

Through Tess's contacts, she had gotten word that a certain millionaire black-market dealer in Syria had come into possession of the seven golden statues stolen five years earlier, and he was preparing to sell them. Once purchased, she feared they would disappear into a private collection, never to be seen again. Or worse, the inscriptions would be deciphered, and their link and information connecting them to Cleopatra would fall into the wrong hands. If there was something there that would hint at the location of her tomb, it could be catastrophic in the wrong hands. She couldn't let that happen.

So, I sat there facing a significant dilemma between the proverbial rock and a hard place, listening to her story and trying very hard to organize the list of all the reasons for turning her down, and it was a long list. She took advantage of my silence and said, "I understand; you need to discuss this with the others. You can meet with them when you get back."

I was about to protest when she said, "Oh, and there's one more thing. He has a book—a book with a solid gold cover and pages made from some kind of crystal-like substance, containing text that bears no resemblance to any known language. According to my sources, the stories floating around about it say it was a volume that was saved from the library at Alexandria. Another says it was a volume from Atlantis." She paused, "To me, it sounds like what you described having seen in Ecuador."

Damn, she had me at the solid gold cover and crystal pages, I thought as I saw her smiling broadly. Where was that damn poker face when I needed it? Could it be possible that this was a volume from the legendary Metal Library in Ecuador? If so, how did it wind up in this guy's possession? More importantly, how the hell could I even be considering her crazy request… but I was, and she knew it.

I still hadn't given her an answer as we walked hand in hand back to our hotel in the cool evening air as the "City of Lights" earned its name before our eyes. She didn't bring up her request again, and I never answered her. That evening, some things were better left unspoken. The next day, she caught her flight back to Cairo, and later, I headed back to Florida, riding an emotional tsunami as the jet engines hummed in the background.

My parting response to her request had been, "I'll be in touch."

When I arrived in Orlando, Joe was waiting for me. I threw my bag in the SUV and got in. After a welcome home and how was your flight, Joe said, "So, how was the vacation?"

"Good," I replied, "Good and interesting," I added.

He looked at me quizzically for a second before returning his concentration to the road ahead. "How was Tess?" he asked.

"Good," I said, "She was good."

"And you said the trip was interesting, like sightseeing and historical interesting?" he asked.

I didn't answer right away, and he followed with, "Okay, Colt, so what's going on? You guys didn't break up, did you? Your mind is swirling, and your mouth is on autopilot," he said in a concerned voice.

I realized then that I hadn't been listening to him, wrapped up in my thoughts. "Sorry, man; no, we didn't break up or anything. It was a great trip and wonderful to spend some long-overdue time together."

"Okay then, what's got you wound so tight and that brain of yours working overtime?"

I really didn't want to get into Tess's request then; I wanted to be able to speak to the whole team about it, but I knew I had to answer.

"Tess asked me a question I couldn't answer," I said.

"Holy cow, she asked you to marry her," he responded excitedly.

I laughed and said, "No, man, no, nothing that easy."

He paused, "Well then, what did she ask you?"

"She asked for my help; actually, she asked for 'our' help."

Another pause, "Okay, so what kind of help did she need?"

"The kind that will require a decision by the team, not just me, and I need to explain it to everyone simultaneously. How quickly do you think we can get everybody together?"

He thought briefly and said, "I think everybody is around, so we should be able to set something up for tomorrow afternoon."

"All right, let's do it," I said, tapping the vehicle's communication system screen. It was programmed to send a priority message to everyone's phone. I gave the voice command and then dictated the message, "Meeting tomorrow at two p.m., main conference room." Our priority messages were, in essence, a "Red Alert" communication, extremely important.

Within minutes, acknowledgments of receipt began coming in and confirmations of attendance. It even went out to Fitz at his Bithlo office and his SAT phone.

"So, you going to give me a hint of what's going

on?" Joe asked.

"Sorry, buddy, you're going to have to wait," I said apologetically.

I saw him tense up at the wheel, "Roger that, Colt," he responded. He knew it was serious.

I had Joe drop me off at home and told him I would be in late the following day, having already received confirmation from the whole team. I needed to try and get over any jet lag before the meeting and figure out how I was going to broach the subject with them. Tess's request was so far outside anything Risky Business had ever done before. I knew we were headed into uncharted waters and was sure it would be dangerous and illegal.

Wow, two of my favorite things, I laughingly thought as I grabbed a cold beer out of the fridge. After a long hot shower, I flopped down on my bed and fell asleep. The dreams came swirling and stayed with me all night. I awoke at nine a.m. the next day, showered, grabbed a cup of coffee, and headed to the office.

As I drove, I decided the only way to approach this question was head-on. Be completely upfront and honest with the team and get their reactions. There could be a lot on the line with an operation like this, a tightrope act at best, and if we accepted, I was pretty sure we would be operating without a net.

CHAPTER THREE

Everyone was seated at the conference table when I walked in. Joe had already established our secure video link with Fitz, who was sitting in his office in Bithlo. I put on a smile as I entered and responded to the round of greetings and pleasantries as I pulled up my chair amongst them. I rarely sat at the head of the table. Yes, I guess I was the boss, as some liked to call me, but we were a team, a unit, and I preferred just to be seen as part of it.

None of them had ever met Tess; they knew about her and our relationship and were familiar with her professional credentials, but there had never been a face-to-face with any of them. There was no particular reason; it had just never happened, so I had no idea how her request would be received. I grabbed a cup of coffee on my way to my seat and took a sip before diving in.

"While in Paris, I had a request for help from Dr. Worthington, a rather strange request," I said. All eyes were laser-focused on me now, even Fitz, peering through his cloud of cigar smoke. "Five years ago, seven golden figurines were discovered in a tomb in Egypt. Tess was part of the group that was working on the discovery." I explained her hypothesis about the inscriptions on them, the fact that they were stolen, and that she had recently received word about the person who now had them in their possession and his plans to sell them.

Doc said, "I remember reading about that and the

supposed Cleopatra connection. It created quite a frenzy in the world of Egyptian archaeology, and then they disappeared."

"Were stolen," I corrected.

"Yes, yes, stolen," he said. "I never put two and two together and realized Tess was part of it."

"A major part," I added. "It was her initial translation of parts of the hieroglyphs that kicked things into an uproar."

"Okay, so now she knows this guy has them; what's that got to do with us?" Dimitri asked.

"Well… she asked if we would recover them for her," I answered hesitantly.

Silence, nobody said a word; they just sat staring at me with disbelief written on their faces, except for Reggie, who was grinning like a Cheshire cat as she said, "Cool."

Doc said, "You know how crazy that sounds, Colt? That's not the kind of stuff we do."

"Actually, Doc, I beg to differ," O'Reilly said. "That's exactly what we have done in the past. Well, not exactly, but darn close."

Doc sputtered as he did sometimes when he got flustered. "I don't see it that way at all," he said.

O'Reilly smiled and said, "Then I guess we'll have to agree to disagree. Not that I'm saying we do this, mind you. It does sound a bit crazy."

"So, where is this guy located? And if she knows he has the statues, why not notify the authorities and let them handle it?" Dimitri asked.

"That would be a little difficult. You see, he's located in Syria."

That brought a resounding "What?" from almost everyone at once. Now, the animated discussion started. Everyone spoke at once except for Reggie and Fitz, who had been unusually quiet.

I held up my hands and said loudly, "I know; I know that does make it a crazy request, but I told her I would bring it to you, and, as a team, we would decide. So, there it is; you know as much as I know. Oh, except for one more thing, he also has a book whose description sounds a lot like the ones we saw in the library in Ecuador."

That quieted everyone down.

"How is that possible?" Dimitri asked.

"I don't know," I answered, "according to Tess, rumors are saying it might be a volume saved from the library at Alexandria or even a volume from Atlantis. I don't know any more than that."

"She wants the book too?" Joe asked.

"No, if we agree to do this, the book is ours."

There was more silence as mental wheels were turning. Dimitri broke the silence, "What do we know about the guy who has this stuff?"

"I didn't get all the details from Tess, but she said he is a multi-millionaire black market art and weapons dealer. In his early fifties, he's an ex-pat from France named Francois Dubois. He has quite a luxurious villa in Damascus and is well known for being a rich playboy type. He likes to flaunt his wealth," I answered.

"I'm guessing he has quite the security team, then," Dimitri said.

"From what Tess said, it's more like a small army."

"Well, that's just freakin' great," Dimitri added.

Fitz's voice came through the speakers, "Colt, I've got a question for you."

"Go ahead, Fitz."

There was a pause, then, "You're not actually considering this lunacy, are you?"

"Hey, I told her I would present the request to you guys and let you decide."

"Well, you wouldn't have let it get this far if you weren't considering it," he said rather tersely. "You've done some crazy stuff in your life; we've done some crazy stuff in our lives, but this, this is beyond crazy."

Doc said, "You know he's right, Colt; this is way out crazy. I mean, if the authorities can't do anything about it, it's got to be bad."

I knew they were both right, and I probably should have said no when Tess asked... but I didn't. Fitz had read my mind; I was considering it—as crazy as it was, but I knew she had no other avenue for help. Tess was desperate, and the recovery of these statues was important on many levels. This is one hell of a mess, I thought, as I tried to keep my personal feelings out of it.

I looked at the faces around the table and almost regretted asking them to become involved, but deep down, I knew we could do this. I was sure of it—well, pretty sure ...okay, let's just say hopeful.

O'Reilly spoke, "When I was still with the agency, my main area of operation was the Middle East, all over the Middle East, including Syria. Let me tell you that is no place you want things to go sideways. An op that did got me stateside and in a hospital for three months. I had support from my people at the CIA and our assets on the ground, and it still almost killed me."

Reggie looked at her and nodded, then at the group, "She's right. You know I did two tours in the "Sandbox" and have the scars to prove it. Even on a good day, shit can go south in a heartbeat, and people can die… just sayin'."

"It's a volatile area, Colt; not much brotherly love for us over there. I would think long and hard about what you're considering—you and your team," Fitz added.

"I am," I said, "that's why I want to hear from all of you. If you think it's too risky, then it's a no-go. I'll accept that and let her know." The room was silent again.

Dimitri finally said, "I don't think we have enough information to make an informed decision. I have a lot of questions that need to be answered before I give it a thumbs-up or thumbs-down."

Everyone agreed that the information was sketchy at best.

"We can arrange a secure video conference with Tess, and you can ask her directly. If that's agreeable, Tony can set it up."

I looked at him, and he nodded, "Can do," he said.

"Fitz, what say you?" I asked.

"I definitely agree; you are going to need a hell of a

lot more intel before a realistic decision can be made, and that's just for starters. O'Reilly, do you have any contacts or assets still in place that could provide us with the current situational climate over there?" he asked.

"Maybe," she said, "I'll have to find out who's still in play or hanging around in the area; it could take a while."

"My sense is that time is not on our side. According to Tess, this guy may already have buyers lined up or lining up to purchase the statues," I said.

"Well, then it sounds like this needs to happen ASAP," Fitz replied. "Can you all get this meeting and info together within forty-eight hours?"

I looked around the table, and Tony said no problem on his communications end. O'Reilly said she would give it her best shot but no guarantees, and I said I would get with Tess and make the arrangements with her.

"Well, then, that's my two cents worth," Fitz said.

"So, we'll meet with Tess in two days," I said.

Fitz nodded, and before he signed off, he said, "I still think you're crazy to be considering this, Colt. Talk with you in two days."

Everyone else stayed seated, and a general discussion began about what an op like this would entail. I sat back and listened and thought, at least they didn't immediately say no. That was something.

CHAPTER FOUR

The forty-eight hours went by quickly, and soon, we were gathered back in the conference room, waiting for Tony to secure our link with Tess. Fitz had come over for the meeting and sat at the table next to me. There were a few beeps, and then Tess's face appeared on the large screen as the secure, encrypted link was established.

I smiled when I saw her face and said, "Hey, Tess, can you see and hear us?"

"Yes, everything is coming through loud and clear; good to see you again so soon, Colt."

"You too, Tess. Everyone, this is Dr. Tessa Worthington. Everyone, go around the table and introduce yourselves."

When the introductions were done, Tess said, "It is a pleasure to meet you face-to-face finally. I've followed your exploits in the media and heard a number of stories from Colt."

"That's scary," Dimitri laughingly replied.

"On the contrary," she replied, "he has had nothing but good things to say about all of you. Even you, Fitz," she finished, smiling broadly.

That got a laugh out of everyone, including Fitzsimons.

Still smiling that engaging smile, she said, "But

let's get down to business. I know you have many questions for me, and I will try to answer them. I've dug up as much as I can about Dubois and his operation, so let me give you what I have, and we can address any questions that arise as we go."

That's my girl: direct and down to business. It was two-thirty in the afternoon our time and eight-thirty in Cairo. An hour later, Tess wrapped up her part as we sat there digesting the information we had just been given.

Dubois was rich, very rich. He started out selling drugs and running guns throughout the Middle East. His business grew exponentially with the regional and international conflicts that sprang up, along with the demand for his drugs. He trafficked in all kinds of drugs, from opium to the new synthetic opioids—all could be found on his menu. He also moved everything from Kalashnikovs to mobile rocket launchers. He was well-connected throughout the Middle East and had several high-ranking politicos in multiple countries on his payroll.

The local government turned a blind eye to his dealings and was well paid for it. He lived in a palace of sorts near Jaramana on the southwest side of Damascus. His compound consisted of multiple buildings in a horseshoe around the main house, all surrounded by a ten-foot stone wall, and there was a large, guarded steel-gated entrance with a circular driveway leading to the main house. The house was two stories with a sprawling layout. Lots of space for entertainment on one side and his office/living quarters on the other. He usually had around twenty to thirty men in the compound area at any given time and another hundred or more a phone call away. Plus, the whole place was protected by a state-of-the-art electronic security system. Tess said she was working on getting details.

On his business side of the house, Tess explained he had his office and a secure room for his art with a vault-type room for his most valuable pieces. She figured that was where the statues would be, along with the book. He sold his art in two ways; one was to host a party for his prospective buyers and hold an auction-type event. The other was more private and usually held in his office area. It could consist of potential buyers coming and inspecting the merchandise or a video link and online auction. It was a "by special invitation only" event and was always a small select group of pre-approved, wealthy potential buyers. She felt this would be how he would sell the statues and book.

Dubois was a narcissist and loved the upper-class notoriety that dealing in the illicit art world provided him. He relished his rise from street dealer to black market kingpin and enjoyed flaunting it at every opportunity. It sounded like the old lipstick on a pig analogy, "No matter how you dress it up, in the end, it's still a pig."

I broke the silence in the room, "How solid is your information?"

"It's solid. I have a good friend with a brother who works as a house servant. He has agreed to provide a layout and schedule for all upcoming events. The wild card is that I don't know when he plans to move the goods yet."

After the silence became deafening, I said, "So to

recap, this black-market egomaniacal dealer lives in what sounds like a fort, with a state-of-the-art security system, guarded by a small army, in a country we are not welcome in, and you want us to retrieve seven gold statues from a secure and probably fortified room in this home?" I said.

Tess replied hesitantly and said, "Don't forget the book."

"Right," I replied more sarcastically than I intended. "And get a gold-covered book as well."

After a few minutes of silence, Tess said, "Well, when you lay it out like that, it does sound kinda crazy, I suppose."

Fitz said, "That, my dear, is the understatement of the century. You are asking to put this whole team in harm's way for these golden statues," he retorted gruffly.

He continued, "I appreciate your historical concern for these pieces, but I have to ask, would they be worth even one person's life sitting at this table? Because that's what you're asking them to do: put their lives on the line for these things. I'm sorry, but from where I'm sitting, I don't see the value in that kind of risk."

Fitz wasn't wrong, I thought. We've all been in dicey situations before, but this is, by far, the most dangerous one we would have ever faced if we accepted. My concern had been growing exponentially as the details had come out. This was far worse than I had been led to believe in Paris. I don't think I was intentionally misled, but Tess's thinking had been driven by the potential historical importance of these things, and she had not thought about their recovery strategically. "Reality rears its ugly head," I mused silently....

I looked around the room; the cordial smiles had been replaced by furrowed brows and a solemn countenance expressed by all, even Reggie.

"Tess, I'm sorry, but a decision can't be made without more information and further discussion with the team. We will get back to you when we reach a consensus. In the meantime, we need any additional intel you can get for us."

"I understand, Colt. Let me see what I can do in that regard. I know DuBois plans to sell the statues soon, but I don't know how soon. I fear time is not on our side, but I'll let you know, and I thank all of you for even considering this. Colt, we'll talk soon," she said as she broke the connection.

I got up from the table, went to the fridge behind the small wet bar in the conference room, and got a cold beer. I held it up and said, "Anybody else want one?" The ladies said yes, and the others got up from the table and availed themselves of their beverage of choice from the fully-stocked bar.

Once we all were seated, I took a long hit on the cold beer and said, "Okay, let's talk… anybody?"

Doc said, "I can see where she is coming from, but I have to side with Fitz. This seems like going out and asking for trouble rather than dealing with it if it crosses our path. We've never gone looking for trouble, but we've dealt with it when we had to."

Joe said, "You're right, Doc; the question is, are we willing to risk our lives for these statues?"

Dimitri derisively laughed, "This whole thing sounds like some *Mission Impossible* shit; that's what this is," and tossed down his vodka.

O'Reilly, rolling her beer bottle back and forth in her hands, looked around the table and said, "It does sound crazy. I've spent a lot of time in that area years back, and I think the real question is, do we think, logistically, that we could pull it off? And in my mind, the answer is yes; I think we could." That revelation took most of us by surprise.

"We've got access to resources that make it a possibility. Having said that, I wouldn't support moving forward without more intelligence—a lot more and a hell of a good plan."

Reggie reached out with her beer bottle, clinked it on the neck of O'Reilly's, and said, "I agree."

Dimitri was pouring more vodka into his glass at the bar when he said, "You know, I always did like those movies."

"What are you talking about? Which movies?" Doc asked.

"*Mission Impossible*," he replied as he walked back to the table, vocalizing his impression of the MI theme song and grinning.

I turned to Fitz and said, "What about you?"

He responded quickly, "You people are crazy; you know that, don't you?"

I knew it was a rhetorical question, so I didn't bother to respond.

"So where does that leave us? I don't hear any firm No, but I also don't hear any of you saying let's do it," I said.

Joe piped up, "I don't see the value added if we do this. I mean, if we were successful, the historical significance could be huge, but is that enough to risk our lives?"

Dimitri looked at him, "Well, that was reason enough before; don't forget Ecuador."

"Yeah, but we didn't go looking for trouble down there, and we weren't operating in a politically hostile environment; we just dealt with what came up," Joe answered.

"True," Dimitri replied. "But we did have fun," he said, grinning.

"That coming from a man who went to Ukraine on his 'vacation' to blow up Russian tanks from horseback," Doc retorted.

"We never blew up tanks from horseback… I don't think. We just used them as transportation."

"Yeah, and remember, Dimitri, you got shot in Ecuador, Mr. 'We Had Fun,'" Joe threw back.

As serious as all this was, O'Reilly cracked up laughing, shaking her head as she quipped, "Now, now, boys.…"

I said, "I think we've gone about as far as we can today. Let's break, sleep on it, and resume our discussion tomorrow. Give it some serious thought. As Tess said, time may not be on our side, so we must have a go/no-go ASAP.

The executive floor of our headquarters, where my office was located next to the conference room, was empty except for O'Reilly and Reggie. They were staying in the guest rooms we had created in the building renovation—not the Ritz, but nicer than Motel 6. O'Reilly had said good night to Reggie as she stopped by the fridge and grabbed some plain bottled water before retiring. "Gotta clear my head," she said with a shrug.

She closed her door, kicked off her boots, and flopped down on the queen-sized bed with the bottle in hand. Her confident air had vanished; she was worried, sipping slowly from the bottle as she closed her eyes. A flood of memories came roaring back, and she couldn't stop them. She remembered the day all too well. It was a simple op. She was to drive to a house in the old part of town, pick up her asset, Hassen, and bring him to the safe house the CIA had set up. He had contacted her, saying he had some vital information he needed to give her right away, in person. As she slowly drove down the dusty, narrow street, she had no idea that Hassan had been compromised. She approached the pick-up address and saw him ahead, standing in the doorway of the house. Scanning the area, she saw nothing out of the ordinary. Finishing up her second year in Iraq, she knew her job always required vigilance, even more so during operations such as this. She stopped the vehicle in the street, looked around, and turned to nod at Hassan, standing no more than eight feet away. A cold chill ran down her spine as she got a good look at the expression on his face... sheer terror.

She started pulling away as she heard the report from the AK-47, and Hassan's body flew toward her as red stains began appearing on the front of his shirt. She hesitated; Hassan was nineteen years old and had been working with her for over a year as an informant. Her hesitation almost cost her life. She watched as his body crumpled to the ground, revealing the man who had shot him standing a few steps back in the open doorway. He immediately opened fire again as she hit the accelerator, but not before hearing the explosive thud as bullets hit the door. A split second later, she felt the burning sensation as they burst through the metal and entered her body. Three times, her body jerked as they tore through the vehicle door and into her flesh....

Her assailant had stepped into the street and continued firing as she sped away, the excruciating pain of her wounds beginning to overpower the adrenaline rush that was keeping her going. Dodging people and other vehicles, she worked hard to control the car with one hand as a bullet in her shoulder made her left arm useless. She had to get somewhere safe. Getting lightheaded, she felt herself giving in to the pain as she dodged men on motorbikes and the foot traffic on the narrow, dusty street. O'Reilly knew that passing out in this part of town would be a death sentence; she had to keep going. Five minutes or five hours later, she couldn't tell—time had become a blur—she found a semi-vacant lot littered with trash and other debris and managed to pull her car in amongst it. She felt herself losing consciousness as she dug into her bag for the satellite phone, her only chance for survival.

Finally, pulling it from her bag, she punched in the four-digit number that would send an emergency distress signal to the Ops Center and activate her locator beacon. She hoped her team would get to her first as the phone slid from her grasp, and she fell sideways across the front seat. The searing pain racked her body as a sea of blackness finally engulfed her.

She came to momentarily, being jostled around in the back seat of a vehicle, and she began to panic until she saw Uri's concerned face peering down at her. Uri was the Mossad agent assigned to her team and had been working with her for over a year. She knew she could trust him as she heard him say, "Hold still, Shannon; we've got you now. You're safe."

She passed out. Her next memory was of bright lights and an antiseptic smell, people moving around her, frantically talking as she lay on a hard surface. She heard a male voice say, "She's waking up…."

A female voice said, "Quick, give her this; we need to knock her out while we try to stop the bleeding." She felt the sting of the needle in her arm and then darkness.

Five days later, she opened her eyes in a military hospital in Ramstein, Germany. Her body was wrapped in bandages, and her career as a covert CIA operative was over.

O'Reilly jerked awake, the water bottle still clutched tightly in her hand, now wishing she had grabbed a beer. She slowly sat up on the edge of the bed and placed the bottle on the nightstand. She cupped her face in both her hands, elbows on her knees, a slight shiver running down her spine as she remembered where she was. She had thought she was over it. It had been seven years since it happened, but sitting here with the attack fresh in her mind, it seemed like yesterday…. With difficulty, she pushed the memory back into the compartment where she kept it locked away. She knew the memories of her two years in Iraq were still with her, but this one, the last one, would haunt her forever.

She went to the bathroom and splashed cool water on her face, now wide awake. She realized that their discussion of actually going back to the Middle East is what had triggered her dream... or nightmare.... As she looked at her reflection in the mirror, the beads of water on her cheeks looked like tears running down, a sad face looking back at her. She picked up the towel as a look of grim determination appeared in the mirror. Wiping her face, she thought, I've shed enough of those, no more.

Now was not the time for regret; now was the time to turn the corner and put the ghosts from the past behind her. Turning off the bathroom light, she crawled into bed as a sense of purpose and strength returned. We can do this; we will do this was her last thought before a restful sleep consumed her.

CHAPTER FIVE

People began congregating in the conference room around one-thirty in the afternoon. I was sitting at the table along with Dimitri and Doc. Joe and Reggie walked in and sat down. Fitz was on the video link as the room filled with small talk. I looked around and asked Reggie, "Have you seen O'Reilly?"

She grinned and said, "Yeah, she said she would be here in a few minutes."

"All right, we'll wait until she gets here to start."

I was talking to Dimitri when I heard Joe exclaim, "Holy crap," and looked in the direction he was staring. There, standing in the doorway, was O'Reilly, only it was not the flaming redhead we all knew. Her hair was now a very dark brown. She walked slowly to the table and took her seat as we all continued to stare.

She looked around the table and said, "What?"

Doc spoke first, "Your hair—it's not red."

"Oh, that," she said rather offhandedly while smiling broadly. "This is how I wore it back in the day. You know, redheads really stand out in the Middle East. This makes me not so noticeable in a crowd."

I saw the surprise registering on the faces around the table. I turned back to O'Reilly and said, "So, I guess this means you're a go on the mission?"

"Sure, why not?" she replied, still smiling. Reggie

had a Cheshire cat grin as she said, "Me, too."

I took another look around the table at the faces staring at O'Reilly and Reggie, thinking, well, the ladies have stepped up; I wonder what the rest are going to say while knowing full well what the answer would be. Fitz's voice came over the video link, "Damnit, O'Reilly, I knew you were going to go for this crazy operation."

"Hey, Colonel, you know I do crazy pretty well," she laughed.

"All too well," he replied.

I waited a bit before I spoke. "Well, guys, what say you?" I asked.

Dimitri turned to Joe and shrugged as Doc sat there looking somewhat uneasy.

"What the hell?" he finally said, "I'm in." Joe nodded as well, and now everyone was staring at Doc.

"Well, against my better judgment," Doc finally said, "count me in."

Tony smiled, saying, "I will provide you guys with as much satellite coverage, intel, and electronic support as I can get my hands on while you're over there."

I nodded. "Guess it's settled then; we are a go. I'll let Tess know and bring her in at our next meeting. She may have additional information for us. Let's start working on some of the details now, and I'll set another meeting tomorrow for all of us, including Tess."

Fitz's gruff voice turned us toward the monitor, "You all are certifiably crazy, but you're pretty ballsy too. I'll start putting feelers out and see what I can come up with to support this insane mission."

"Appreciate that," I replied. "We'll need all the help we can get."

"You got that right; I'll be back in touch tomorrow." Fitz broke the video link.

Tess was ecstatic at the news. She assured us we had made the right decision. I'm not sure we all agreed one hundred percent, but no one commented. I told her we would gather as much information as possible and start formulating a plan. She said she would work through her contacts and let us know what she found out. We signed off, and calls and emails began flowing from our headquarters to contacts around the globe. Responses were less than I had hoped, and what we did get painted a very dangerous picture for us.

Fitz reported that there were a number of covert military operations either in progress or in the preparation stages but couldn't provide us with much more than that. However, he confirmed that JSOC (Joint Special Operations Command) was active in the area. He also said those operations had a tight lid on them for obvious reasons. We thanked him and said we would proceed with our planning. He agreed to let us know when more intel came in.

Three days later, we were all back in the conference room with maps, satellite imagery, and other information spread out on the table, putting together the framework of a plan. We had been there for a few hours when O'Reilly came in, smiling. Walking to the table, she said, "I may have hit paydirt, guys."

That got our immediate attention, and Dimitri said, "That would be a nice change from what we have so far."

She pulled up a chair and laid some papers on the table; after taking her seat, she began. "So, I reached out to some of my still-active contacts and discovered that a good friend was still operating in the region. His name is Uri, a Mossad agent assigned to work with my CIA unit."

She continued, "Uri had been an operative back in my day. He has advanced over the years and is now coordinating all their operations in Iraq, Iran, and Syria."

"That's great," I said. "Do you think he can help?"

"I don't know for sure, but I've reached out to him through my contacts and haven't heard anything yet," she answered.

"Well, at least there's a possibility of his help; that's more than any of us have had so far," Doc replied.

"And you're sure we can trust him?" Dimitri asked.

O'Reilly looked at him seriously and said very slowly, "Yes, I'm sure we can... he saved my life."

Dimitri grinned and said, "That's good enough for me, but I had to check. No offense meant."

O'Reilly smiled slightly. "None taken," she replied through slightly pursed lips.

"Until we hear from him, we need to keep putting this plan together. Our hardest part will be getting into Syria. With any luck, this Uri might be able to help with that," I said.

"I'll let you know as soon as I hear something, Colt," O'Reilly said.

"Good, now, I don't see a problem with us at least getting to Egypt. We'll take the jet, but from there, I'm sure things will become more difficult."

"What about gear and weapons?" Dimitri asked.

"We can put them into those secret compartments we installed on the plane; it shouldn't be a problem," Joe added.

"We can do that, but I don't see us crossing any borders armed. We may have to rely on what our friends in Syria can provide," I said.

"If Uri comes through for us, I'm sure firepower will be least of our worries," O'Reilly said. "I'm going to guess that he will try to get us into Syria through Israel."

"Then, all we have to do is get through Egypt to the Israeli border," Doc said. "I don't think that will be much of a problem," he added. "I'll bet Tess can help with that."

"I'm pretty sure she can, but we'll need to confirm that next time we talk with her," I said.

Four days later, Tess confirmed she could get us transport to the border, and Uri had contacted O'Reilly. He was very surprised to hear from her. She gave him a quick brief on what we were up to, and he told her she was crazy… but said he would help. She told him she would get back to him as soon as we had a time frame, and he said to give him at least a week's notice, more if possible. He could start putting things in motion now, but it would take him several days to devise a safe transport plan.

Three weeks later, we had crossed Egypt, met up with Uri's fixer, and crossed into Israel, heading for the Syrian border. Our flight to Egypt had been uneventful. When we arrived, Tess informed us that the sale of the statues was imminent, so we had to move quickly. She said DuBois was having a big party in two weeks and didn't know if that's when he planned to sell them. Through her connections, she had acquired an invitation with a backstory of being a wealthy American art collector with a somewhat checkered past. The first we heard of this plan was when we landed in Cairo.

I was not happy. She had put this plan into motion without telling us, and it was too late to make any radical changes, so it was up to us to adapt to it and try and make it work. The Syrian border crossing was easier than expected. Once across, we were taken to a safe house on the outskirts of Damascus, where Uri was waiting for us. It was an emotional reunion for Uri and O'Reilly. We could tell there was a special relationship there when, after a long embrace, O'Reilly said, "You've gotten grayer."

Uri replied, smiling broadly, "And you are as beautiful as ever."

Uri was around six feet tall with salt-and-pepper black hair. He was lean, maybe two hundred pounds, and very fit. O'Reilly introduced us, we sat down, and she began briefing him on our plan. He said nothing as she went through the details, listening intently. O'Reilly finished up, and after a few moments, Uri spoke.

"So, you need my men to stage an attack on the DuBois compound under the guise of a competitor wanting to take over his business as a diversion so you can enter and retrieve these golden idols? How do you plan on getting inside?"

"Tess will already be inside. She has an invitation to the party he's throwing. Doc, Dimitri, and I will be with your group, and Colt and Joe will infiltrate from the opposite side of the compound with Reggie on overwatch," O'Reilly answered. She laid out the floorplan we had drawn up from the information Tess's contact had provided and some of the satellite images we had gotten. She identified the side for the attack and the location of his office, our main target.

Uri studied the floorplan and the areas of attack and ingress O'Reilly had pointed out. "It's not a bad plan, but it is crazy, you know?" he said.

She laughed, "As I recently told my old boss, I do crazy pretty well."

"You do indeed, lady; you haven't changed a bit," he replied. "Not one bit," he quipped. "I will tell you, DuBois has been on our radar for some time now. He has been funneling money, drugs, and weapons to groups participating in terrorist activities and attacks throughout the Middle East. The CIA has taken the lead in monitoring his activities but has not taken or planned any direct actions against him. We have protested their inaction and offered our assistance in any planned operation to no avail. Since he is so well connected within the government, they seem concerned about political ramifications."

"This 'false flag' plan of yours just might be a way of delivering a significant blow to his organization without revealing our involvement." Uri paused again, thoughtful, and then continued, "As I said, this is a crazy plan, but it just might work. But I am pretty sure it will upset the powers that be in the Agency."

"I could care less," O'Reilly said. "Their inability to act is not our problem."

There was another pause as they looked at each other, smiling. Uri ended the moment with, "I'm in."

I turned to Uri and said, "If that's the case, we're going to need weapons, and we can pay for them," and handed him our list.

He let out a low whistle as he looked at the list and said, "This may take a day or so, but I believe I can handle it."

"Not a problem; the party is a week and a half away, so we have a little time, but the sooner, the better," I said.

"I understand," he answered, handing the list to one of his men standing behind him. The man took the list, looked at it, nodded, and quickly left the room. We spent the next few days doing a recon of the area and identifying our strategic locations with the help of the vehicles and drivers Uri provided. We found a vacant house about two miles from the compound, took it over, and Joe and I decided to make it our point of departure and return for the infiltration. The street on the back side of the compound was perfect for the main force to attack.

The rear wall of the compound ran along one side of it for over one hundred feet or so. Dimitri informed us that if Uri came through with our weapons and explosives on the list, he would have no problem setting at least three breaching charges along the wall. The more noise and multiple points of entry we could create, the more DuBois's forces would be spread out—away from his office. At least, that's what we hoped.

As the day approached, the tension began building, and adrenaline began flowing. Uri had about forty men; all would be dressed in traditional outfits, as would

Dimitri, Doc, and O'Reilly. Their primary weapons would be AK-47s. Only Reggie, Joe, and I had special weapons. Joe and I had silenced Glock-19s, and Uri had procured for Reggie an Israeli suppressed M89SR sniper rifle that she fell in love with immediately. Joe would also be carrying an AK.

When the night of the party arrived, we did a weapon and Comms check... we were ready. Before leaving, I pulled Tess aside. She looked amazing in a very revealing cocktail dress, and I grimly said, "No heroics, just get in, locate the statues, and let us know. We'll be ready to come and get you as soon as you have them. Let me know if anything goes sideways before you find them, and we'll get you out."

She looked at me, smiled, and said, "Got it," as she touched her finger to her lips and then pressed it against mine. "Don't worry; it will be fine." I clenched my teeth as she departed.

We all loaded up and went our separate ways, a feeling of dread building in the pit of my stomach as Joe and I were dropped off at the vacant house. An hour later, we were all in place. Tess had entered the compound, and the party was in full swing. I looked at my watch; it was eight-thirty, and nine o'clock was our go time. The minutes seemed like hours as the second hand slowly dragged its way around the watch face. Tess said she had spotted DuBois; he was surrounded by a group of his guests and was involved in an animated discussion. After watching for a few minutes, it was apparent he wouldn't be leaving them anytime soon. She said she was making her way to his office. It was ten minutes to nine.

CHAPTER SIX

Against my strenuous protests, Tess had insisted she would be the only one who could identify the statues, so she should be the one on the inside. The plan was for her to make her way to Dubois' office and locate the statues. When done, I would use the amazing, futuristic portal device that had come into our possession in our search for the legendary Metal Library in Ecuador. This advanced alien device allowed me to create a connection or doorway through space from my location to any other place I could visualize in my mind. The key was that I needed a mental visual image of my destination, either having been there or through a photograph. Our extraterrestrial benefactor had told me during our Ecuador expedition that image details were of the utmost importance to transit safely from one point to another. That was our plan to extract her. Tess's inside person had gotten her pictures of the hallway outside DuBois' office, which I had committed to memory. Simple? Nothing could be further from the truth.

We were able to communicate with Tess through our Comms systems earpiece, and Joe had insisted we put a mini-button camera on her dress. That was a challenge since her gown was a diaphanous, shimmering, gold-threaded long cocktail gown that hugged her figure like a second skin. It was very sheer, and it had a slit up the side that, in my opinion, went entirely too high. She had chided me as being overprotective and prudish, saying, "The goal is to get DuBois' attention and pretend to be a wealthy American collector interested in buying the statues." I did not doubt that her choice of garments and stunning beauty would certainly get her the attention she was looking for and possibly more....

All the teams were in place. Joe and I were in the vacant house, ready to use the portal device to get to the hallway outside DuBois' office. Reggie had taken a position on a rooftop overlooking the street leading to the front gates of the compound, providing overwatch. Her job was to notify us if DuBois' backup troops showed up. She could hopefully slow them down with some well-placed rounds from her perch. Dimitri, Doc, and O'Reilly were with Uri and his men, some forty strong, at the rear outside wall of the compound, waiting for my signal. They were dressed in local garb, which we hoped would confuse the guards inside when they were spotted. Our goal was not to take over the compound but to create a significant enough distraction to make them think a rival militant faction was breaching the compound.

We could see and hear the party was well underway, with approximately fifty guests in attendance. Tess had notified us that the host was involved with a group engaged in a loud, boisterous conversation, so she would make her way to his office. She only ran into a couple of guards and told them in perfect Arabic that she was to meet DuBois in his office, acting a little tipsy and saying he was on his way. This must not have been unusual behavior for their boss as they allowed the beautiful woman to pass. We could see that the hallway in front of the office was empty, and the office door was not locked. She slipped in, surveyed the room, and began looking for the objects. Tess had gone through most of the office when we heard her surprised voice saying, "Mr.

DuBois, I have been waiting for you." She had turned toward the door, and we could see him entering the office. He was not happy.

"Who are you, and what are you doing in here?" he demanded.

"Did you not get my message that I would be waiting for you up here?" Tess replied coolly. Easy Tess, I thought. She only hesitated momentarily before going into her story of being a wealthy art collector who wanted to make him an offer for the statues she had heard he had for sale. He was slowly approaching her. His predatory gaze covered her from head to foot. Her looks and assured demeanor took him slightly aback, but his eyes narrowed to slits as a cloud of doubt began to grow on his face.

"How do you know about the statues?" he brusquely asked as he continued his approach.

Tess stood her ground and confronted him in a confident, regal way, saying, "I told you; I am also a collector of rare art and artifacts. The word is out among certain circles that you have acquired something I am interested in and am willing to pay handsomely for them."

Now seemingly interested, he stopped two steps away from her and said, "How handsomely?"

She smoothly replied, "Five million for all the statues."

He laughed, "That is too bad; not only is your offer too low, but I have already sold them to another for eight million dollars."

Tess sounded slightly flustered, "You have already

sold them? To whom?"

"That is none of your concern. They are gone, and if we truly traveled in the same circles, you would have known that." I saw his hand come out from inside his jacket, holding a very nasty-looking curved knife as he pulled her toward him. The camera view was blocked. "Tell me who you really are now, or I will slit your pretty little throat and watch the blood ruin your beautiful dress. What a shame that would be."

I heard the sadistic tone in his voice and knew we had to act. Over the comm, I said, "Dimitri, Tess is in trouble. Go, now." Seconds later, I heard the series of explosions coming from the rear of the compound as Dimitri, Doc, and O'Reilly, along with Uri's team, began their assault.

I had moved my hand to the silver cuff on my wrist, touching the center stone, visualizing the hallway outside DuBois' office, when I heard him shouting, "What the hell is going on...?" a pause and then, "Is this your doing?"

"I have no idea what you're talking about," Tess replied in a concerned tone.

I had formed the portal and was stepping through with Joe right behind me as I heard Tess say, "Get your hands off me," and then there were sounds of a struggle. I stepped out of the portal's mist right outside the office door, my silenced Glock 19 in hand. In one motion, I kicked the door open and saw DuBois with his knife raised.

The sound of the crashing door made him pause and spin around. He took one look and immediately pulled

Tess in front of him, placing her between himself and his date with the Devil. The knife was at her throat, and he shouted like a madman, "Take one more step, and this pretty lady will die." My blood boiled as the creep had the nerve to brush his lips against the back of Tess's neck while pressing his dagger even more tightly against her throat.

As the explosions and gunfire continued, now inside the compound, I hesitated, and through clenched teeth, I said, "Drop the knife, or you are a dead man."

"Maybe so, but she will die first," DuBois threw back. I looked at Tess, standing there with no fear showing on her face as her right hand came out from the folds of her gown, holding a thin six-inch silver dagger. She looked at me, gave a slight nod, and then drove it to the hilt in Dubois' right thigh. He screamed in pain as he moved the knife away from her throat. The next instant, her left elbow crashed into his ribcage in a bone-shattering blow that drove him two steps back as Tess dropped to one knee.

No more hesitation, DuBois stood there, exposed, as I fired twice—a double tap, one to the heart and one to the head. He was dead before he hit the ground. I rushed to Tess, still on one knee with her hand to her throat, took her shoulders, and gently pulled her to her feet. I immediately moved her hand and saw the wound bleeding, asking, "Are you okay?" as I wiped some of the blood away with my hand.

She looked at me and gently smiled, "Better now."

Frowning, I said, "I never should have let you get into this situation."

Tess looked deeply into my eyes and, squinting slightly, said, "Let me? Colt, you know I rarely ask permission to do whatever I think needs to be done. Nonetheless, I appreciate your knack for being in the right place at the right time." Feeling admonished, I was surprised when her two hands pulled me close, and her warm lips met mine. It was a short but passionate kiss that ended way too soon. She whispered as our lips parted, "Thank you, my love." And with a wink, she lightly kissed me on the cheek. I smiled slightly and thought this is one hell of a woman.

Joe's voice broke the spell of the moment when he said, "Okay, you two, time for that later; sounds like the party is headed our way," as more gunfire could be heard echoing in the halls.

"Right," I said. "Hand me your med kit; I need to stop this bleeding."

Joe slid his backpack off without speaking and pulled the small emergency kit from it. I inspected Tess's wound more closely and saw that if it were half an inch longer, it would have hit the carotid artery. Damn, I thought as I wiped more blood away; that's too close for comfort. The wound was deeper than I had first thought, and I realized the tape butterfly sutures wouldn't be enough to stop the bleeding.

I said, "I'm sorry, but I'm afraid this is going to leave a scar," as I took the medical super glue from the kit and applied it to the length of the wound. I carefully pressed the wound closed, and minutes later, the glue had done its work; the wound was sealed, and the bleeding stopped. She only flinched slightly from the burning sensation of the glue.

As I quickly applied a gauze bandage over it, she looked at me, smiling broadly, and said, "That's okay; I hear guys dig scars."

I couldn't help but laugh and replied, "You're one crazy lady."

She gave me another quick peck on the cheek and said, "Thanks, big guy, we've got work to do," and turned to DuBois' desk. Spotting the laptop with the small external drive attached sitting there, she immediately scooped it up, saying, "I hope this can give us some information on who purchased those statues." She handed it to Joe, and he stuffed it in his backpack as I continued to scan the office. Tess leaned over DuBois' body and pulled her blade from his thigh. Wiping the blood off on his pants leg, she sarcastically said, "Mess with the bull, you get the horns, asshole," and replaced the blade somewhere in the folds of her gown.

"Didn't your inside person say DuBois had two large vaults in his office?" I asked.

"Yes, he did," Tess replied, looking around the room and not seeing any evidence of them. Her eyes landed on the two large tapestries hanging about twelve feet apart on the wall behind the desk. She hurried over to one and lifted the edge, "Bingo," she said as she jerked it down from its hanger, revealing a sizeable vault-type door. Moving to the other tapestry, she ripped it down, revealing a second vault door.

The din from the assault was getting louder as Tess said, "I need to see what's in them." They both had combination dials and large, spoked wheels for opening.

"Well, no time for subtleties," I said, "Joe, you're up."

Opening his backpack, he removed the other device we had been given by the friendly alien being we had met in the Andes of Ecuador.

CHAPTER SEVEN

We called it a drilling device, which was a misnomer. It didn't actually drill; instead, it disintegrated the material it was aimed at. No noise, heat, or bright light—the material just vaporized. This and my portal cuff were advanced technology that "Jeannie," the being we had met in Ecuador, had given us. This thing could penetrate any material and be set to any depth. The size of the opening it could create was unbelievable, from a pinpoint to one big enough to drive a truck into. It was limitless in its effectiveness and ability, with its power coming from harnessing the mysterious Zero Point energy that is everywhere in the universe. Joe had been practicing with it since we had acquired the tool, and his skills were becoming rather proficient.

He pulled the device from his pack and tapped the top. A set-up display came up. "Okay, Colt, what do you want to do?" he asked.

"Aim it at the combination lock and open a twelve-inch-wide hole."

"Roger that," he replied and set the adjustments on the device. Seconds later, a twelve-inch hole appeared where the combination lock and the metal surrounding it had been. I grabbed the spoke handle, spun it, and pulled the door open.

"Joe, do the same thing to the other door," I said as I peered inside. Tess was right behind me and let out a low gasp. Before us was an array of ancient artifacts.

"Look at this, Colt," Tess said as she walked into the vault, inspecting the rows of shelves filled with artifacts. "Egyptian, Turkish, Iraqi, and even Sumerian," she said almost to herself. The glint of gold could be seen coming from all areas of the ten-by-twelve-foot room. It was an unbelievable assortment of artifacts: statues, vases, plates, and so much more.

Momentarily mesmerized, I turned when I heard Joe call out, "Hey, Colt, you need to see this." I left Tess to examine the artifacts and went to the next vault. Joe had opened the door and stood there, the light from the room showing pallet-sized stacks of bills. I let out a low whistle as I stepped inside. Bundles and bundles of American one-hundred-dollar bills were everywhere, stacked almost to the ceiling and filling nearly the entire vault. Joe stepped beside me and said, "There must be millions of dollars in here."

"Possibly more," I added.

Then, Dimitri came bursting through the door, out of breath, and putting a fresh magazine in his AK 47. He looked around, quickly took in the scene, and said, "Holy crap." Our plan had been for Dimitri to hook up with us in DuBois' office, and the four of us would portal out to our safe house, our departure point at the start of the raid, about two miles away.

"You guys get the statues?" he asked, breathless.

"No, they're not here," Tess answered.

"Not here," he stammered. "I thought your intel said he had them here."

"It did," she replied, "but he has already sold them."

"So, this whole operation was for nothing," he blurted out. Then, seeing the bandage on Tess's neck, his countenance became very concerned, and he said, "What happened... are you okay?" as he looked at her, then the body on the floor.

"Fine, just a scratch," Tess said, "and no, I don't think it was for nothing. We have his computer, so I'm hoping it will give us information on the purchaser of the statues. Oh, we've also discovered a few more interesting 'things' in those vaults."

Joe had moved to the open office door and peered out into the hallway. "Guys, I think we have company approaching; we need to adios on out of here."

"We can't leave these artifacts," Tess protested.

"We have no choice," I said. Hopefully, Uri and his team will be able to recover some of them if they do actually take the compound.

Our Comms came to life as Reggie said, "Colt, you're about to have company. We've got three vehicles hauling ass down the street toward the front gate. Looks like reinforcements for the bad guys."

"We need a little more time," I answered.

"Roger that," she said, "I think I can slow them down a bit." She leveled her Israeli suppressed M89SR sniper rifle, supplied by Uri's people, and fired off six rounds in quick succession. Two each into the cab of the three approaching vehicles. The effect was immediate; the lead vehicle careened to one side, crashing into a parked car and flipping over. The second vehicle slammed into it, bursting into flames, and the third vehicle rolled to a stop. Men began pouring out of the wrecked cars. Some were stunned, and others started running toward the front gate of DuBois' compound. Reggie picked her targets and dropped the first three men, sending the others for cover, not knowing where the shots had come from.

Back in the office, things were getting tense. Tess still wanted to salvage some of the artifacts. Seeing all the money in the second vault, Dimitri said, "Even if you did take out the leader, there is enough money here to finance a new regime under some other dude."

"I know," I said, "Not sure what we can do about it."

Joe's voice interrupted us; peeking out the door, he said, "We have bad guys at both ends of the hall headed our way."

"Can you hold them off? We need a couple more minutes," I said.

"Don't think so, but I'll try," he said as he opened fire with his AK47. I turned to see Dimitri digging into his pack. He pulled out some small canisters, pulled the pins on top, and began tossing them into the money vault. They exploded, and a bright white light began emanating from the room. He continued with four more. Just inside the door of the vault were two large duffle bags. He had pulled them out, and one was partially open, revealing them to be stuffed full of money. He grabbed the bags before tossing two more canisters into the front of the vault.

"Hey, we don't want the bad guys to have access to this money," he stated with a chuckle, dragging the two duffels into the office away from the flames. "I figure a good dose of 'Willie Pete' should take care of the rest of the money." That's the military slang name for White Phosphorus, one of the hottest burning and hardest to extinguish compounds out there. Its 5,000-degree temperature could literally burn through metal. The withering gunfire brought our attention back to Joe at the door, who was slamming another magazine into his AK.

"This is my last mag," he said as we heard multiple blood-curdling screams coming from one end of the hallway, followed by an unearthly roar.

I looked at Joe and said, "What the hell...." Most of the gunfire had ceased as the men's screams and horrific sounds continued in the hall. Joe cautiously peered out the open door.

"Holy shit," Joe exclaimed, "I don't believe it."

"Believe what?" I asked as I moved to his side and looked down the hallway. He was right; I couldn't believe what I was seeing. The massive Dire wolf, who had become my protector in the New Mexican desert last year, inexplicably stood in the middle of the gunmen, tearing flesh and savagely dismembering bodies, impervious to the intermittent gunfire hitting him. Within seconds, the eight gunmen were dead, and the beast stood amongst the torn bodies, looking down the hall toward the other group of men, its bloody maw and yellow eyes glistening in the hall lights as it took steps toward them.

I had forgotten about the other attackers and quickly turned toward them. They stood there, frozen in place, eyes wide and mouths agape, their guns held loosely at their sides. I turned back to the Dire wolf, slowly stepping out of the gore and moving down the hall, its massive paws leaving bloody prints on the floor.

Terror struck the gunmen. As the beast slowly advanced, they began screaming and running away, many dropping their weapons as they fled down an adjoining hall.

The beast was now passing the open door where Joe and I stood. He paused, looked at us, and let out that low guttural woof sound we had heard him make before in New Mexico. Having heard it a number of times in the past as he approached us, we deduced it was his acknowledgment of our presence. He stared at us momentarily, eyes glowing, lips rolled back, revealing his huge teeth, then turned away and ran down the hallway after the departing gunmen. Joe and I stared after him for a few seconds in disbelief. Joe turned to me, eyes wide, and softly said, "Was he smiling?"

Still staring down the hall at the departing beast, I said, "Maybe...."

Dimitri joined us, saying, "Time to go, boys; things are heating up. I just added a couple of Thermite grenades to the mix." He was right; I could feel the heat from the burning money vault on my face as I stepped back into the room, which was rapidly filling with smoke. Tess had been standing behind me during the wolf's attack. She was staring at me wide-eyed and, in a quivering voice, said, "Was that the...?"

"Yes, that was him," I answered.

She replied, "Oh my God, I had no idea...."

I quickly surveyed the room and, over the Comms, said, "All teams ex-fill now; I repeat, ex-fill now."

As I was touching the center stone on my silver cuff, visualizing the room in the safe house clearly in my mind, Tess shouted, "Wait, Colt, we didn't get the book." She turned and hurried back into the artifact vault. Damn, in all the excitement, I had forgotten about the book. A few seconds later, I heard her voice from inside the vault, "Found it." She ran back into the office with a large book, its golden cover shining in the firelight from the inferno in the money vault, and said, "Okay, now we can go."

The Comms came to life, and I heard "Roger on exfill" from Doc and O'Reilly, followed by a "Copy" from Uri and a "Boogieing out now" from Reggie. The portal had formed, and we stepped to safety, leaving behind the blazing inferno and slaughterhouse.

CHAPTER EIGHT

I have thought about that night numerous times since returning home, wondering whether the wolf continued its rampage or, once we were out of danger, did his vanishing act as he had done in the deserts of New Mexico. Guess I'll never know. The information we received from Uri was positive. There were only a couple of wounded men; luckily, none were severe injuries. With the help of O'Reilly's and Uri's connections, we got out of the country, and seven days later, we were back in Cairo, where we had left the corporate jet.

According to the intel we received in the after-action report, we had been successful in completely disrupting DuBois' operation. The local government had moved in and secured the artifacts along with what little money had not been destroyed. The museum in Cairo was trying to negotiate with the Syrian government for the return of some of the antiquities, with little success, and the attack was being blamed on a fringe ISIS group. We had turned the duffle bags of money over to Uri—a few million dollars, we estimated, and told him to use it as he saw fit. He assured us it would be used wisely as he bid us a safe trip home.

Tess stayed in Cairo to try and help with the negotiations. We had DuBois' laptop and drive. If anybody could extract data from it, it would be Tony. We contacted him *en route*, and he was anxiously awaiting us. The flight back was uneventful, and we had time to review the raid thoroughly. Doc and O'Reilly wanted to hear everything about the wolf showing up, and Joe filled them in on the gory details.

"So, the old medicine man was telling the truth," Doc said. "The wolf protects you wherever you are. That's pretty damn cool."

I sat there staring, still trying to wrap my head around this whole spirit world, wolf guardian thing. "Yeah, I guess he was," I replied. "He did get us out of a tight jam. With the time he bought us, we were all able to get out of there safely."

"You didn't have to call or summon him; he just showed up?" O'Reilly asked.

"No, nothing like that. I didn't even know he was there until Joe saw him in the hall and alerted me," I answered.

Dimitri chimed in, chuckling, "I wonder if he knows when you're in trouble and pops into our reality to save your ass?"

"Kind of looks that way," I said. "But I'm not sure I want to go around staking my life on it."

"Well, when he shows up, he is definitely a force multiplier; I like it!" Dimitri added.

"I agree," Joe said. "We know we can depend on each other, but I'm still not comfortable relying on him to bail us out of every dicey situation we may get into."

"I go along with that," I replied. "We cover each other's six, and if he shows up, fine; if not, we do what we always do."

"Kick ass, and to hell with the names," Dimitri

laughed.

"With any luck," I said, smiling.

We arrived in Florida late in the evening. We had caught up on some much-needed sleep on the flight and left the airport for our headquarters building on US-1, a couple of miles north of Tico Airport, around 10 p.m. Tony was there waiting for us in the lobby.

"Welcome home," he said with a big smile.

"I didn't expect you to be here this late," I replied.

Grinning, he said, "No big deal, I wanted to get started on that laptop as soon as possible."

Joe pulled it out of his backpack and said, "Here you go; do your magic."

Tony grabbed it like a kid with a new toy at Christmas. He shouted over his shoulder as he headed to his lab, "I'll let you know as soon as I get something."

We went to my conference room on the top floor of our building and pulled up seats around the table.

"So, what's our next move?" Doc asked.

"Until we hear something from Tony on the laptop, I guess we have time for some R&R," I answered.

"I hope it doesn't take too long; I hate waiting," O'Reilly said.

We all agreed... luckily, it didn't. Late the next afternoon, Tony called me to say he had gotten into the computer and the hard drive. I told him to meet us in my conference room in an hour and notified the rest of the team. We were waiting for Tony an hour later. O'Reilly got there last, wet hair and all. It was good to see her as a redhead again, having washed out the dark brown temporary dye.

Tony arrived and hit a key on the tabletop, bringing the big seventy-inch monitor on the wall to life.

"Okay," he said, "this was interesting and challenging. DuBois' computer was not only password protected, but the files were also encrypted and in Arabic. Once I got through his password, I was able to use my software to break the encryption and then had to run a translation program to see the files in English."

We had been watching the process unfolding on the screen as he described it. He split the screen; the Arabic files were on one side, and the translated files in English were displayed on the other. "This guy seems to have kept pretty good records. I found arms shipments, contacts, storage, and delivery locations." He tapped the keyboard again, and the screen changed, "But this is what I think you're looking for. It's a list of art and artifact sales. He's been in business for a while. At least three years of purchases and sales are listed, and I believe this is the one you are interested in. The entry said gold statues, sold, eight million U.S. dollars."

"That has to be it," I said.

"Then let me introduce you to Mr. Conrad Jorgensen—multi-billionaire, entrepreneur, and world-class recluse," Tony said, smiling. That elicited a surprised response from most people at the table.

Doc said, "I've read about him; he is quite the story."

"Isn't he the head of Jorgensen Industries, that multi-national corporation?" I asked.

"One and the same, it would seem," Tony replied. "I did some digging and found an eight-million-dollar cash withdrawal from a Swiss bank connected to one of his overseas companies," he said as he put up a picture of an old *Fortune 500* magazine cover on the screen with a distinguished gray-haired man on it. "This is our guy."

Dimitri added, "He's the one who's such an eccentric recluse that he makes Howard Hughes look like a party animal. I heard he lives on his yacht and never leaves it."

"It's more of a super yacht; It's four or five hundred feet long, and he always stays in international waters. It keeps him out of any country's jurisdiction no matter where he goes," Doc added.

"Yeah, I found out he and a lot of his corporate dealings are pretty shady and under scrutiny by several governments."

O'Reilly said, "He has corporations worldwide and keeps tabs on them from his yacht. If he doesn't do business virtually, he will anchor the yacht off the closest coast of whatever country he has business in and then fly the principles out for a face-to-face meeting. He's got a nice bird, an Agusta Westland A109, Mk 2, that he keeps on the yacht."

I looked at her quizzically, and she said, "Hey, remember I worked for the CIA, and I do like to keep up with the aviation industry."

"Got it," I replied, smiling.

"You think he has the statues on board the yacht?" Doc asked.

"I don't know," I replied. "But one thing is for sure,

this job just got a whole lot more interesting."

CHAPTER NINE

The meeting the next day was productive. Tess was ecstatic at the news of our willingness to continue to help recover the statues. She let out a low whistle when we told her who we thought the buyer was. "That name is too familiar. He operates in similar circles as DuBois. I know people who have had dealings with him over the years. He's extremely wealthy and a shrewd businessman but an unscrupulous jerk."

"We came to the same conclusion from our research. The big question is, where is he keeping the statues?" I asked.

Tess paused and then thoughtfully said, "That's a tough one. He has real estate all over the world. He has villas, chateaus, and penthouse apartments; he even has a castle in Switzerland. I'm afraid they could be anywhere."

"Hey, Tess, Doc asked a question earlier. Is it possible he has them on his yacht?" I asked.

Again, she paused before answering, "That is a possibility. I recall hearing about a collection he keeps on board, but I have no idea how extensive it is. Let me put out some feelers, and I'll let you know what I find out."

"Good; in the meantime, we'll see if we can track down his vessel's current location. We need to start monitoring his movements."

"Good idea, Colt; I'll be in touch as soon as I have any information," Tess replied and then signed off.

I turned to Tony, "Okay, I need to know everything about this super yacht and its current location. Once we have that and hear back from Tess, we can start exploring our options. No moves until then, so everybody take a break and stay in communication."

A week later, Dimitri and Joe were sitting in my office when Doc and Tony came in. I looked up and asked, "You got something for us?"

"Yeah, we do," Tony replied, pulling up two chairs next to Dimitri.

As he and Doc sat down, Joe continued, "I've been digging into Jorgensen's businesses and information on his boat."

Doc laughed, "Colt, you'll have to forgive him. He has been calling Jorgensen's five-hundred-foot-long mega yacht, *The Pangaea*, a boat for the last week."

We all chuckled as Tony got red-faced, "Hey, it's made to float in the water, carry people, and has an engine, so yeah, it's a boat," he retorted defensively.

"Boat, yacht, whatever," I said. "What did you find out?"

"A lot," Tony said and continued, "This guy is a real piece of work. His businesses are global—everything, including manufacturing, real estate, oil and gas, technology and mining, and that's just the shortlist. I finally was able to track down his boat," he said, looking squarely at Doc. "He's been traveling around the Med for the last few months and has made stops off the coasts of Spain, France, Italy, Turkey, Syria, Egypt, and Libya. He has business interests in all those countries. As we talked about before, he always stays in international waters and never stays longer than a week in any one area. I also found out this guy is under investigation by Interpol, the FBI, and law enforcement agencies in many of the countries where he has operations."

"That's interesting," I said. "So, these agencies must think he's up to no good."

"Yes," Tony said. "From what I could tell, some of his businesses are pushing the envelope of legality for multiple reasons. And his cash flow is unbelievable."

"It would have to be to afford a twenty-billion-dollar 'boat,'" Doc added, smiling.

Tony continued, "I've got the specs for his boat here," as he opened his laptop. "He had it constructed in the Netherlands about seven years ago."

Doc jumped in, "Yeah, he went from his old three-hundred-foot vessel to the new one, *The Pangaea*—a major upgrade."

"It's a state-of-the-art boat," Tony continued. "It has every electronic and computer-controlled system you could order. The crew is comprised of five elements, each with its own staff: the captain, who has overall responsibility for the yacht; the chef, who is responsible for the cuisine; the interior staff, which creates a hotel-like environment; the deck crew, which operates and maintains the vessel; and the engineers, who ensure the proper functioning of its many systems."

"And I'll bet we can add a security team to that list," Dimitri added.

"So, how many crew members are we talking about?" I asked.

"It varies," Doc interjected. "We don't have an exact number, but you can figure between 60 and 80, given the situation."

"Situation?" I asked.

"Yes," Doc continued. "If you are cruising at sea or anchored and throwing a big party on board, the staff or crew size will vary."

"I was also able to get the construction plans and electrical/electronic schematics. The company keeps all their mega yacht information on a secure server for obvious reasons, but it wasn't that secure," Tony added, smiling.

"Have you been able to pinpoint his location?" I asked.

"Sort of," Tony replied. "Unlike aircraft, these guys aren't required to file any kind of flight plan or cruising plan. So, I'm having to try and compile that information from a variety of sources and build a picture of his movements on anecdotal information. Things like where his major corporations are located and the closest major port to them that could provide access for him offshore. I'm trying to figure out his next move by digging into personal appointment books, if you will, which is not easy. I've had to try and get into his business's computer systems, but they are protected by some unbelievable encryption and security systems."

"So, you haven't been able to break into their systems?" Joe said.

Tony gave him a withering look and said brusquely, "I said they are very well protected; I didn't say I couldn't get in."

Dimitri cracked up laughing and said, "I guess he told you, Joe." Doc was smiling broadly, as was I at this exchange. It was not uncommon for team members to chide one another over their skills and abilities—all in good fun.

Joe smiled and said, "Well, excuse me, Mr. Wizard; I didn't mean to cast aspersions on your computer abilities."

Tony was grinning now and said, "Just don't ever let it happen again. As I was saying, this guy's companies are electronically very well protected. They even have spider traps in case someone breaks their encryption to gain access to their systems."

"Spider traps?" I asked.

"Yeah, that's what I call them. They are programs that can detect an intrusion or attempted hack, block it, and send an alert to their computer techs. It would be possible for them to backtrack the hack and find out information about the intruder. Some traps will send a malware program to the hacker's machine and shut it down or completely corrupt his system."

"And you know this how…? You didn't get us busted, did you?" I asked, suddenly feeling very concerned.

"No, we didn't get busted; I know what to look for. I helped create some of these kinds of traps for previous customers years ago. I've used the same type of trap on security systems I've designed and set up. We even have a few on our system, but ours are much more sophisticated. When I got ready to go snooping around, I figured they might have something like that, so I used my algorithm that knows how to detect those traps and disable them before an alert is sent without tripping any other security traps that might be present."

"So, you were able to get in and out undetected?" Dimitri asked.

"Yep, no problems. I began looking for any information about meetings the company's CEO had scheduled in the previous six months and tried to match it with the locations I had of *The Pangaea*. It took some doing, but I was finally able to see a pattern developing. There were meetings, annotated as very important, scheduled at times when it looked like his boat was in the area. Finding that, I jumped into some of his other companies and began looking for upcoming important meetings their CEOs had on the books and found a number of them scheduled. Using the dates of the meetings, I've been able to put together what I think is the route he'll be following."

"Nicely done," I remarked. "You have been busy."

"Actually, it has been kind of fun," Tony replied. "I haven't done this much hacking in a while. Not since I got us into that Cray during our Ecuador expedition a few years ago."

"So, you're sure you were able to get in and out of these other company's systems without being detected?" I reiterated.

"No problem; once I cracked the first one, I found that his other companies were basically using the same software and security devices, so piece of cake. I even left myself an easy access backdoor to their systems so I can get in and out anytime I want to."

"Sounds like you may be able to track him now,"

Dimitri said.

"Yes, and not only that, now that I can get an idea of his location or potential location, I should be able to find a bird that I can start tracking him with in real-time. Before, it would have been like looking for a needle in a haystack, but now I can really narrow down my search. Once I find him, he's mine, and his track and destinations will be easier to follow."

"Good job. Doc, will you contact the ladies? We'll set up a meeting two days from now. That will give me enough time to connect with Tess and bring her into the discussions. I think we are making some real progress—now, let's see where we go from here. This is going to be a tricky situation: finding this guy and then coming up with a plan to recover the statues. We're going to have to get real creative with this one," I added.

"Hey, getting creative in dicey situations is how we roll," Dimitri laughingly added.

"That's true," Joe replied. "But this time, maybe we won't have to blow anything up or risk getting shot."

"Well, now, what fun would that be?" Dimitri chided. "Seems like everything we do is risky one way or another. Hell, that's half the fun."

Doc sat there, shaking his head, and said, "Your idea of fun is slightly different than mine."

"Yeah, but it's never boring, Doc; you have to admit that," Joe added.

Doc threw up his hands and said, "I give up; you two are certifiable."

That brought peals of laughter from all of us. What

a team, I thought. We're laughing now, and I hope we can keep that attitude through the rest of the mission.

CHAPTER TEN

The meeting was in full swing; Fitz was on video link as well as Gus Falconetti, the captain of the *Falcon*, our main treasure recovery vessel, now working off Amelia Island, Florida. I felt it was important to have him part of this meeting. He and his crew were all ex-UDT Navy, so I figured his seafaring skills and expertise would be a plus in our planning. I wasn't sure how just yet, but under the circumstances, I knew he would be an asset.

Tess was linked in as well. Tony had brought the newcomers up to speed on the latest information he had gleaned from his research. As soon as Tony was done, I addressed the group. "This is the information we have so far. Tony is still working out a potential travel route and destinations for *The Pangaea*."

"So, what's the plan?" Fitz asked.

"As of now, we don't have one," I answered. "That's what I'm hoping will come out of this meeting. We think the statues we are looking for are onboard the vessel, but how we obtain them is the big question."

"I hope you're not planning on an armed assault," Fitz said.

"That would not be my first choice, but everything is potentially on the table," I responded.

"We're not even really sure the statues are on the vessel," Doc added.

Tess jumped in, "Guys, I think I may have confirmation that they are. I heard from one of my reliable sources that someone had recently been shown them on board Jorgensen's yacht. That was within the last three weeks."

"Well, then, that pretty much confirms our target," I said. "Now, the question is, how do we get them?"

Silence filled the room. You could almost hear the gears turning in everyone's heads as we sat there staring at each other.

"You're sure the assault isn't a viable option?" Reggie asked, looking somewhat disappointed.

"Not my first choice, Reggie, but not off the table either," I answered. With a furrowed brow, she became silent again.

The silence was broken by Gus's voice coming from the monitor, "Trying to board that vessel while it's underway would be crazy. I think your only chance for success in this operation is if you can get to her while she's at anchor, and even then, it will be dicey—just my two cents' worth."

"I appreciate your perspective, Gus, and you've got a great point. Determining when and where she will be stopping should be a top priority."

"So, with that, how do you propose we get on board if we can find her at anchor?" Dimitri asked. "And if we do get on board, how long is it going to take us to recover these statues and get the hell out of Dodge?"

"And what do we do about the crew if we run into them? I'm thinking getting into a shooting match onboard would be something we should avoid," O'Reilly said.

"If at all possible," I said, "but we know there will be security. That means we need a plan that eliminates or at least minimizes our contact with them."

"That sounds all well and good, but how do you propose to make that happen? With a vessel that large, not running into a crew member while searching for these statues seems highly unlikely," Doc added.

My mind was swirling, trying to take all these factors into account while attempting to piece together a plan that would accommodate them and still lead to a successful outcome… I wasn't having any luck… yet.

"Let's shift gears for a moment and let those other questions percolate. Do we know where on the vessel this art gallery or display area is?"

Tony said, "I think so," as a cross-section layout of *The Pangaea* came on the screen. "I need to dig into this a little more, but I'm thinking this large stateroom here might be the place."

An area on the plan lit up red. It was a large stateroom on the third deck.

"The reason I say that is when I was going through the electrical blueprint of the boat, I found a lot of additional wiring in this stateroom, along with sensor locations noted throughout. If you'll notice this comment below, it states, 'owner will provide additional security.'"

When Tony enlarged the print on the screen, we could easily read the notation he was talking about. He continued, "This is the only room I could find with that kind of electrical service and notation."

"Then my bet is that's our target," I said. "How long before you can give us a better idea of the vessel's location and course?" I added.

Tony was thoughtful for a few moments, then added, "As I said earlier, I've been checking meeting schedules with his corporation's CEOs, and it looks like he had one yesterday with a shipping company he owns in Lisbon, Portugal. In my opinion, he has made a loop of his companies in the Med. This last meeting in Lisbon kinda gives me the idea that he may be heading out to sea. If so, he could be heading to South America or the States. It's forty-five hundred miles from Lisbon to Miami. His boat's range, fully loaded with fuel, is right at eighty-five hundred miles, and its cruising speed is between twenty and twenty-two knots; that's about twenty-three miles per hour. That could put him in Miami in around eight days. Of course, that's an estimate since the weather could become a factor in that timeline. Plus, he may be heading further north, say New York. He has major business interests in both places. My next move will be to get into the computer systems in both those locations and see if I can find a meeting scheduled—say within the next ten days. I'll start with Miami and New York first, and if nothing comes up, I'll look into his South American holdings."

"We need to know as soon as you can nail that down. If he is headed for the States, it sounds like we will need to have a plan in place and be ready to implement it, at the very least, within a week," I said.

"Are you kidding?" Doc blurted out.

"You heard the man; that's the time we have if his hunch is right. We need to be ready in case it is," I added.

"We'll be lucky to have a plan put together, let alone ready to implement in that time," Dimitri said.

"Hell, you boys are going to need a lot more than luck on this one," Fitz said. His dour expression added to the impact of his statement.

I knew he was right, and my level of concern had just hit the roof. I looked at Tess's face on the monitor and saw her crestfallen expression as she saw the hope of the recovery of the statues evaporating. I had no real words of reassurance for her, so I kept quiet. The silence in the room was broken every now and then by side conversations amongst the team. I was afraid we may have heard the death knell for this operation.

We had been sitting there for over half an hour when suddenly, as if a bolt of electricity had run through her body, O'Reilly sat upright in her chair and slapped both her palms on the table in front of her. Her sudden movements startled everyone and got our attention immediately. I looked at her and saw the Cheshire cat grin and sparkling eyes looking at us.

"What?" I asked.

"Guys, we've been so wrapped up in this thing that we've blown right by our answer without slowing down," she said.

"What the hell are you talking about?" Joe asked.

She scanned the room and the monitors before speaking. "We know this guy is a major recluse and probably paranoid as hell if he stays on his vessel and never comes to port, staying in international waters."

"Yeah," I replied.

"So, how does he get his fuel and supplies?" she asked, still smiling.

Tony lit up like a neon sign as he looked at O'Reilly and said, "He has them delivered!"

Still smiling, she said, "Exactly, and…."

"He would have to be at anchor for delivery," Tony added.

"And…?" O'Reilly asked again.

Now, Tony was as excited as O'Reilly had become. "Only major ports of call could provide those kinds of services, especially with the level of quality a multi-billionaire would require in his supplies. I'm pretty sure he would want more than hamburgers and bottled water," Tony continued, his voice colored with his excitement. "All I have to do is determine which ports have the capabilities of very high-end supplies and re-fueling, then cross-reference them with his route, and we should be able to get a pretty good idea of where he will be anchoring for re-supply."

"Exactly," O'Reilly said, "and if he doesn't have a meeting scheduled at the ports you identify, then that could be his re-supply port, and there may not be a corporate entourage on board."

Now, I was smiling. "Except for the crew on the refueling and the supply delivery vessels," I added.

"Bingo," O'Reilly said. "We now have an anchored vessel and potentially two ways for us to get on board without raising suspicions."

I looked around the table and at the monitors and saw that the despondent faces that had been there had been replaced by thoughtful expressions and, in some cases, grins. I exhaled deeply, not realizing I had been holding my breath while listening to the interchange between O'Reilly and Tony. Gus's voice filled the room, "Now, that has some possibilities," he said, smiling. "I think our chances of success just went from forget it to a strong maybe."

As I sat there looking at my team, I thought, with this crew, I'll take a strong maybe any day! The discussion became very animated and fast-flowing. Progress was being made. I said, "All right, gang, I think this is going to be a long night. Tony, your information on this guy and his travel is critical. I need you to get to it."

"Roger that, Colt," Tony said as he slapped his laptop closed and jumped up from the table. He said over his shoulder as he left the room, "I'll be in the computer center if you need me."

Tess said, "Colt, I'll be there the day after tomorrow." Before I could say a word, she broke the connection.

I looked around the table and said, "Okay, guys, we have one hell of a plan to put together; let's get to it. By the way, Gus and O'Reilly get the gold stars for the day."

CHAPTER ELEVEN

The next seventy-two hours flew by. Not much sleep was had by any of us. Catnaps on the couch in the conference room were about it. Some just slept in their chairs, but in the end, it was worth it. We had the framework of a plan. We were all exhausted, so I told everyone to take a break, go home, and get a few hours of rest. It was two p.m. of day three. I told everyone we would reconvene at eight p.m. I was the last one to leave and stopped by the computer center on my way out. Tony was busily typing on his computer, and I could tell by what was on the five large monitors that he had a number of programs running while data kept changing on his main screen.

"Hey, Tony," I said, "it's time to take a break, man; we're getting back together at eight tonight."

He threw up his hand, never turning around. "Gotcha, Colt; I'll have something for you by then. Can't stop now, but I will see you at eight."

I knew better than to try and argue with him when he got this way. He was like a runaway locomotive, not slowing down for anything, typing furiously on his keyboard. I turned and left without further conversation.

As I pulled into my garage and got out of my vehicle, the tired really hit me. I got into the house, stopped by the fridge, grabbed a bottled water, and headed to the bedroom. I quickly set my alarm for 6 p.m., kicked off my shoes, took a long hit from the water bottle, and fell on the bed, clothes and all. I don't remember anything until my alarm woke me up four hours later.

Surprisingly, I didn't feel too bad as I got undressed and headed for the shower. I turned on all the jets in it, placed my hands on the wall, and leaned my head against the cool tile as the big overhead rainforest showerhead pelted my back with hot water, the room filling with steam. I have no idea how long I stood there and never heard the glass shower door open.

I momentarily flinched when I suddenly felt a soft hand slowly sliding down the middle of my back and realized I had company. Without moving, I said, "You should have called; I would have picked you up."

There was a chuckle, and then, "That would have spoiled the surprise," Tess said as she slid both arms around my chest and pulled her body tightly against my back. I was smiling now, turning slowly with her arms still around me, and wrapped my arms around her. Looking into her eyes and also seeing her wet hair and glistening skin from the water, I said, "Well, this is one surprise I'm glad I didn't spoil," as I placed my lips firmly against hers.

The ringing of my phone drew me out of my slumber. Picking it up, I looked at the caller ID, noticed it was Tony, and saw it was eight-fifteen. I realized I was late for our meeting. I answered and immediately said, "I know, Tony, I'm late. I'm on my way," and hung up. Sliding out from under the sheets, I dressed quickly. Before leaving, I leaned over the sleeping visitor in my bed, kissed her bare neck, and smiled. Fifteen minutes later, I hit the front door of our headquarters, nodded to the security guys, and took the elevator to the third floor, still smiling and not feeling any guilt for being late....

As I entered the conference room, I said to everyone seated, "Sorry I'm late, guys; something came up." I chuckled internally as I sat down and thought to myself, That was a hell of a choice of words, Colt. Still smiling, I looked at Tony, who was fidgeting in his chair. I could see his bloodshot eyes from where I sat. Damn, I'll bet he hasn't slept since the last meeting. "So, what have you got for us, Tony?" I asked.

He was totally caffeinated and exhausted, a combination that only amplified his normally animated behavior. He jumped to his feet and, as he typed into his laptop, said, "I've got some good news and some better news."

The big monitor on the wall came to life as Doc said, "Well, that's a nice change; I wasn't expecting to hear that."

Tony said, "We may have caught a break. Jorgensen is not headed for South America; I'm pretty sure he's headed to Miami."

"How does that help us?" I asked.

Tony continued, "From what I've found out, there's a big meeting scheduled with the CEO of a Miami import/export company that Jorgensen owns right around the time his boat should be arriving in the Miami area. If his pattern stays the same as what I saw in the Med, that could mean he will be in the Miami area for around a week, and I found out they aren't scheduled to take on fuel or provisions there."

"Okay, that buys us a little more time for planning," O'Reilly said. "What's the other good news?"

"A manifest page showed up on the monitor from a company called EDI. This is the company called Exquisite Dining, Inc., which will be providing the provision resupply for the boat, and it's located in Jacksonville. I'll call it the 'Shopping List' —it was extensive and very gourmet." Tony typed into his laptop again, and another bill popped up, this time from a Marine fuel company located at the Port of Jacksonville, showing a refueling appointment for *The Pangaea,* scheduled for a week after the Miami meeting.

"Now, that is good news," I said. "That puts them almost in our backyard, and it gives us a little breathing room," I said, "not much, but every little bit helps."

"Now, it's time to get down to the basics," Dimitri chimed in. "How are we going to get on board and retrieve the statues?"

Reggie spoke, "It's obvious; we either use the fuel boat or the food boat to get us there and infiltrate the vessel undetected."

Gus's voice came through the video link monitor. "The young lady's right; one of those vessels should be our way in. The refueler will have a minimum crew—most of the work will be done by deckhands on the yacht. Probably none of its crew will go aboard. The food boat, on the other hand, may have more crew, and some may even be required to board the yacht. I'm thinking that should be our way in."

"Good point," O'Reilly said. "We need to find out more about that boat, its crew, and the delivery procedures."

"That shouldn't be a problem," Gus added. "Mac and

I will go ashore, hit the port, and do a little recon on their whole operation. Not much going on here, so I'll leave Nils in charge on board to maintain our visual presence, and once ashore, we'll grab a rental car and head to Jax in the morning, if that's okay with you, Colt."

"Absolutely, Gus; take one of the SAT phones and stay in touch. We'll start working on a search and recovery plan here."

It was then that the conference room door opened, and Tess walked in. "Hey, gang, just got in a bit ago; what did I miss?" she asked, smiling as she walked across the room and pulled up a chair next to O'Reilly and Reggie. Yes, most everyone looked at me, then back at Tess and her smile.

I cleared my throat, "Glad you're here, Tess; we'll fill you in." Over the next fifteen minutes, Tony and Doc brought her up to speed on what we knew thus far.

"So, now, you're just waiting for the information from Gus to determine how we're going to use the food boat to best access the yacht undetected," she said.

"That would be optimal, but it remains to be seen if it's possible. What we do need to figure out is how to gain access to Jorgensen's art gallery, get the statues, and get out," I said. Tony put the cross-section of *The Pangaea* on the screen, and I continued, "We're pretty sure the red area is the gallery. It's amidship and on the third deck adjacent to that large entertaining area. Looks like there are three entryways into the room. One large main door from the party area and one each on the port and starboard sides of the room. Give us the top-down view of that deck, Tony." The image shifted, and we could see the gallery centrally located with the two side doors opening into passageways. This view showed an exterior deck with a jacuzzi toward the stern, then large doors opening into the party room, and then the two side doors going into the gallery, one from an inside corridor and the other from the deck on the port side.

"It looks like our entry will be through one of the two side doors," Joe said. "We need to know about the security system and how we're going to disable it."

I looked at Tony, who was sitting down now, almost looking dazed; he was exhausted but managed to say, "I'll figure something out, but not tonight."

"Go home, Tony," I said. "Get some rest; you can tackle it again when you're rested, and that's an order." I didn't need to add the last bit, but I wanted to drive my point home.

He stood up and said, "Roger that, Colt. I'll leave my laptop here, so you'll be able to access any of the deck plans." Then he turned and left the room.

Reggie frowned and asked, "Is he going to be all right?"

"He'll be okay; he just gets really focused on a task and won't let up until he completes it. This was a real challenge for him, but he came through as he always does," Doc said. "He'll get some rest and then be chomping at the bit to get back into it. That's just the way he works."

Joe added, "That's true; he's a real genius, and once his brain gets into high gear, there's no stopping him until problem solved."

I looked at the monitor and said, "Gus, you know

what to do; get back in touch as soon as you have any information."

"Will do," he said and signed off.

I looked around the table and said, "Okay, folks, let the plotting begin...."

CHAPTER TWELVE

The next five days were a flurry of activity. As expected, Tony returned, rested and ready to go. He found us a couple of weather satellites that gave us a visual image of Jorgensen's yacht and was able to confirm his course. He arrived in international waters off Miami two days later.

Gus and Mac had gotten us the information we needed, and Mac even got hired as a part-time dock worker for EDI. Gus had set up an observation post, monitoring the company's dock and loading procedures, and from what he observed and the information Mac provided, he felt comfortable that he knew their routine. Tony and Joe had put their heads together and come up with a solid plan to disable the security system in the art gallery. Now, it was time to fine-tune the details.

We reviewed the fueling schedule that *The Pangaea's* captain had arranged. It was set for early afternoon, five days from now. The provisions company was set for later the same afternoon. After discussions, we agreed that a nighttime boarding would be best. The question now was how to arrange that. O'Reilly provided us with a viable solution.

"You know, if we somehow delayed the supply boat leaving port and made their rendezvous with Jorgensen's yacht occur late afternoon going into the night, that might give us the opportunity to board."

"That's not a half-bad idea, O'Reilly," Gus responded. "We would need to delay the boat or take her over and then come up with a believable reason she would be late getting to *The Pangaea*," he added.

"We're all going to need to be on board, so taking over the vessel might be our only option," Dimitri said.

"From what I've seen, the vessel usually has about eight to ten crew. The size of the load would dictate how many we have to neutralize." Gus went on, "She's about eighty-five feet in length and looks like a mini-container ship. The supplies are packed in large plastic containers that are six by six by eight feet. They stack them on the deck like a container ship and have a boom hoist that lifts them off and sets them on the deck of the receiving vessel."

"The takeover would have to be non-lethal if we go that route," I said.

"Absolutely," Doc added, "we certainly don't want to be involved in harming any U.S. citizens during this operation."

"So, how do we do that?" I queried.

Gus spoke up on the video link, "I may have a solution to that problem."

He immediately had our undivided attention. "And that would be?" I asked.

"Mac says all the workers there are part-time, and they've been told their employment will probably only last until the end of the month."

"How does that help our situation?" I asked.

"I'll have Mac do a little more digging, but it seems

there's not a lot of goodwill being spread around the docks. There are a lot of disgruntled workers, and a little cash incentive might keep the crew quiet about additional people hitching a ride with them to the yacht, especially if we can assure them they would only be a taxi and not involve them in anything that could cause them trouble. It's an eighty-foot vessel, so there would be plenty of places for our team to remain out of sight and not have any interactions with the crew."

Doc said, "Now, that could be a viable solution to one of our problems. That's the crew, but what about the captain?"

"Mac said from what he's heard, the captain isn't very happy with the company either, so a little more money might be all it takes to get him to go along. I'm guessing ten thousand dollars apiece for the crew and twenty for the captain could buy us a ride," Gus said.

"I like that idea; have Mac test the waters with the crew and see if he feels like they would be willing to accept an offer like that. Ten thousand dollars for just looking the other way just might be something they would go for."

"Will do, Colt; I'll be in touch," he said, and the connection was broken.

"Okay, if that works, we've eliminated the need for violence on the cargo ship. What about once we get onboard the yacht? There's still a potential problem with us running into crew members and security. I would still like to avoid violent confrontations, if possible," I said.

Doc was grinning now, "What if we incapacitated any we run into with tranquilizer darts? I'm sure I could get my hands on what we would need to take someone out within five seconds of being hit."

Reggie was grinning now and said, "Doc, you devious devil, you."

He nodded in mock recognition and said, "A combination of a neurological blocker with a strong animal tranquilizer mix would immediately block any muscular response, incapacitate them, and give the tranquilizer time to work. I could mix it so they would be out for at least an hour."

Dimitri was looking at him now and said, chuckling, "Remind me never to piss you off, Doc."

"What about the delivery system?" O'Reilly asked.

"There are several sources for any system that you would want—rifle or pistol. They are used in zoos, animal control, cattle ranches, and other large animal wildlife capture and containment organizations. No problem getting our hands on what we need."

"You got the stuff to mix up the knockout cocktail you're talking about?" Dimitri asked.

"No, but I can easily get what I need locally. Wouldn't take any time at all," Doc replied, still smiling.

Fitz had been quietly observing the meeting via the video link and finally spoke up, "I wasn't sure this whole operation was a nut you could crack, but it sounds like you finally may be on to something."

"Have some faith, Fitz," I said.

"Doc, if you're sure you can make this work, then do it." I added that we didn't need any more details than what he had provided. It's best to let Doc do his thing his way. In a situation like this, the less we knew, the better. Just as long as it worked.

"So, we may have a solution for the crew on the cargo boat and taking care of any crew members we run into on the yacht. The next big hurdle will be the security system in the gallery," I said.

Reggie asked, "Before we get to that, what if the tranq idea doesn't work or something goes wrong with it?"

Dimitri laughed, "You're always itching for a fight, aren't you, Reg?"

She was smiling, "Not really, I just want to be clear on the rules of engagement for any unforeseen situation we may run into. If it happens to include some level of violence, I'm okay with that," she said, rocking back in her chair and clasping her hands behind her head, still smiling broadly.

"All right, everyone, we don't use lethal force if at all possible, but if a situation arises, I will leave it up to you to decide how best to neutralize it." I wasn't giving them free rein, but I knew they needed a definitive answer.

"Thanks, Colt, that's all I needed to know," Reggie replied.

Dimitri continued to rib her and, laughing, said, "So, now you know you can kick ass if you have to. Happy now?"

"I am," Reggie replied, "and remember, big boy, if you get into a jam and need someone to save your butt, just give a holler."

Now, everyone was laughing as Dimitri shook his

head with an "Are you kidding me" look.

"All right, you two, time to get back on task." Sometimes, I feel like a schoolyard monitor with this group, I thought... but in reality, I wouldn't change a thing.

O'Reilly had been sitting there looking very thoughtful before she spoke, "I think we're missing the elephant in the room. This Jorgensen is a really bad dude. Say we are successful; do you think a man with his money and power will let us get away with it? I'm pretty sure he will deploy whatever resources necessary to find out who the thieves were and get his stuff back, and I don't think the use of lethal force would be a problem for him."

"So, what are you saying?" Doc asked.

"Think about it, Doc; the statues get stolen from him—who are the suspects? He would eliminate any of his rival collectors right off the bat, and then that leaves him what? Who made the discovery? The Cairo Museum. And who made the possible Cleopatra connection that was front-page news? Dr. Worthington. He would eliminate the museum from being involved in an operation like this. So, where does he look next? ... Tess. But how could she pull off a job this sophisticated? Does she have connections or associates that might be able to help her? That would lead him to you, Colt, and, by extension, to us. We haven't exactly kept a low profile with our adventures and activities these past couple of years. It wouldn't take a rocket scientist to connect the dots. The next thing you know, his men are hitting our front door with guns blazing.

"He will find us, no matter what it takes, and there

will be hell to pay if we don't mitigate his response," she paused. "Unless we figure out a way to take him out of the picture permanently, we will be putting our entire team, including Tess, in danger."

There was silence in the room. O'Reilly was right; we were so wrapped up in the execution of our plan that we had missed the possibility of its future ramifications.

"You mean kill him?" Joe asked, somewhat taken aback by her comment.

"Well, I'm not necessarily advocating that, but I don't see any other options we could employ to get rid of him… but I'm open to suggestions."

Tony had been listening to the exchange and spoke up, "We know this guy is wanted all over the world; I've seen the charges that some of the agencies have against him, and he is definitely not a nice guy. In fact, he makes that DuBois character look like a choir boy. INTERPOL wants him for allegedly providing chemical weapons to Boko Haram, and the FBI wants him for supporting, with money and weapons through some of his companies, a number of terrorist groups. He's allegedly big in the illicit drug trade. Basically, if it's illegal, this guy seems to have his finger in it and is making tons of money."

"That's why he's always on the move and stays in international waters," O'Reilly added. "Even though he and his organization have been accused of these things, the authorities haven't been able to touch him. If he ever broached the twelve-mile limit, and the authorities knew about it, they would be down on him like a bird of prey."

"The authorities must have some solid evidence, or there wouldn't be warrants out for his arrest," Doc said.

"So, this slimeball stays one step ahead of them and keeps supporting these other slimeballs," Dimitri said, "from the safety of his floating palace in international waters."

"That's about the size of it, I'm afraid," O'Reilly said.

Tony had been staring at his computer screen and looked up, smiling, and said, "What you're saying is, if he came into the territorial waters of the United States, he could be arrested."

"If the authorities knew about it, yes, they would grab him in a heartbeat," O'Reilly confirmed. "Why?" she asked, now looking at Tony intently.

Still smiling, Tony said, "I think I have an idea."

CHAPTER THRITEEN

"What are you thinking?" I asked. Tony was busily typing on his laptop. The diagram of the yacht on the monitor was replaced by a screen showing electronic representations of gauges, dials, and buttons—all labeled. Then, a second and third page came up, and on them, I recognized an electronic compass, fuel gauges, and temperature gauges.

My mind was racing as I turned to Tony and said, "Are we looking at what I think we're looking at?"

"What would that be, Colt?" he asked, smiling broadly.

"It looks like an electronic representation of the controls for a vessel."

"Right you are," he said, laughing. "When I downloaded the specs, plans, and schematics for *The Pangaea*, I was also able to download its digital control system software. I told you this boat had the latest electronic systems controlling it; this software package controls every aspect of the boat: engines, the helm, and all ancillary operations that would be operated from the bridge."

Joe asked, "Does that mean you could control the vessel from your computer?"

"Theoretically, yes," Tony responded. "The biggest problem I see would be connecting to the boat's system remotely."

"Well, you guys just may be in luck," Fitz's voice boomed through the monitor. "One of my teams has been working on a new gizmo, a plug-in interface that would allow for a solid and stable remote connection to any computer system, kind of a skeleton key for computers. We think JSOC would be interested. A covert team could infiltrate an enemy's computer center, plug this in, and get out undetected, and they could monitor any and all traffic without the knowledge of the bad guys. This gizmo would be completely undetectable on their system. The only way to get rid of it is to physically unplug it. Its size and innocuous design make it easy to hide in a computer room. It has a built-in self-destruct system if removed improperly. It also provides us access to the entire system; the main computer would not see the access with this device as an intrusion. So, no alerts or warnings would be sent. The biggest problem I see is someone would have to find the computer room and physically plug it in."

Without hesitation, Reggie said, "I'll take care of that; Tony can show me where I have to go and what to do, so not a problem."

Tony said excitedly, "I can definitely work with that. What's the proximity requirement of the device, Fitz?"

"It will vary with this prototype, depending on the location of and any shielding around the main computer room, but on a vessel like this, I would think ten miles would be a safe guess. I can talk to my guys and get more specific information for you."

O'Reilly chimed in, "I can get you close enough in the *Raven* if Fitz will let me borrow it again."

"Only if you bring it back with a full tank of gas," he said, laughing loudly.

"I think I can do that, Colonel; I'll even have them clean the windshield and check the air in the tires," O'Reilly said, laughing as well.

"Then, she's all yours, and if this crazy plan of yours comes together, I think I can arrange to have a welcoming party for this guy and his crew once he enters U.S. waters," Fitz added.

Spirits had been lifted dramatically. This was the most jovial mood I'd seen this team in for quite a while, I thought. The joking continued amongst them as smiles blossomed around the table. Tess looked at me, her eyes sparkling as she mouthed, "Thank you."

I returned her smile, nodded slightly in acknowledgment, and winked. Now, all we had to do was put all these parts of the plan together and make it happen... no problem. As my grandaddy used to say when faced with a monumental challenge, "Ain't no mountain for a climber."

The days flew by as the final pieces of our plan were put into place. Gus and Mac had come through, and the five-man crew and captain agreed to our financial arrangement for providing a seventy-thousand-dollar water taxi ride. According to Mac, the supply ship would take about an hour and a half to offload the ten supply containers and retrieve the empty ones. The captain had agreed to fake engine trouble about six miles offshore and delay his rendezvous with the yacht until around dusk. Under the cover of darkness, we would board her. Mac would be the sixth crew member on the supply ship and the one to go aboard with the manifest and papers that had to be signed by the ship's purser.

Doc had outfitted Reggie, Dimitri, and me with tranquilizer pistols in addition to our standard armament. Reggie had Fitz's gizmo box, and Tony had briefed her on the location of the ship's computer room and where to install it once she was there. We estimated we would have about one hour on board before the supply ship headed back to port, and we had no idea how long it would take us to break into the gallery, retrieve the statues, and be ready to disappear into the night stealthily. If the supply ship left before we were done, we would be stranded onboard the yacht.

Luckily, Gus offered a solution to eliminate the need for the supply ship as transport back. His vessel, *The Falcon,* was operating about thirty-five miles north of the port of Jacksonville—around Amelia Island. He would move her south and into international waters and anchor about four miles from *The Pangaea* on the day of our operation. We would contact him by radio, and he would pick us up in the twenty-four-foot RHIB (rigid hull inflatable boat) that stayed with *The Falcon.* We no longer had to depend on the supply boat for a ride.

The plan was set: ride out to *The Pangaea* on the supply ship, slip aboard after dark, break into the gallery, and get the statues while Reggie installed Fitz's computer gizmo. All rendezvous on deck and ex-fill on the boat Gus would provide. Once the gizmo was installed, O'Reilly, Doc, and Tony would be in the *Raven,* hovering some distance away. When given the signal, Tony would use the gizmo to hack into the yacht's helm, take control of her, and head for U.S. territorial waters, where Fitz would have a law enforcement welcoming committee waiting.

Simple, I thought... that is, if we weren't detected sneaking aboard, didn't have any problems with the gallery security system, found the statues, the gizmo got installed, we didn't run into any crewmembers or security, got off the yacht, and Tony was able to hack into the yacht's computer and move it into U.S. waters. Simple, yeah, right.

On the final run-through the day before the operation, we decided that it would be good to have some kind of distraction that would draw security and crew members away from the gallery area to minimize the possibility of our contact with them. Mac was the one who provided the solution. Each of the large plastic supply containers contained specific items. Two for frozen food, two for dry foodstuffs, two for fresh meat and vegetables, and two for general paper goods and serving supplies. Mac had seen cases of Sterno listed among the serving supplies on the supply list. While the supply ship was on its way out, he said he could slip into that container, open a few cans of Sterno, rig an incendiary device that would ignite them, and ensure there were paper supplies close enough to catch fire. It was set to be the third container loaded on the yacht; there were eight containers in all.

We agreed that could provide the necessary distraction and told him to proceed with his plan.

The night before the raid, Tess and I had a quiet dinner at my house. I grilled some Mahi fillets and threw together a Caesar salad and some steamed asparagus. Add a bottle of white wine, and we had a nice dinner, even if I did prepare it. Things were quiet at first, small talk about the meal and my cooking and some gentle ribbing about the crunchiness of the asparagus, then silence. Tess picked up her wine glass and looked at me over its rim. "Colt, do you really think we can pull this off?"

I finished my bite of Mahi and washed it down with some wine. I didn't answer her immediately, but when I did, I chose my words carefully. "If things go as planned, then yes, I do. I think we have prepared for all contingencies—well, all the ones we could think of," I added quickly.

"And if things go sideways?" she asked.

"Then we abort and get everyone out," I said.

"And the statues?" she asked.

"Nobody's life is worth those statues," I said emphatically. "Nobody's!"

That night, as we lay there in the dark, Tess's head on my shoulder, I stared at the almost invisible ceiling fan over my bed, listening to the nearly inaudible clicking sound it made on each rotation of the blades, feeling its cool breeze blowing across my body and the warmth of Tess's laying against me. What if things did go sideways, I thought. We had a contingency evac plan, but... There were a hell of a lot of moving parts to our plan, and this was no lightweight criminal we were dealing with.

Yes, Syria had been dicey, but there we had help. This one, we were pretty much on our own. I was worried; no, let me rephrase that, I thought—I was concerned. I knew my team; they could handle themselves and have done so in unbelievable situations, but....

Somehow, this one felt different, and yes, I was

worried about Tess's safety. Even though she had proven to be as tough as any member of my team and capable of taking care of herself, I was still worried. I leaned over and kissed her forehead without waking her. It will be fine, I told myself and forced my brain to shut down for at least a few hours, falling asleep while convincing myself the clicking sound overhead was not the sound of a time bomb preparing to explode.

CHAPTER FOURTEEN

We had gotten onboard undetected. It was full-on dark as we began working our way to the gallery, two decks above us. Reggie had already headed for the computer room, and O'Reilly, Doc, and Tony were in a slow orbit in the *Raven* about six or seven miles away. When the time came, O'Reilly would bring the *Raven* to within three or four miles of the yacht before Tony attempted to take control of the vessel's computer system.

We had hoped that everyone would be having the evening meal at this hour in one of the dining areas or their staterooms. Imagine our surprise when we got to the gallery deck and found the doors to the outer party deck wide open and music coming from the gallery. We could see four men seated on the couches inside, drinking and smoking cigars, while two security guards stood watch at the large open doorway.

We had no idea who three of the men were, but from the pictures we had, the fourth was definitely Jorgensen. The stairs we had used to get to this deck brought us out on the port side of the gallery, and luckily, we saw the men through the large windows that lined the exterior gallery wall, the low wall that was providing us cover for the moment as we sat with our backs against the wall. Dimitri said very quietly, "Well, that really screws things up."

My mind was racing as I said, "No kidding."

Joe whispered, "So, Colt, what's plan B?"

"Give me a second," I said as I furiously tried to devise a plan B. Finally, I said, "Dimitri and I can take out the two guards with the darts; they will definitely be armed, so they need to go first. But it will take us a few seconds to re-load a new dart, and there is no way to get a clear shot at the guards from cover. We are going to have to step out into the open to ensure a hit."

Joe whispered again, "And hope like hell those guys in there aren't quick on the draw."

I cautiously peeked through the window. The men were relaxed, laughing and talking, dressed very casually. I saw no sign of guns and dropped back down. I looked at my watch; we had been on the yacht for thirteen minutes. There was at least another thirty minutes of loading left, and Mac's device wasn't set to go off until the supply ship had left. We were sitting in the main exterior walkway, exposed, and could be discovered at any minute by a crewman.

"We can't wait for Mac's device to ignite; we have to do something quickly. We need another distraction." Tess quickly looked around and spotted the door we would use to enter the gallery from our outside deck area.

She leaned over and said, "Work your way down to the outside party deck doors where the guards are," as she pulled off her tactical vest and began pulling off her black long-sleeved top.

"What the hell are you doing, Tess?" I whispered excitedly.

"I'm going to give you guys the distraction you need; now, get in position." Under her shirt, she was wearing a tight-fitting black tank top, and with the black pants, she was quite a sight as she slowly crawled to the door. She turned when she got there and motioned for us to get moving. I said I would take the guard on the left, Dimitri the one on the right, and Joe would enter the gallery prepared to neutralize the man closest to us as we reloaded.

I looked back at Tess, standing with her hand on the door handle. We were in position, and I gave that striking blonde in the black tank top a thumbs up. What happened next was a blur.

Reggie had already dodged two crewmembers on her way to the computer room, moving silently, still undetected. As she entered the hallway where the computer room was located, she felt confident in completing her mission until the young crewman stepped into the hallway from an adjoining passage.

His surprise at seeing this person dressed all in black gave way quickly to his challenge to her, "Who are you, and what are you doing down here?" he blurted out.

Reggie quickly responded with a smile as she continued walking toward him. Raising her hand in greeting, she said, "Oh, hi, I was just looking for the ladies' room," still moving and still smiling. The crewman stood still, a puzzled look on his face as Reggie, now fifteen feet from him, pulled her gun and placed the tranq dart in his chest. The look of surprise was still on his face as he glanced down at the dart protruding from his body, looked back at Reggie, and collapsed to the floor.

Reggie stood on alert in the hallway, waiting to see if anyone had heard their exchange. Hearing nothing, she tried to decide what to do with the unconscious crewman. Not seeing any good options, she decided to leave him as she saw the computer room door immediately to her left. Time to move, get in and get out before anyone else shows up. Tony's instructions proved remarkably accurate, and she had no problem installing the gizmo. The green LED lit up three seconds after plugging it into the computer patch panel. Tony said that would be the sign that the installation was successful and the device had been integrated into the main system. She said over her Comm, "Installation completed."

"Roger that," came Tony's reply from the *Raven*. "The connection looks good from here."

"Copy, heading for ex-fill now," she said as she left the computer room. She closed the door and saw a crewman blocking her path as she turned to retrace her steps. He had the same type of crew uniform as the one she had neutralized but in a quadruple X size. This guy was huge, looking like Andre the Giant—at least six foot six and well over three hundred pounds. His body literally filled the hallway. Now, Reggie paused, unsure of her next move, when "Andre" asked in German what was happening. Luckily, being fluent in several languages, German included, allowed her to answer readily.

"I found this man unconscious and was checking the area for intruders," she replied, trying her best to sound official. It didn't work as this mountain of a man, scowling, continued approaching. She had reloaded the dart gun after her encounter with the other crewman and quickly fired a dart into the new threat's chest. Nothing happened as he continued his advance. Reloading quickly, she fired again; he was still advancing but looked really pissed. He was only ten feet away when she fired the third dart. Even though his chest looked like a pin cushion, he never slowed.

He reached down, grabbed her by the shoulders, and lifted her off the ground. His grip felt like her shoulders were in a vise as the dart gun fell from her hand to the floor. Her arms and hands were locked to her sides; there was no way she could throw a punch, not that it would do any good. A quick mental assessment of her situation left her with only one option. She began swinging her body slightly and delivered a kick to the big man's groin, making solid contact with "the family jewels." This elicited a response.

The crewman dropped her and immediately grabbed the injured area with his hands, bending slightly at the waist. This afforded Reggie the opening she had been hoping for, and she unleashed a brutal punch to the center of the man's face, crushing his nose and making solid contact with his cheekbones. She immediately grabbed her hand in pain; it felt like she had just punched a concrete wall. But her actions had their desired effect as the man dropped to his knees, nose bleeding profusely and eyes glassing over as he fell face-down on the deck in front of her.

Reggie realized then that it had been Tony's frantic voice she had been hearing in her ear. "Are you okay, Reggie? What's going on?" he asked.

"I'm fine; it's all good," she replied, still nursing her sore hand.

"What happened?" Tony asked.

"Long story," she said, "I'll fill you in later, and boy,

do I have a bone to pick with Doc. Heading to ex-fill now." She had to walk over the big guy's back on her way out. She quickly moved down the corridor, heading for the upper decks and her rendezvous with the rest of the team.

CHAPTER FIFTEEN

Tess strode confidently through the gallery door and loudly said, "Excuse me, gentlemen, can you help me?"

Her entry had the desired effect as all eyes turned to her, and the guards turned their backs to us as they reached for weapons. Our darts did their job, and the guards went down within seconds. We reloaded and hit the two men closest to us while they were still seated. Joe had rushed in with us and grabbed the third man by the front of his jacket, holding his silenced Glock against the guy's head.

Jorgensen, whose attention had been on Tess, only slightly noticed what was happening in the room around him and, showing little surprise, arrogantly said, "Lady, do you have any idea who I am?" Tess was still approaching the seated man who had turned in his chair to address her.

Smiling, she answered, "Actually, Mr. Jorgensen, I do."

During their exchange, Jorgensen had slowly opened a drawer on the side table next to his chair and reached for the gun inside. He glanced down at it as he was bringing it to bear and never saw Tess's spinning sidekick coming until it made contact with his head. The gun dropped from his hand as he was propelled out of his chair and collapsed unconscious on the floor.

Tess walked to the table, took the gun out of the drawer, rolled Jorgensen over, and began binding him with our zip-tie handcuffs. We were busy doing the same with the rest of the men in the room. The roll of duct tape came out of Dimitri's pack, and we bound their legs together and covered their mouths with it.

We began checking out all the exhibit cabinets for the statues; they weren't there. I could tell Tess was frustrated as she looked in the last one and slammed her hand down on it. "Not again," she exclaimed. I looked around the room and saw nowhere they could have been stored out of sight.

Tess was fuming as I said, "Hang on for a minute," and walked over to Joe's detainee, the only captive still conscious, and ripped the duct tape off his mouth. Tess came over and looked at him, seated in his chair, and asked, "Have you seen the seven gold statues that Jorgensen has in his possession?"

He had watched her in action, and I guess he didn't want any part of that, so he answered quickly, "Yes, he showed them to us earlier."

"Where are they now?" Tess asked.

It was then we heard the excited chatter between Reggie and Tony. I looked at my watch and saw we had been onboard the yacht for just over an hour. I said over the Comm, "Mac, you there?"

A few seconds later, he replied, "Roger that, Colt; I'm undercover below and about to make my way to your location. I've been following the activity on Comms; it sounds like everyone is having fun."

"Yeah, a regular party going on. Are you ready with

the diversion?"

"I am, and the supply ship is gone, and most of the loading crew have left the area. I want to wait another five minutes before I light things up. The rest of the crew should be out of here and heading to their normal duty stations. When the smoke is visible, all hell should break loose."

"Copy, let us know when you light it up and head our way."

"Will do," Mac replied.

The man in the chair, not having his hands free, was shrugging toward the gallery's back wall, "Over there," he said, "There are doors in the wall."

Tess rushed to the back wall in the gallery; she scrutinized the molding on the wall and the wall itself, tapping on it at regular intervals. Moving a statue on a tall pedestal revealed a handle and locking mechanism. "There's a door here," she said. Joe replaced the tape over our guest's mouth, and we all moved to the back wall.

The Comms came to life as Mac said, "On my way up, she's smoking,"

Moments later, the ship's fire alarm went off, and as the crew members scrambled everywhere, I said, "Joe, we need this door opened." The locking mechanism was interesting—there was a handle, a keyhole, and a combination dial. So, it obviously was a double lock.

I turned to Joe, who was rummaging through his pack, when Dimitri said, "I got this one, Colt." I turned to see him slap a grey glob onto the area of the locking mechanism, stick a detonator in it, and move to the side.

Before I could say anything, he said, "Fire in the hole," and squeezed the trigger device in his hand.

Tess had moved to the far side of the room, and Joe and I just had time to dive over the couch behind us before the explosion blew a hole in the door. Now, on a "Dimitri scale," this blast was only a one and a half or two, with a ten being destroy the whole building, but it was enough to break the glass cases in the gallery and cause our ears to ring. Laughing, Dimitri went to the door, carefully grabbed the hot metal where the locks had been, and pulled it open.

Tess immediately went inside; there was no light in the room as it had been destroyed by the blast, so she was shining her flashlight across the shelves. Two crew members came running into the gallery and stood frozen at the sight before them. Neither Dimitri nor I had gone inside the room and were able to take them out with the dart guns.

"Damn, I don't see them," I heard Tess exclaim. I went inside and added my flashlight illumination to hers. There were pieces of art, ceramics, and paintings around the room. In one corner, I saw a metal box and opened it. The light reflecting from inside lit up the seven statues, looking like Oscars waiting to be awarded.

I called Tess over and said, "I believe this is what you're looking for."

As she peered into the box, I heard her gasp. "It's them," she said and began taking them out of the box. Joe stood guard at the door in case other crew members entered the room.

Dimitri had joined us at the box and said, "Finally,

we found the little suckers," as he reached in and picked one up.

"Yes, we did," I said. "Now, it's time to get to the ex-fill and get out of here." We took the statues, heavier than they looked, into the gallery, where Tess tore down one of the drapes on a window. Tearing the gauzy material into pieces, she began wrapping each statue individually. I started helping and said, "We're all going to have to carry these, guys; they're too heavy and won't fit in one pack." After wrapping them, we put two statues in each of Tess, Dimitri, and my packs. Joe got the last one.

Then, Tony came over the Comm, "You guys need to get out of there. I have control of the boat, engines are running, and I am about to engage the emergency anchor release and head this bad boy into U.S. waters."

We took a last look around the gallery; all our guests were still unconscious on the floor. "Let's go," I said and headed for the door. We had to go down two decks to get to the main deck and our ex-fill point by the boarding ladder. Crewmen were running around everywhere; most didn't give us a second look, and the couple that did were treated to the last of our darts and collapsed on the deck. I heard my radio squawk as we got to the main deck.

It was Gus. "Colt, do you copy?"

"I copy, Gus; we're almost to the external gangway on the port side." This was a set of stairs that ran down the side of the yacht in a zigzag pattern to a level where personnel from smaller vessels coming alongside could board the yacht. We saw Mac and Reggie standing by the railing. Three crewmen were sitting with their backs against the wall, unconscious. As we approached, the fire alarm still blaring, I asked, "You guys okay?" as I took another look at the unconscious crewmen.

"Yeah, we're fine," Reggie answered. "Don't worry about them, Colt; I didn't shoot anybody. It's just nap time; they'll wake up soon… maybe," she said, flashing a grin.

The radio crackled again, and Gus's voice said, "Colt, I'm two hundred yards out."

I keyed my mic, "Good, copy," I said as Tony's voice came over Comms.

"Guys, we've got a problem; I can't get the bow anchor to release."

Okay, so here's the situation: You can't just turn a five-hundred-foot yacht to the left and move forward. Turning something this big is a process, a somewhat slow process. To facilitate the turn, Tony would employ the thrusters on the port side to help turn the vessel more quickly. Thrusters are nothing more than props mounted below the waterline, built into the hull of large ships to help them turn and maneuver when a side-pushing force was needed. There were three on each side of the yacht—bow, midships, and stern. Employing them to max while having the rudders full to port and the engines at full throttle should make turning this beast a little easier, that is, if the anchor was released.

"Tony, give me an update," I said.

"I've got complete control of all the other systems, but the remote emergency bow anchor release isn't working. You guys are making the turn, kind of pivoting on the anchor, but I won't be able to head her in with the anchor still attached.

"Can you use the power of the engines to pull the anchor loose from the bottom?" I asked.

"Maybe," Tony replied. "But if the captain figures out what's happening, he could get the crew to shut down the engines manually. It would take some time, but it's a possibility."

"Bloody hell," I exclaimed, best-laid plans... I thought.

"What now, Colt?" Dimitri asked as more crew members began showing up on the deck. We were out of darts, so it was back to brute force as Mac, Reggie, and Joe began dispatching them.

I got on the radio and said, "Gus, we have a problem. Tony can't get the bow anchor to release. We may have to try and do it manually from up here, and we're running out of time."

There was no reply for a couple of minutes, and then Gus said, "Tell Tony to shut down the bow thruster."

"What? What for?" I asked.

"Just tell him to shut down the bow thruster until I tell him to restart."

"Copy," I said, then over Comms, I gave the order to Tony.

Luckily, there was no debate as he came back, "Bow thruster shut down."

Smoke was billowing from the stern cargo area now. It looked like Mac's device had done its job and more. I looked at my watch; ten minutes had passed, and no word from Gus. At eleven minutes, Gus came on the radio, "All right, if you don't want to swim home, get your butts down here."

We looked over the railing and saw the inflatable moving to the gangway. We were halfway down when a large explosion went off at the ship's bow. We had all clambered aboard the boat as Gus said to me, "Tell Tony to engage the starboard bow thruster, full power—the anchor has been released, and give those engines hell. With the fire, standard procedure is to seal all watertight doors, so everybody will be locked down for a bit. If Tony has shut down ship-wide communications, then that may buy us the time we need."

While we were moving away from the yacht, we could tell she was coming about—slowly but coming about. We decided to keep her in sight for the time being. Tony confirmed that not only had the ship-wide communications been shut down, but he also shut down the fire mitigation system. So, all the crew had were pumps, pumping seawater on the fire. The yacht had been anchored only sixteen miles offshore to facilitate fueling and provisioning. It normally had been staying twenty miles offshore. We had four miles to go. I looked at Gus and said, "Four miles."

"I know," he said. "If Tony can get her turned and running full-tilt, that's about seven or eight minutes to reach our territorial waters." That is if nothing else happens.

The Comms came alive; it was "O'Reilly, "We've got you in sight; we'll be following you. Tony says it will be about five more minutes before he can have a due-west heading. The captain is trying to gain control, but he's got him blocked out for now."

We were about a hundred and fifty yards off the yacht's port side; O'Reilly, in the *Raven*, was another hundred yards away. It seemed like hours, but finally, Tony came on Comms, "Okay, she's on a due-west course, and engines are running wide open. Everything looks good, and I turned the fire suppression system back on."

I was smiling as I looked at the smiling faces in the boat and turned to Gus to speak when I heard Doc's excited voice. He was on the *Raven* as a spotter for O'Reilly and Tony.

"Colt, the helicopter on deck is spinning up."

CHAPTER SIXTEEN

I grabbed the binoculars, looked toward the ship's helipad, and saw the helicopter's rotors starting their slow spin to start up. "O'Reilly," I said over Comms, "somebody is trying to get away in the chopper."

"I see it," came the reply. "I'll take care of it," she said as the nose of the *Raven* turned toward the yacht and headed that way. The rotors on the chopper were getting to lift-off speed when I heard, "Man, I really hate to do this; that's such a nice bird." Then, the twenty-millimeter cannon barked in two short bursts. The tail rotor and rear of the Augusta flew apart as the rounds from the *Raven* tore through it.

O'Reilly came back on Comms, "Nobody is leaving in that bird." We could see three men scrambling to get out of the incapacitated helicopter. As I watched through the binoculars, I recognized the men from the gallery encounter as they ran back into the safety of the yacht's interior.

I looked at the others in the boat and said, "Looks like Jorgensen and the others from the gallery have gotten loose and were the ones who just tried to get away in the chopper."

"Good luck with that," Dimitri said, laughing, as we could see flames coming from the rear section of the helicopter. "Nice shooting, O'Reilly," he added.

"Thanks, big guy. Tony tells me they have two boats stored in bays on the stern of the yacht: two forty-footers, one Go-fast, and one fishing boat. That might be their next try at escaping. I'm going to swing around and take a look. He also said they have about two miles to go to break the twelve-mile threshold."

"Roger that, keep them boxed up and keep those throttles pushed to the firewall," I replied. I got an affirmative response from Tony and O'Reilly as the *Raven* banked and headed to the yacht's stern. I looked at my watch; the operation had been going on now for a little over two hours—just a bit longer, I thought. I turned my attention to the west, and, through the binoculars, I could see at least a half-dozen groups of flashing lights, red and red and blue. Well, it looks like Fitz has come through on his welcoming committee promise, I thought as I keyed the mic on the radio. "Fitz, do you copy?"

A few seconds later, I heard, "Good copy, Colt, Sit Rep?"

"Things got a little dicey, but we're bringing the big boy to you. May want to have some patrol craft standing by to search for anyone who decides they would rather swim than be arrested."

"Understood; we have a smorgasbord of vessels waiting to welcome these guys. The Coast Guard Cutter, *Valiant*, a couple of LCS Navy vessels (Littoral Combat Ship), at least a half-dozen armed patrol craft from other agencies, and two helos. When word got out that this guy might be within our grasp, everybody wanted in on the action."

I laughed as I said, "You always did know how to

throw a party, Fitz."

"Go big or go home," came his reply.

Tony's excited voice broke in over Comms, "Colt, they've shut down one of the engines."

"What?" I exclaimed. "How did that happen?"

"I told you it was a possibility if they figured out something was wrong. They did a manual shutdown in the engine room. I still have control over the computer, but they bypassed the system with the manual override."

"What about the second one?" I asked apprehensively.

"Still operating at full throttle, but I'm sure they're working on a manual shut-down there too. It's only a matter of time before she's dead in the water."

"How much time?" I asked, now a little frantic.

"No telling, but it probably won't be long," Tony answered.

"How close are we?" I asked.

There was a pause. "According to my calculations, less than a mile," he said.

The flashing lights of the awaiting law enforcement vessels were shining brightly ahead. They weren't moving, just waiting like vultures waiting for their prey to die. I knew they had to stay within the twelve-mile limit, and they looked close, but not close enough. The sound of the *Raven's* minigun broke my train of thought. I said, "O'Reilly, what's happening?"

Seconds later, another burst from the gun was heard. Then she said, "Tony was right; they were trying to launch those two boats, but not to worry, those boats aren't going anywhere."

"That's for sure," I heard Doc say, "they both look like Swiss cheese."

We had slowed and were close to the stern as the *Raven* banked and moved to our port side about fifty yards away.

"Are we going to make it?" I asked over Comms to no one in particular. It was kind of an out-loud thought.

"Ha! Take that," I heard Tony saying, laughing almost manically.

"What's going on?" I almost shouted.

"I think we're going to make it," Tony replied. "It won't stop them, but it will damn sure slow them down."

"What?" Now, I was shouting.

"I just activated the fire suppression system in the engine room." Tony was laughing wildly. "They have a new fire-suppression foam system. They're not going to be able to see squat now. We've got less than a quarter mile to go. Even if they did shut down the other engine, they would have no way to stop their forward momentum with both engines off. The boat is ours, Colt."

We must have crossed into U.S. waters during our exchange as the waiting vessels began swarming around *The Pangaea*. One of the Sea King helicopters came in at a low hover over the foredeck as we watched an assault team of about twelve men fast rope down to the deck, guns at the ready, and head to the bridge. The second helo came in and deposited another team. It looked like things were well in hand. "Gus, I think it's time to adios on out of here. All right, everybody, time to head home."

I keyed the radio mic. "Fitz, I can confirm that Jorgensen is on board. Just look for the guy with a gray beard and a swollen left side of his head."

"Copy, Colt; everybody is moving in; we'll find him—good job."

"Thanks, man, see you back at the ranch," I replied as Gus made a hard turn and headed back out to sea. After dropping us off on Amelia Island, Gus and Mac stayed with the *Falcon* while we made our way back to the port where we had parked our two SUVs, loaded up, and headed south. O'Reilly was dropping Doc and Tony off at our headquarters and then returning the *Raven* to its hangar at Fitz's airfield. Tess, Reggie, and Doc were in my vehicle; Dimitri and Joe followed close behind.

Spirits were soaring; not only had we recovered the statues, but we also delivered an international criminal into the hands of law enforcement. We had a two-hour drive back to headquarters in Cocoa, or the "Lair" as Dimitri had named it, and that was plenty of time for Reggie to read Doc the riot act about his darts not being able to stop the German "King Kong." It was all in good fun, but Reggie laid it on thick—that he put her life in danger by not planning for the takedown of Andre the Giant.

Doc sat there quietly, taking all her abuse in stride, and after a ten-minute tirade, finally said, "I do apologize, young lady; next time, I promise to make my potion strong enough to take down two water buffalos and a giant." Then, he burst out laughing.

Reggie smacked him on the shoulder and said, "I'm

serious... well, sort of," and started laughing as well, her mock indignation melting away.

Tess and I had been listening quietly, chuckling under our breath at the exchange. It was quiet now as the adrenaline dissipated, and our exertion began taking hold. We were all mentally and physically exhausted. Tess reached over, placed her hand on my thigh, and squeezed it. I turned to her as she said, "You did it, Colt; you actually did it," with that beautiful but weary smile across her face.

I returned her smile, "We did it," I said, "We did it."

"I know," she replied. "Your team was incredible; that's what I meant. It was indeed a team effort." Then she leaned toward me and quietly said, "But you made it happen," and squeezed my leg again as she looked down at the packs on the floor containing the statues.

"Two things, lady," I said, smiling, "Neither you nor the statues are leaving my sight. We'll set you up in our conservation lab, and you can continue your work there. We should have everything you need, and if not, we'll get it."

"Yes, sir, Dr. Burnett, anything you say, sir," she said as she gave me a mock salute. "And the second thing?" she asked, smiling.

"We'll discuss that when we get home," I replied, glancing her way and seeing her eyes sparkling. No further comment was made, nor was it necessary.

"I'm glad we understand each other," I replied, laughing. We finished the ride back to our headquarters just north of Cocoa in silence. We were all wrapped up in our personal thoughts of our recent adrenalin-charged adventure and enjoying the quiet respite.

CHAPTER SEVENTEEN

We spent the next few days getting Tess set up in the lab and beginning the removal of the material on the statues' bases and their conservation. She got settled into my place, and I will admit, I was enjoying having her around after all this time apart. There was a kind of routine setting in, a very pleasant one.

We had gotten an update from Fitz, who said the raid went very well. Jorgensen and his henchmen were in custody, his yacht was impounded in Jacksonville, and all the law enforcement agencies involved could care less how he got into U.S. waters and were ignoring his wild claims of being hijacked and forced against his will into our waters and being robbed. It was being chalked up to the ravings of a cornered madman.

All good news for us, and it earned Fitz some brownie points for bringing the information of Jorgensen's arrival to the attention of the authorities. He assured us he had just banked a few favors owed because of it. "Always good to have on hand," he quipped. With our tech's help, Tess had been making good progress removing the black material from the bases of the statues. After analyzing some of the first fragments, she found that it was indeed a type of resin with a pigment added to give it the black color. The removal was a slow process, but the bases were indeed covered with hieroglyphic text. The workmanship was beautiful, worthy of a queen. The bases were square, about two inches high by four inches long. All four sides of the bases were filled with writing, none of it the same. Now that she had figured out what the black material was, our techs took over the removal and cleaning while Tess began working on the translation.

It was not easy, even for her expert eye. She was trying to figure out a context for the inscriptions and wasn't having any luck. Doc had volunteered to help her, and the two of them had been working on them for a week and a half. The hieroglyphs were small and intricate. She was using our optical scanner to enlarge the glyphs and project them on the monitor in the lab. She was able to photograph them and then place the images from each statue end to end in seven groups, trying to understand what the glyphs on each statue were saying; it was slow going. Trying to make sense of seven groups of four sides each for a total of twenty-eight photographs would be enough to drive anyone crazy. She had given each statue an arbitrary reference number—one through seven, grouping the photos of the four sides under each statue's number. Nothing had revealed itself.

The statues were solid gold, so we moved them to our vault for safe keeping once the bases were cleaned and photographed. A day later, I got a call from Doc around 5:00 p.m., saying he had something I had to see. Tess and Doc had moved their research to one of our small conference rooms. When I arrived, they had all the photos spread out on the conference table. He turned as I walked in. "Ah, Colt, you need to look at this," he said, sliding the photo he had been studying toward me.

I looked at the hieroglyphs in the photo and, after

a couple of minutes, said, "You know, I don't know much about Egyptian hieroglyphs."

"I know," he said, "but look here," pointing at one of the glyphs. I looked closer—something was nagging me. "Look familiar?" he asked.

"I don't know," I replied.

"How about the obelisk we saw in Ecuador, in 'Jeannie's' city?" he said.

"Are you kidding me?" I mumbled as I recognized three more glyphs from the obelisk. Last year, we were involved in quite an adventure in Ecuador. In the Andes Mountains, we found a lost city that had been built millennia ago by an advanced race that had come to inhabit our planet. They had arrived before Homo habilis appeared on Earth. In this magnificent city stood an obelisk with strange carvings on it. Six of the hieroglyphs on it were also in this group from the base of one of the statues. I looked at Doc and said, "What the hell?"

"I know. I just realized where I had seen them before and called you. I have no idea what they say, but what I think this means is... Contact!"

Tess was now looking over our shoulders and asked, "What are you guys talking about?" I had never really gotten into details of our Ecuador adventure with her, so this was new stuff. We spent the next fifteen minutes giving her the CliffsNotes version on "Jeannie," our otherworldly acquaintance and benefactor, the obelisk in the plaza, and the carvings we saw on it. She was staring at us, wide-eyed, as the enormity of what we were saying hit her.

"So, you think somehow the Egyptians had contact

with 'Jeannie?'"

"Well, not necessarily her, but she told us her race had established outposts all over the world. I'm thinking someone from one of them may have made contact," I said.

Now, Tess paused with a furrowed brow. "I wonder... I've found a reference to an emissary or visitor from Ra, the 'sun god,' but didn't think much of it until now," Tess replied. "So, what does it say?" she asked.

"We don't know," Doc answered.

"Well, how can we find out?"

Doc and I exchanged glances, and he turned to her smiling and said, "I believe that would require a trip to Ecuador."

"I want to go," Tess said immediately.

It had been a long day, and I was tired; the beginnings of a headache were building, and this conundrum wasn't helping. The trip to the lost city might be the only way to get the answers we sought. The quickest way to get there would be using the portal device I had gotten from Jeannie. But I had never tried to portal that great of a distance. According to what she had told me, it should be possible, but... I still had some trepidation thinking about it. We studied the rest of the photographs but found no more of the strange, out-of-place glyphs.

I left for my office with them still studying the pictures, leaving the two researchers to their work and me with multiple questions bouncing around inside my head. I knew the two of them would keep at it late into the night and decided I would stay, too. I had a lot to think about. Darkness fell as I sat at my desk, and I watched as my view of the Indian River disappeared into its inky blackness. As I often do on late nights, I went to the wet bar in my office, poured some single malt into a glass, added two ice cubes, and returned to my desk and my thoughts.

My headache had gotten worse. I sipped my scotch, leaned back in my chair, clasped my hands, and placed them over my closed eyes, blocking out the office lights and hoping for some relief from the pain. After what seemed like only a few minutes, I felt the pain quickly melting away. I was startled upright in my chair when I heard the familiar voice ask, "Is that better, Colt?" Not believing my ears, I slowly removed my hands and opened my eyes.

Standing in front of my desk in all her glowing blue glory stood Jeannie. Her beautiful blue aura was lighting the area around her. She laughed her soft crystalline laugh when she saw the expression on my face and blithely said, smiling, "Why so surprised, Colt?"

Somewhat at a loss for words, I stammered a bit and said, "I am surprised; I had no idea that something like this was possible."

She laughed even more as she replied, "I told you when you visited my city and helped restore our energy source that it would provide me with capabilities beyond your comprehension."

"Yes, you did," I managed to get out, "But I guess I never considered something like this."

Smiling broadly now, her majestic beauty radiated

across the room as she spread her arms in an encompassing gesture. "This is nothing; this is only a small portion of what is now available to me. Moving through space and time is how I keep track of you and your activities," she said, her laugh punctuating the fact that she enjoyed the experience.

"So, you have been keeping track of us?" I asked.

"Of course, I have, you silly man," her offhandedness was surprising and refreshing—like two old friends meeting again after an extended separation.

"Well, that's what we are, Colt, right? Old friends…?"

A slight jolt ran through me as I remembered she could read our thoughts. Although not intrusive, she could keep track of our thoughts if she wanted to. I shook my head slightly as if trying to shake off a lingering sleepiness.

"I'm sorry, Jeannie; I had forgotten about you being able to read our thoughts when you wanted to, and, yes, I do consider us old friends."

Her lovely angelic smile remained as she said, "That pleases me, Colt. You must remember that you are the first person I have revealed myself to and interacted with in hundreds of your years. It was an extraordinary moment for me to do so—a moment I have not regretted."

As I looked at the lovely glowing figure draped in a gown reminiscent of Greek goddesses, I said, "And neither have I," instantly thinking… of all the lame statements. She is a being composed of energy we do not understand and hundreds of thousands of years old, and that's the best response you could come up with, Burnett? You dolt!

Jeannie laughed again. "Don't be too hard on yourself, Colt; being in my presence does present a person from your world with some challenges. I do understand. I have expanded my knowledge of your civilization immensely since we last met. Your repair of our power system has allowed for that."

"And, what do you think?"

"I'm afraid I'm very disappointed. We had such high hopes for this planet. You may still survive, but there are not enough people like you and your friends. I'm not optimistic... but there is still hope."

Her next comment took me aback, "I sense you have a new friend."

I think I stammered a bit; I'm not sure why, but I said, "No, Tess is not a new friend; I have known...." She held up her hand, stopping me in midsentence.

"I am not talking about the female; I am talking about your other new friend."

I was puzzled and not sure what she was getting at and said so.

She looked at me with those piercing eyes and slowly said, "The wolf."

I was shocked to hear that and quickly looked around the room, not knowing if he had materialized somewhere. "Oh, that. I guess he is a new friend, but how did you know?"

"We are aware of many levels of existence and parallel worlds. I have the ability to transcend this world and am aware of things that go on in other realms, especially when they have to do with you."

Okay, I was officially speechless and sat there gawking at her, mouth open, not knowing what to say. She's interested in things that have to do with me?

I was confused as she waved the comment off and said, "I would meet him."

I didn't get a chance to reply. Within seconds, the massive Dire wolf materialized right there in my office, his yellow eyes glowing, but I sensed no malice in his posture or expression. He looked at me, then back at Jeannie as she raised her hand, palm toward him in what looked like a greeting. The wolf dropped his head slightly and then looked back up—a sign of recognition, I thought.

They stood perfectly still, looking at one another for several minutes. Then Jeannie nodded her head; the wolf dipped his again and vanished. I sat unmoving, spotted the scotch still sitting on my desk, and took a long drink, hoping the strong liquid would jolt me back to reality, but then I realized... this is my reality.

Jeannie stood there staring at me and finally said, "He feels you are a strong and worthy warrior and have a good heart. He knows he made the right choice when he chose to bond with you.

"You had a question for me, Colt?"

I gathered myself and said, "Yes, Jeannie, we think we have found something you may recognize." I picked up the picture of the strange glyphs and showed it to her. She looked at the picture on my desk for a couple of minutes before speaking.

"Yes, I do recognize this; it is old—very old."

"We found it as part of an inscription on golden statues in an ancient Egyptian burial. What does it say or mean?" I asked.

"It venerates the one known as Ra and says you will find everlasting life in his temple or presence," Jeannie replied.

"So, the Egyptians did have contact with your people."

"As I told you before, in the beginning, we built outposts all over this world. No doubt some of our people did make contact with other emerging civilizations."

"And the rest of the hieroglyphs?" I asked.

She smiled at me and said, "That is for you to discover," then added, "You must place the statues in the right order. Each statue is not a statement but part of a longer narrative when viewed in the proper sequence." She paused, then answered a question I had not yet asked, "Yes, you could easily use the portal device to travel to my city. It has no limitations, and I believe Eduardo would be pleased with your visit, as would I." Before I could speak, she vanished.

I sat there, pondering what had just happened: Jeannie shows up, she wants to meet the wolf, he shows up, they say hello (I guess), he disappears, Jeannie answers my question about the glyphs, and then she vanishes. I took another swallow of my scotch, shook my head, and thought, just another day at the office.

I called down to the conference room; both Tess and Doc were still there. I told them I would be right there; I had some news about the glyphs. I hung up and headed down.

CHAPTER EIGHTEEN

I arrived to expectant faces as I entered the room. The pictures of the statue bases were spread on the table. "A trip to Ecuador won't be necessary. Jeannie stopped by the office," I said.

"She what?" Doc blurted out in disbelief.

"She appeared in my office and told me about the glyphs," I replied while studying the photos. "Have you found a starting point yet?" I asked.

Tess, who had been standing there quietly, said, "No, not yet. What did she have to say?"

"A couple of things; she confirmed the glyphs are from some of her people. They refer to the sun god or Ra, and she said the statues must be read in sequence."

"In sequence?" Tess asked.

"Yes, have you found anything that might indicate some kind of sequence with the statues?"

"You mean like statue one, two, three kind of thing?" she asked.

"I doubt it will be that easy," I answered. "Wait here; I'll be right back."

Ten minutes later, after a quick trip to the vault, I returned with the statues on a rolling cart. "I don't think the photos are going to work. Let's stand these guys out on the table and see if we can see anything like a sequence."

We stood them facing us, side by side, and Doc and Tess began turning them and examining them closely. After ten minutes, I asked, "Well, anything?"

"There's lots here, but I can't put my finger on the starting point," Tess answered.

"I don't know much about Egyptian hieroglyphs, but many of the ceremonial carvings and stela in Central America that I have seen will start with a date or official title of the personage being venerated. Have you found any date on these?" I asked.

"Yes, this one has a date," and Tess pointed to the fourth statue on the table. I picked it up and moved it to the number one position.

"What's the last thing it says on it?"

"Something about a journey," Tess replied.

"Okay, is there one that starts with a reference to a journey or travels?" I asked.

"I think this one says something about some kind of preparations," Tess said. It was the number six in the statue lineup.

I moved it to the number two position and asked, "What was the last thing the hieroglyphs said?"

Tess was getting excited as she began moving the statues on the table like chess pieces on a board. She stopped when all the statues were lined up again. Now, she was smiling. "This is beginning to make sense," she said, "but the last statue's text ends abruptly."

I looked at the statues on the table and repeated

what Jeannie had said, "They must be read in the proper sequence." Then, it hit me. I went to the first statue on the table and turned it ninety degrees to the left, showing its second side.

Tess had moved next to me and, in almost a whisper, said, "That's it; it picks up where number seven ended." She quickly studied it and then rotated the second statue and, after a couple of seconds, looked at me, grabbed my face in her hands, and kissed me.

That took me by surprise as she let me go and said, "You figured it out, Colt. You have to read each side as part of a sentence, starting with statue one and continuing to seven. Then you go back to one, rotate as you did, and the sentence continues." Tess had been rotating the statues, and as she spoke, she turned number seven, studied it for a minute, and went back to number one and rotated it again, revealing its third side. "Yep, that's it exactly," she exclaimed, grabbing her pad and starting to make notes. "This will take some time, but I think it's the key... to what, I'm not sure."

I looked at my watch; it was almost midnight, so I said, "Now that we seem to have found the sequence, and since you've been at it all day, let's call it a night, and you can start fresh in the morning."

Tess turned and looked at me like I was some three-headed monster and said, "You're kidding, right? This could be the key to a discovery as big or bigger than finding Tut's tomb. I'm not stopping now," and turned back to the statues on the table.

I raised both hands in submission, "Hey, I just thought it was a good idea, but never mind. You do what you have to do."

She didn't take her eyes off the statues and said, "You know I will, Colt."

Doc took the opportunity to say, "I'll put on a fresh pot of coffee and see what we have to munch on."

I looked at him and said, "You're staying too?"

"You bet I am," he replied. "You heard the lady; this could be big," as he left for the small kitchen on this floor to forage.

"Well, since I can't see myself being much help, I'm going to head home and get some rest."

Tess did turn to look at me then and said, smiling, "Colt, you have been of immense help. You found the key. Now, it's up to me to find the answer."

I returned her smile, nodded, and left the room. On the way out, I told our night security supervisor they had the statues in the conference room and to keep a close eye on them.

"Will do, Dr. Burnett; I have a man I can post outside the door."

I walked out of the building, feeling better about leaving them working. As I got to my vehicle, I looked back at the building and said to myself, "The game is afoot, Watson; the game is afoot."

I woke the next morning to an empty bed; she must have pulled an all-nighter, I thought. I grabbed a shower and headed out. When I got in, I saw a security guard still at the conference room door.

"They still at it?" I asked.

"Not sure about that," he said, smiling. "But they're still in there, haven't left."

I nodded and opened the door. They were there, Tess asleep with her head lying on her crossed arms on the table, a large pile of notes in front of her. Doc was kicked back in a chair, sound asleep as well. He woke up when I closed the door. Stretching and rubbing his eyes, he asked, "What time is it?"

"Eight ten, time to wake up, sleepyhead," I chided. Our voices roused Tess, who went through the same stretch and rubbing of eyes.

"Ah, Sleeping Beauty has joined us," I laughingly added.

She looked at her watch, at Doc, and then at me.

"Well, aren't you Mister Yippity-Skippity this morning," she said through a yawn.

"That's what a good night's sleep will do for you," I replied jovially.

She put her hand up to silence me and said, "Okay, enough of Miss Merry Sunshine; that's too much until I've had at least two cups of coffee."

I placed the box of donuts and Danishes I had picked up on the way in on the table and said, "You guys find the coffee; I've got breakfast."

Doc got up, grinning, and said, "You're a lifesaver, Colt." He grabbed a donut as he was heading for the door. "I'll take care of the coffee," he said as he exited the conference room.

Tess had taken a Danish from the box and, between bites, said, "We got it."

I looked at her quizzically as she continued, "The translation—we figured it out."

"Fantastic, fill me in," I said, somewhat wide-eyed.

"In a nutshell, it was written at the behest of the high priest in whose tomb we found them. It tells of a journey that Cleopatra embarked on."

"Where to?" I queried.

"That's one of the interesting things; it doesn't really say, but the journey takes place during the year she died."

I thought for a moment, then said, "Maybe he was referring to her trip to the afterlife after she died."

"Maybe," Tess replied, "but I'm not sure about that."

"Why not?"

"There were no references to the gods or the afterlife —Osiris, Isis, nothing."

"That does seem strange," I said.

"What seems strange, Colt?" Doc asked as he brought the fresh pot of coffee into the conference room.

"I was telling him about the lack of mentions of gods of the afterlife," Tess answered.

"Yeah, we thought that was kind of strange since the story seems to be about Cleopatra's death."

"Interestingly, there is a mention of Ra, the sun god, and it seems to say that Cleopatra believed him to be the one god."

"Wait a minute; I thought that died with Akhenaten. He introduced monotheism, the belief in the

Aten as the one God. After his death, the Egyptians returned to a polytheist religion and re-introduced all the old gods. As I recall, that was long before Cleo's reign."

"Glad to see you've stayed up on your Egyptian history," Doc said, smiling.

"You're right," Tess answered. "He didn't take the throne until around 1353. That's one of the things that makes this text so confusing; things seem out of place or time, at least as we know it. There's also a cryptic reference to a meeting one night with an emissary of Ra. He told Cleopatra, and this is where the strange glyphs that Jeannie deciphered for you [JP1]appear in the text, that she would have everlasting life in his presence or temple. That's just not making any sense."

"What else does it say?" I asked.

"It talks about making preparations with her handmaidens for this journey and says something about the end being close. As I said, it's not really making much sense."

Now, Doc jumped in, "It's been stated that she committed suicide after Mark Antony, her husband, killed himself rather than being taken a Roman prisoner by Octavian. His army had defeated Cleopatra's, and he was about to become ruler of Egypt."

"Isn't there a lot of debate about the timing of these events, who died, when, and where?" I asked.

"Yes, there are several stories about how this happened, but none are really verifiable," Tess said. "That just adds to the confusion of this message, but the exciting part is that it mentions Cleopatra's tomb and hints at a location."

"Now, that is something," I said. "And you're confident about the accuracy of your decipherment of the hieroglyphs on the bases?"

"I am," Tess answered. Doc added his agreement to her statement.

"Well, why don't you guys get some sleep? I'll have the statues placed back in the vault, and we'll work on figuring out this mystery a little later when everyone is rested. I'll have all your notes moved to my office, and we'll reconvene there."

There was no argument this time, and they headed out after another donut or two.

CHAPTER NINETEEN

I spent the day reviewing the notes, and later that afternoon, I got a call from Tess. She said she was rested but thought a meal and a good night's sleep were what she needed to be back to one hundred percent.

I told her I agreed—that was a good decision, and I would leave word for Doc and be home within the hour. I sent Doc a text informing him of the plan and that we would meet in my office the next morning at eight, then headed home.

Tess wanted to be outside for the evening, so she put the top down on her Jeep Wrangler and insisted on driving. Over the years, I learned that arguing with her was usually a no-win situation; besides, I didn't mind being the passenger for a change. We hit the Beeline Expressway (I just can't bring myself to call it the Beachline, its new name) and headed east to Port Canaveral.

The early evening air felt nice as it enveloped us. Tess had pulled her hair back in a ponytail, and I was enjoying her profile as her hair danced in the wind. This was cathartic for both of us. We had spent the last couple of weeks stuck in the offices of our headquarters, and while necessary, we both preferred the outdoors and the feeling of freedom that came with it.

After a relaxing dinner, sitting outside in the salt air, watching the boat and cruise ship traffic in the port, and engaging in light conversation, we headed back to the "Mainland." On the way, the discussion turned to the statues and their enigmatic message. We both agreed there was something we had not discerned yet and were hoping that taking our minds off the problem for the evening and getting a little more rest would bring clarity in the morning.

A glass of wine when we got home and a hot shower seemed to revive and relax us both. The cool sheets of my king-size bed were refreshing, and it wasn't long until the enigmatic message was the last thing on my mind as we were both intent on more pleasurable thoughts.

Later, as I lay there, Tess's body nestled comfortably against mine, I let my mind wander, letting the thoughts of this evening wash away the mental baggage that had been piling up in my head. As the ceiling fan made its customary, almost inaudible, click on each rotation, this time, it wasn't the tick of a time bomb getting ready to explode as I had once imagined. The repetitive sound became footsteps progressing toward a revelation, one that could be of substantial historical significance. With that thought, I fell asleep and rested peacefully until the alarm woke us at six-thirty the next morning.

We arrived at my office by eight, and Doc appeared with O'Reilly in tow shortly after that. As they entered, Doc said, "Hey, folks, I wanted to bring O'Reilly in on our work. I'm hoping her analytic skills will be helpful."

"Fine by me," I said. "The more eyes on this, the better. This has turned into the proverbial conundrum."

We gathered at the conference table with the photos of the hieroglyphs laid out in their proper sequence.

Tess gathered her notes, looked through them, and said, "Okay, here's what we have so far: some of the glyphs are unusual, slightly different from ones I have worked with in the past. So, when reading the text, we sometimes have to guess about some of it, based on contextual elements we can identify."

"I'll give a brief overview, and then we can get down to the strange or confusing parts. Doc, chime in at any time. The high priest, whose tomb held the statues and seems to be the author, had his death date as two years after Cleopatra died, which we now know as 28 BC. The date on the statue text refers to her death in 30 BC, as we would know it, the preparation for her long journey prior, and her meeting an emissary of Ra, the sun god, or as Akhenaten called him, the Aten, who appeared to her through a heavenly mist one night. She may have secretly shared in Akhenaten's belief in the one God, but there is no reference to this belief in any information we have about her reign as Pharaoh Queen.

"This revelation was very strange. I wasn't sure I had read it right, so I had Doc check it, and he came up with the same thing. The other strange passage talks about her departure for the house or temple of the sun god, but it does not mention any of the gods of the afterlife. Then, there's a section that talks of her handmaidens and their journey. There, Osiris is mentioned along with Isis and their judgment by Maat in the final phase of their trial before passing into the afterlife."

As Tess paused, O'Reilly spoke up, "I'm no expert in Egyptology, but from what you have said, I see the disconnect in the story. Cleo's preparation and the handmaidens' preparation seem to be completely different. Even though we're talking slaves and royalty, the passage or journey into the afterlife is the same for all."

"It is, and therein lies one of the problems. He also states that he eagerly awaits his Queen joining him in the presence of Osiris. All very puzzling," she said.

"Okay, wait a minute," O'Reilly said. "This priest guy died two years after Cleo, right?" she asked.

"That's what it says," Doc answered.

"Then why does he say he will be waiting for her to join him instead of just meeting him in the afterlife?" O'Reilly asked.

We sat silently for a few minutes, stunned at her question; then a thought hit me like a bomb going off, and I said, somewhat incredulously, "It sounds to me like he is saying he died before her...."

"That's not possible," Doc spit out. "He died in 28 BC, two years after her death."

"Why isn't it possible?" I asked.

"Well, all the history books tell us...." his sentence trailed off as he realized the folly of his statement.

I chuckled, "With all we've seen and been through, you think our history books are a reliable source?"

He smiled slightly and said, "You're right; I wasn't thinking."

Tess had rustled through the pile of notes in front of her. She pulled out one page and then looked through the photos of the statue bases. She studied them intently and then looked up, and as she slid both to Doc, she said, "I'll be damned; how could I have missed that?" Looking at all of us somewhat perplexed, she added, "What the hell does that mean?"

As Doc finished looking at the pages, he said, "Don't worry, Tess; I missed it too. It seems our accepted written history may have colored our interpretation of the text. If that's true, I think we need to revisit everything and see if we missed anything else."

Tess nodded in agreement, not speaking as she began arranging her notes. She finally said, "I think we need to go back to the photos and retranslate what's there. There very well may be other things we misinterpreted, based on our traditional understanding of the historical record."

This revelation was indeed a mystery whose scope was mind-boggling. As I sat there, my thoughts swirled in my head... where do we go from here? I asked myself. After a few moments, an idea began to form. What if I approached it as any detective would, or at least as the ones I've seen in the movies or on television might? Not that that's the best anchor for critical thinking. I began by asking, "What facts do we have, and what clues can be found in the priest's text?" I'm not comparing myself to Sherlock Holmes or Phillip Marlowe in my deductive skills, but I have done my share of mystery-solving over the last couple of years. I quickly ran through what we knew. As I did, one unbelievably unlikely conclusion began coalescing and came to the forefront. After a few moments, I looked at everyone seated at the table, hoping now my movie and television detective education wasn't coloring my thinking.

I took a deep breath and finally said, "It sounds to me like the only conclusion that can be drawn from this guy's text is that Cleopatra, Queen of all Egypt and last of the Ptolemaic rulers... faked her own death."

Tess and Doc sat there with mouths agape and eyes wide. O'Reilly was sitting there smiling.

O'Reilly said, "I'm glad you said that, Colt; I'm no expert on ancient Egypt or anything, but based on the translation, I came to the same conclusion, implausible as it may seem."

"But why?" Doc asked. "To what end?"

"She didn't want to be paraded around in public as the defeated ruler of Egypt and a captive of the Roman Empire by Octavian, so she found a way out," Tess said almost breathlessly.

"Or was provided a way out," I added.

"What do you mean?" Tess asked.

"Faking one's own death is not a plan you come up with overnight, and pulling it off successfully so that it withstands extreme scrutiny and the test of time would be beyond difficult. This obviously was planned very well and in advance of her defeat by the Romans."

"So, you're intimating that she knew of her impending defeat in advance, Colt, or at least had a contingency plan?" Doc asked.

"I really don't know," I replied, "but I think it's something we have to consider, and I say that only in light of her visit by an emissary of Ra."

"What's that supposed to mean?" Tess asked.

"Who was this emissary, where did he (or she) come from, and why the visit?" I asked.

"It could have been another believer or priest of Aten," Doc added.

"It could have been, or it could have been something much different," I said, smiling slightly.

Doc paused, then said, "You don't think he could have been...?" He didn't finish his sentence as his eyes narrowed and his brow furrowed.

Still smiling, I said, "Why not? She said they had outposts around the world for tens of thousands of years and interacted covertly with emerging civilizations." The "she" I was referring to was, of course, "Jeannie," the technically advanced being we had come in contact with during our search for the Metal Library in Ecuador. "Remember—in the text, the priest said the emissary appeared to her out of nowhere at night in a mist. Now, what does that sound like to you?"

Doc's eyes widened as it dawned on him, "A portal device."

I just sat there, smiled approvingly, and said, "I believe so."

CHAPTER TWENTY

Silence filled the room as we all tried to process the possibility of this fantastic idea, each in their own way. Finally, Tess, staring at me, spoke, "I think we need to talk this through before we jump back into the translation of the text. If what you're saying, Colt, in any way resembles what may have taken place in 30 BC, we need to look at all our information in a new light."

And so it began, a marathon meeting of facts, supposition, and guesswork. No idea was too radical to put forth. Some could be easily discounted; others demanded further consideration and investigation. After three hours of discussion, we arrived at two possibilities: one, this was a syntax error on the part of whoever carved the text, or two, Cleo did fake her own death with the help of this priest and others. This begged the question, why and where did she go?

Tess and Doc went back to translating the text in light of these new revelations, and O'Reilly and I left them to their task. As we walked down the hall, I said, "I could use a cold beer right about now."

She laughed and said, "I'll drive."

Ten minutes later, we were sitting in a little joint on the river just south of Titusville with two cold mugs of beer on the table and a beautiful view of the Indian River in front of us. After a few sips and quiet contemplation, O'Reilly said, "I'm glad you came to the same conclusion

I did about the text. I hesitated at first, worried it was a crazy thought."

I chuckled and said, "So did I, but the text pointed to that conclusion. All the detective movies I've seen say the solution to the mystery or crime is more than likely right in front of you."

She laughed out loud, "So, you used detective movies to arrive at your conclusion, and I used my years of analytical experience to arrive at the same place. Guess that speaks highly of the movies you've watched, or... we're both wrong."

I took another sip and thoughtfully said, "I don't think we're wrong. Now, all we have to do is figure out why and where the hell Cleo went."

"I stick by my idea that she didn't want to be seen as a defeated ruler and a trophy for the Romans. So that might cover the why, but your idea of assistance she may have received from one of the outposts of Jeannie's people certainly seems like a possibility. Everything we saw and learned in our earlier encounter with her definitely opens the door to that possibility. I think pulling off a disappearing act like that would take some kind of 'unusual' intervention."

We ordered a second beer and decided to have lunch. I ordered us both the "house specialty," the Wineburger. The rustic appearance, some might call it rundown, of this place belied its excellent food. We sat silently, staring across the river with the Vehicle Assembly building at the Kennedy Space Center barely visible in the distance. Our food arrived, and we began enjoying this local culinary delight. After a few minutes, O'Reilly spoke, "I think the answer to our 'where' question may be hidden in the meeting with the emissary."

"I agree, but there is still more that we don't know," I said, thoughtfully staring out over the river.

We finished our lunch and headed back to the office, where we found Tess and Doc still at it. On the big monitor was a photograph of the inside of a burial chamber. Their discussion was animated and punctuated by pointing at various sections of the pictures. Tess looked up as we entered the room and said, "Glad you guys are back; we've got a couple of things we need your opinion on." We took our seats at the table, and she began.

"We first went back to the priest's reference to Cleo's meeting with the emissary of Ra. His statement does mention a light and the emissary appearing in what he calls a heavenly or divine mist. That seems to support your portal idea."

"And you missed that the first time you translated the text?" I asked.

"Well, we didn't miss it exactly, more like glossed over it, not recognizing the importance of his description at the time," Tess said. "Then there's a strange section that seems to say Khepri will lead to or point the way to or provide answers."

"Answers to what, and who is Khepri?" I asked.

"As to the answers, I have no idea, but Khepri was a solar deity, depicted as a scarab, whose task was to move the sun from sunrise to sunset across the sky like the dung beetle rolls dung across the ground."

"So, there's another solar reference," O'Reilly said.

"Yes," Tess agreed as she pointed to the monitor and said, "This is a photo of the inside of the priest's tomb. Look closely at the paintings on the wall. There are more than a few sun symbols and direct depictions of Ra."

"Is that unusual?" I asked.

"Yes, it kinda is, and their location or placement within the wall murals also seems a little strange. Unfortunately, the tomb photos don't give me the detail I need."

I leaned back in my chair, smiling, and said, "This sounds like a trip back to Egypt might be in our future."

Tess laughed and said, "If we want to solve this mystery and get answers to our questions, then you are absolutely correct."

"Well, then, it's time to get the rest of the team together and bring them up to speed on what we have found so far and tell them to grab their go bags."

Tess smiled broadly and asked, "How soon can we leave?"

"We can get everybody briefed this afternoon, and I'll have them get the jet ready, so how's tomorrow morning?"

"Fantastic," she said. "I'll make some calls and get the permissions we need to visit the site. There shouldn't be any problems there."

"Then, that's the plan. Doc, will you contact the others and get them here as soon as possible?"

"You bet, Colt, I'm on it," he said as he got up from the table.

I turned to O'Reilly, and before I could say anything, she said, "I'll get with the ground crew and have them prep the jet."

"Thanks; see you later this afternoon." She nodded in assent and followed Doc out of the conference room.

Tess smiled broadly as I said, "Kind of nice having a boyfriend with a private jet at his disposal." She laughed loudly. "What's so funny?" I asked.

"You are," she said as she got up from her chair and came over, leaned down, and kissed me firmly on the lips. Standing there, eyes sparkling, she said, "Colt, you passed boyfriend status a long, long time ago," as she headed for the door. I was the one now smiling broadly. She turned as she got to the door and said, "But don't let that go to your head, you big palooka," and left the room.

Still smiling, I shook my head and thought, she certainly has a way with words and went about my preparations for tomorrow's departure.

The afternoon meeting went fine, and the team was raring to go. Dimitri and Reggie asked if we really needed them on this trip. After some consideration, I said, "Well, we don't need anything blown up or anybody shot, so I guess we can manage without you."

They laughed, and Dimitri said, "But remember, we're only a phone call away if things change."

"I certainly will," I replied.

We covered most of the material and told them about our working theory. They were as incredulous as we were when we first came up with it, but I told them we would answer all their questions on the flight and sent them on their way to prep.

Tony would also be staying here, manning our computer/communication center. Once again, he would be our global eyes and ears while we were in Egypt.

We met at the hangar at eight a.m. the next morning and boarded the jet. As we were taking off, I leaned back in my seat. Some words from *Alice in Wonderland* popped into my head as I thought this mystery just keeps getting "curiouser and curiouser."

CHAPTER TWENTY-ONE

I had no idea how prophetic those words were.
Joe had been somewhat skeptical of our theory about Cleo in our initial meeting, so he asked us to review how we arrived at it one more time on our flight. Tess, Doc, and I started with the beginning of the research. We recounted finding anomalies in the text and strange references to Khepri, usually depicted as a scarab in burial mural paintings and carvings.

"So, why is that unusual?" Joe asked.

"Well, not so much unusual, but what the text seems to say about him is what's puzzling. That's why I want to take a closer look at the interior of the priest's tomb. I'm hoping there will be answers there, and if not answers, maybe more clues that will help us understand what this is all about," Tess replied.

"Got it," Joe said, "so this is all hypothetical stuff for now?"

"Sort of, but very intriguing stuff," Tess answered with a furrowed brow.

Thirteen hours later, we landed in Cairo.

Tess had done an excellent job of "greasing the wheels" for our visit to the tomb with the museum and authorities, not saying anything about our theory but stating she needed more information for her research, which was true. Arriving at the site, we were greeted by the archaeologist in charge, an old friend of Tess's, Dr. Bahadur Shehata. He was delighted to see her but also curious about her interest in the tomb after all these years. He said he was afraid she had abandoned the project after the statues were stolen. Tess assured him that was not the case; she just needed a break after the devastating theft. She asked him if there had been any progress in locating them, and he said no.

He stated, "There were rumors they were on the black market, but no solid evidence." Tess shook her head dejectedly and said that was too bad. His response confirmed our anonymity and no public knowledge of our raid on the yacht, its reason, and its outcome. Tess told him she felt that if she closely inspected the tomb, it might give her some clues as to her theory of a possible Cleopatra connection with the priest.

He was pleased with her renewed interest and hoped she could gain the information she needed from her inspection, adding that he would gladly do anything he could to accommodate her. She thanked him and assured him that her investigation would not hinder his ongoing efforts at the site.

Smiling, he led us into the tomb. All the burial artifacts had been removed, and special lights had been set up to help with the documentation of the interior murals.

The interior was more spacious than I had expected—probably fifteen feet wide by thirty feet long with seven-foot ceilings. The entire chamber was covered in painted murals, even the ceiling. The paintings were in excellent condition, and the colors were still vivid. I was blown away by the attention to detail in the artistic renderings. I had seen pictures of burial chambers before, but this was my first actual visit, and it was impressive.

Doc, O'Reilly, and Joe were silent as they surveyed the interior, and then Doc almost reverently said, "This is amazing."

Joe and O'Reilly quietly agreed.

"So, where do we start?" I asked.

"I want to do a quick scan of the whole room and see if anything jumps out at me; then we'll take it wall by wall and see if we can find any clues that might help us," Tess replied.

"Then, we'll stay out of your way and let you and Doc do your thing. We'll shoot video and take digital photos of the interior, so we have a permanent record."

"Perfect," she said as she and Doc began their search.

Even though fresh air was being blown into the chamber by a ventilating system, the heat was oppressive, and time seemed to pass slowly. After an hour and a half, we needed a break and retreated to the slightly cooler environment outside. Taking shelter from the sun under a large tarp set up for Dr. Shehata's team, we were able to cool off a bit and discuss what Tess and Doc had ascertained from their first look at the tomb.

They had both been taking notes as they examined the murals. Referring to them now, Tess said, "As I noticed in the initial photos I saw, several sun symbols were interspersed throughout the paintings. Some seemed out of place. What do you think, Doc?" she asked.

"Some did indeed, not as if they were adding anything to the narrative being created, but as if they were part of a recurring motif—almost like they were sending a subtle message through their presence."

Tess was smiling broadly now and asked Joe for the digital camera. She began scrolling through the pictures and pointing out what they were discussing. With Tess's help, I began to understand her statement.

"And that means…?" I asked.

"I believe the priest is sending a secret message confirming his following of or belief in Akhenaten's one god, the Aten deity," Tess said.

"Then that would definitely put him in cahoots with Cleo and could support your theory of his involvement in her so-called suicide/death," Joe said.

"I think it does," Tess replied.

"I concur," Doc added.

"The other thing I noticed was the large depiction of Khepri on one wall. He is usually depicted vertically, but in this instance, he is horizontal."

"Do you think that is significant?" O'Reilly asked.

"I don't know," Tess replied as she looked at the photo of that wall on the digital camera screen. "His head is pointing toward the rest of the murals on that wall. Behind him, there are very few images," she said, staring at the photo. After a few minutes, she leaned toward Doc, handing him the camera and saying, "Doc, there are sun symbols on either side of the text on the wall behind Khepri. Can you make out what it says?"

"Something about the royal path or road, I think,"

Doc responded.

"Or the royal way," Tess added.

"Could be," Doc said, "but there's nothing else. It doesn't seem to make sense."

"Remember, the text on that one statue said Khepri would lead or show the way, but never said to what?" Tess queried.

We all sat there in quiet contemplation, bewildered by these strange, disjointed statements as the Egyptian sun beat down on our overhead covering and the hot wind stirred up small dust clouds around the tomb entrance in the distance. The level of frustration was almost palpable as the heat added an uncomfortable distraction to our thinking.

I finally asked Tess for the camera and looked at the picture causing this increased confusion. I zoomed in on the prominent symbol depicting Khepri and stared at it, almost looking out of place due to its size and location. A thought began forming as I mentally ran through everything Tess and Doc had said about him and his context in the Egyptian pantheon of deities.

I looked at Tess and said, "So, Khepri, this scarab, is a solar deity and rolls the sun across the sky from sunrise to sunset, just as the dung beetle rolls its little ball of dung across the sand."

Tess looked at me and said, "Yes."

"The dung beetle uses its hind legs, as I recall, rolling his little ball in the direction he wants to go, correct?"

Tess again replied, "Yes."

I was getting a little excited as I said, "So, his

backside, as he is rolling the ball, is always pointed in the direction he wants to go, in essence guiding him."

Tess's eyes widened as she blurted out, "So, in reality, his butt is pointing forward."

I smiled broadly now and continued, "What did you say you thought the translation of hieroglyphs between the two sun symbols behind Khepri said?"

Tess jumped to her feet and almost shouted, "We've got to get back in the tomb now."

By then, the flow of logic I had been following had dawned on everyone as we all sprang to our feet and headed to the tomb entrance. Approaching the entrance, I heard Joe saying in disbelief, "I can't believe a bug's ass is going to lead us to treasure…."

I laughed and again thought, "curiouser and curiouser."

CHAPTER TWENTY-TWO

Inside, we all gathered in front of the scarab painting. Standing there, Tess began inspecting the wall next to it—the one with the text on it. The large scarab painting was horizontal on the wall, with the text appearing behind it. Looking at the text, Tess said, "I don't get it; there's nothing here."

I walked to the wall, tapped on it with my knuckle, and then did the same on the scarab painting. I heard no discernable difference. I turned to Joe and nodded. "Got it," he said as he pulled one of our presents from Jeannie, that we affectionately called our drilling device, out of his backpack.

The three Egyptian scholars were at the other end of the tomb, involved in a discussion and paying us no attention. Joe set his pack down and activated the device. Pointing it at the scarab painting, he looked at the screen and said, "Nothing, Colt." He then moved to the wall section with the hieroglyphs on it. "Whoa," he said, quietly turning to me and smiling. "Bingo, there's a huge void behind that wall. Looks to be about ten feet high, twelve feet wide, and twenty feet long."

He made an adjustment to the device and said, still smiling, "There's another wall at the end of the passage and a very large room beyond it."

Tess turned to me, eyes wide, and said, "We have to get in there."

Doc was running his hand over the wall with the text on it and quietly said, "The royal path."

We still had not drawn any attention to ourselves from the other researchers, so I quietly said, "We need to get back outside and talk." Joe put the device in his pack, and we left the chamber. Outside, we returned to the shaded work area, still uninhabited, and sat down.

"I guess we're all thinking the same thing," I said.

"If you mean that passage may lead to Cleo's tomb, then, yeah," O'Reilly said. "The big problem is, how will we get to it?"

I turned to Tess and asked, "Do you think your buddy would allow us to take down that wall?"

"Not without good reason," she replied. "We would have to tell him we found something behind it, and I can assure you the higher-ups would take weeks to approve the decision to take it down. Plus, we would have to reveal how we knew something was behind it."

"Yeah, that would be a problem; we can't let word get out about our 'nifty device.' It would raise too many questions."

"Could you say it was a plausible hypothesis based on your research?" Doc asked Tess.

She paused before answering, "I could, but it might be a hard sell, and even if they bought it, it would still take time for it to get approved. Same problem."

"And I don't suppose your friend Bahadur would give you permission or look the other way while we took it down?" I asked.

"No chance," Tess replied. "He is a strictly by-the-book kind of guy. He's a great archaeologist but a stickler about rules and permissions when it comes to dig sites."

"What other legal options do we have?" O'Reilly asked.

No one spoke for a few minutes, then Tess said, "I can't think of any."

"Well then," I said, "I guess that only leaves us with one option: we get in there 'our' way."

Joe perked up. "Can you portal in there?" he asked.

"I thought about that, but I'm afraid there are too many variables to contend with, like air and air quality inside, plus I have no good visualization of what it looks like in there. As you recall, Jeannie was adamant about that being one of the main criteria for safe portal travel—be sure you knew exactly where you were going."

"Other than blowing a hole in it, what's left?" Doc asked.

I looked at Joe and asked, "How thick was that wall?"

"About ten to twelve inches. Only the thickness of the bricks and the stucco covering on our side, which is less than an inch thick."

I sat there thinking and finally said, "Can you see the individual blocks that make up the wall?"

"Sure, I just have to scale back the penetration levels," Joe answered.

"So, you can see the mortar lines?"

"Yep, easily."

Tess looked at me with a furrowed brow, "What are you thinking, Colt?"

I didn't answer but continued with Joe, "If you narrowed the beam of the device, could you follow the mortar lines and remove just a tiny bit of the mortar?"

"Yeah, I believe that I could. It would take a little finesse, but it's doable."

"Could you make it look like a crack on our side?"

"Not sure I could do that, but if I removed enough of the mortar and spaced my entry points about an inch or an inch and a half apart, you could probably hit the block with a blunt object and cause a crack to occur in the plaster on our side following the mortar seam."

I looked at Tess, "If a crack were to occur in the wall, do you think you could convince your buddy that there was something behind it worth looking into?" I asked.

"Maybe," she replied, "but I'm still afraid he would want permission to physically excavate it to see what's there."

I returned to Joe, "How long would it take to create a significant crack?" I asked.

"How significant?" he asked.

"One from top to bottom diagonally across the opening."

After a few seconds' pause, he said, "Uninterrupted, I could probably get it done in an hour or so if you want to be real precise."

"I want to be precise," I answered, "so I think we need to do a small-scale test to see if my idea will work."

Joe and I re-entered the tomb chamber, still just passingly noticed by the two remaining workers inside.

We moved to the wall, and I took out the digital camera and began photographing it as Joe went about his covert task. After ten minutes, he called me to his side. I could easily see the stones making up the wall on the screen. On three of them, there was a red line following the mortar seam.

"The line indicates the seam I have been weakening. Do you need more?" he asked.

I pointed to one stone and said, "Go around this whole stone." He nodded and went to work. The stone I had picked was waist-high and in the middle of the wall.

Two minutes later, he quietly said, "Done." I walked to the wall, which showed no damage, and asked him to guide me to the stone. Once I had my hand on the middle of it, I balled my hand into a fist and hit the stone, watching to make sure my actions weren't noticed. They weren't. I looked at the plaster; there were no cracks, but my hand sure did hurt. I looked at Joe, who only smiled and shrugged.

I tried once again, this time with a little more force and the side of my fist. When I looked at the wall, I was rewarded with a slight crack in the plaster—almost unnoticeable. I looked at Joe and quietly said, "Okay, man, it's all you." He nodded and continued his work as I rubbed my throbbing hand. I continued with the digital camera, now and then consulting with my colleague over the camera screen while looking at his progress on the device's screen. An hour and a half later, Joe said he was done.

The two Egyptian workers had left, so we were alone. I went to the wall and began hitting it with the side of my fist, watching a crack appear with each blow in the plaster, just as I had hoped. Within a few minutes, the barely visible crack ran diagonally from the top to the bottom. "That's it," I said to Joe. "That's exactly what I wanted. Let's get out of here." It was hot, and we were sweating profusely. We were in definite need of hydration by the time we returned to the crew awaiting our return.

Tess got to her feet and said, "Well?"

I took a big hit off the offered water bottle and said, "The wall now has a serious crack in it." The afternoon sun was setting, its long shadows being cast over the entrance to the tomb. "I do believe Ra is telling us our work here is done for the day," I quipped. "Let's get back to our campsite, get something to eat, and I'll fill you in on the plan for tomorrow."

My plan was greeted with a certain amount of skepticism, but not really seeing any other possibility that could provide immediate results, the team agreed. The next morning came, and it was game time. Everyone headed for the tomb except me. I was the lynchpin for the plan's success or failure. A few moments later, one of the workers came running out of the tomb in a panic, calling loudly for Dr. Shehata as I sat waiting for my signal.

Moments later, the worker and Shehata were running into the tomb. I took a few deep breaths and waited. Within minutes, Joe was at the mouth of the tomb and then disappeared back inside; that was my signal. I hurried to the tomb entrance, took another deep breath, and ran in. The team had strategically placed themselves in front of the wall. Shehata was standing with Tess, examining the crack she was pointing out.

I ran up to the group, shouting, "What's going on?" in my best excited voice, and as everyone turned toward me, I tripped, launching my six-foot-five, two-hundred-and-ninety-five-pound frame forward, hitting the wall with my left shoulder at the predetermined spot. I hit it with enough force to make an NFL linebacker proud, and it hurt like hell as I burst through the wall and blocks tumbled around me.

CHAPTER TWENTY-THREE

I don't remember what happened next as one of the falling blocks caught me upside the head, and the lights went out. I came to, looking up into Tess's concerned face as she placed a cold, wet rag on my head. Dr. Shehata was also there, looking concerned and shouting orders to the workers who had gathered. As my head cleared, I became aware of the bedlam that had taken over the tomb. Remembering my part, I groggily asked what had happened. Tess began explaining that I had fallen against the wall, which collapsed, exposing a passage behind it. One of the blocks from the wall had hit me on the head, and I had been unconscious for five minutes.

Everyone was asking if I was all right as I wiped blood from my face, and I assured them I was fine except for the lump forming on my head. However, the head wound bled profusely, covering my face with blood and making things look much worse than they were. I was helped to my feet, and Doc, Joe, and O'Reilly helped me exit the tomb. Tess was with us, continuing to wipe my face. "Are you sure you're all right?" she asked. I could hear the concern in her voice.

"I'm fine," I said, "honestly, go back inside and get Shehata to buy into exploring the new chamber."

"If you're sure you're okay," she said as she wiped my face once more. "That was a dumb plan, Burnett."

Giving her my best sheepish smile, I said, "But it got

the job done."

She tossed the bloodied rag at me and turned back to the tomb, saying as she moved away, "You scared the hell out of me, you big dummy; I hope your head hurts." It did, but it would pass; now, for the new room....

Tess and Shehata became engrossed in the discovery of the passage. Joe said, "Well, Colt, you really sold that one, especially with that unconscious thing."

My head was still spinning a bit as I relied on Joe and Doc to steady me as we got to the shaded area. I sat down, and Doc went to our campsite for his medical kit. I looked at Joe and said, "Believe me; that knock on the head was not part of the plan, and couldn't you have made that wall a little easier to knock down? My shoulder is killing me."

Joe laughed, "I did, Colt. If I hadn't, I think you would have just bounced off."

O'Reilly was sitting there, shaking her head as she said, "You guys are nuts—completely and totally nuts."

"You just now figuring that out?" I retorted, laughing a bit even though I felt like I had been run over by a freight train.

Joe laughed, "We're not crazy, but the crazies leave us alone."

Doc arrived and said, "Okay, everybody, give me some room. I need to see if this numbskull has given himself a concussion." Fifteen minutes later, my head checked, the bleeding staunched with some butterfly sutures, and my shoulder examined, Doc gave me a clean bill of health, more or less. I wanted to get back in the tomb, but he insisted I take it easy for at least an hour before trying to walk around. He said I hadn't broken anything, but I bruised the hell out of my shoulder and would suffer with that and a sore head for a few days.

Ten minutes later, Tess exited the tomb. As she sat beside me and moved the rag on my head to inspect the damage, she grimaced and said, "You bonehead, your idiot plan scared the hell out of me."

I smiled at her, "As I said earlier, it worked pretty well."

She punched my shoulder, the good one, and said, "Don't ever do anything like that again. I was sure your brains were going to be splattered all over the tomb when I saw that block hit your head and the blood."

Still smiling, I sarcastically replied, "That would presuppose I had any."

"Sometimes I wonder about you, Dr. Burnett, and if that might be the case," she said, smiling.

"Well, the jury's still out on that one, but enough of the small talk; tell me that all my pain wasn't for naught."

"Oh, no," she replied. "Shehata is having the workers remove the debris. I only got a quick look in the passage but saw another door at the end blocked by a single piece of stone and two large wheels or discs that had been rolled in front of it. I'm guessing they were put in place to hold the door closed."

"That sounds pretty impressive," I said. "Anything else?"

"The walls are covered with murals, but I didn't get a good look at them. There was so much dust, and the air in there was over two thousand years old. I wasn't about to chance breathing it. They were running the air system into it as I was leaving."

"Well, mask up before you go back in, and Joe, go with her and take the 'Sniffer' with you and check out the air."

"Roger that, Colt."

The "Sniffer" was an air analyzing device that not only tested air quality for dangerous gases but also identified any microbial or particulate matter in the air. They headed back to the tomb, and Doc handed me a cold bottle of water. "Do you think it's safe in there?" I asked him.

"I think so. We all had our masks ready when you broke through the wall, so I don't think we were exposed to any nastiness. At least, I hope not," Doc replied, not smiling.

"Well, you just fill a fellow with a load of confidence, Doc," I replied.

"No, Colt, I'm sure it's fine; we masked up right away, so I'm sure we're all okay, but do let me know if you start coughing up blood," he said as he broke out laughing. "Just kidding, Colt, just kidding," he dodged before I could get to him.

"Doc, sometimes your sense of humor and timing is worse than Dimitri's."

Still laughing, he walked away and sat down next to O'Reilly, who was just shaking her head as she said, "Crazy, you're all bat-shit crazy."

"Maybe so," I answered, "but we're never boring!"

O'Reilly, shaking her head in disbelief but smiling,

got up and headed back to the tomb, mumbling, "Crazy, just plain crazy."

She left the rest of us laughing uncontrollably. I got the go-ahead from Doc a short time later and went back inside the chamber to find that things had settled down, and a serious inspection of the new passage was underway. The ventilation system had been shifted; one vent tube evacuated air from the passage area while another introduced fresh air from outside. Masks were no longer necessary, and lights had been set up, illuminating the whole area.

The wall murals gleamed in their pristine condition; the colors and detail were breathtaking. I saw Tess at the end of the passage examining the two large wheel-type discs that had been rolled from the side walls to cover most of the huge cut stone (slab) that filled the end of the passageway. These discs were around eight feet or more in diameter. They had been rolled out of the side walls until their edges touched, effectively blocking most of the stone slab behind them.

Joe and Doc had followed me in and were staring at the scene before us. Joe finally said, "That's some serious engineering. My guess would be they were meant to keep that slab behind them in place."

"But how?" Doc asked. "And why?"

We had walked to the end of the passage and joined Tess and Dr. Shehata in examining them closer. Dr. Shehata saw me and immediately and, in a concerned voice, said, "Dr. Burnett, are you all right?"

"Yes, yes, I'm fine, but it looks like I made a mess of things," I said, adding a level of concern to my voice that I didn't really feel.

He was very animated, saying, "Yes, yes, but no, you didn't. If you hadn't fallen against the wall as you did, we might not have discovered this passage for months, if ever. But look at these marvelous wall paintings and amazing stonework," he said, pointing at the walls and the stone wheels. He was beside himself with excitement. "I'm sorry you were injured, but a very fortuitist accident it was," he continued.

I looked around and then, in my most professional voice, said to him, "It would seem that way."

Tess looked at me with just a hint of a smile and said, "Fortuitous, indeed."

I winked and smiled back as I said, "I guess the pain was worth it," and moved closer to examine the two large wheels or discs. As I examined them, I had to agree with Joe; this was some engineering. Imagine a one-inch square drawn on a piece of paper, then take two quarters and place them side by side on the square, their edges touching. Part of the square would still be visible, but the quarters would block most of it. That's what we were looking at here on a much larger scale.

Joe was examining the wall the wheel had been rolled out of, exposing only about two-thirds of its size. The rest was still in the cavity that had been carved out for it. "This is very cool," he said. "This is one hell of a locking device."

"No kidding," I replied, "but how did they move these things?"

Joe continued his inspection, focusing on its smooth stucco covering. He ran his hands over it from its center to its edge, then positioned himself to look across its flat surface. Minutes later, he pulled out his six-inch Gerber Gator knife and began tapping the stucco with its butt, about a foot from the wheel's outer edge, listening intently at every blow. After some fifteen strikes, he turned the point of the blade and began chipping away at the stucco.

Dr. Shehata saw what was happening and began shouting for him to stop. He didn't, and within a couple of minutes, had chipped away enough stucco to reveal a circular hole about six inches in diameter and four-to-six inches deep. He moved above that hole about three feet and began chipping again, revealing a similar hole. Smiling, he turned to look at me and said, "It had handles."

CHAPTER TWENTY-FOUR

Standing next to me, watching the desecration that Joe was performing, Dr. Shehata had his mouth agape. Joe returned his knife to its sheath and said, "I think you will find similar holes on the other wheel and that they are spaced equally around their circumference. I believe a few men with three or four-foot-long round timbers could easily roll these guys in and out of their niches without much effort."

Still looking stunned, one of the Egyptian archaeologists looked at Joe and then me and said, "How did..." he never finished his sentence.

"Basic engineering," Joe replied, "just basic engineering."

An hour later, workers had uncovered most of the holes around the circumference face of both wheels. Some holes were still inaccessible as they were on sections of the wheels still inside the carved-out niches in the wall. Round timbers were brought in, and it was time to test Joe's theory. Placing two poles in the wheel on the left, one low and one above it, two men grasped the lower one and two men the upper. Four more men were standing by with two more poles.

Dr. Shehata stood next to Tess and me as Joe gave the order for the men to lift. Amazingly, the wheel began slowly rotating back into its nesting place in the wall. As it rolled and the upper pole became ineffective, it was removed; another pole was inserted in a lower hole, and two more men began lifting. It became almost a dance as the two men reaching their maximum lifting point would remove their poles, step back, and let the others continue lifting and rolling it inward, waiting until another hole came around, and the men continued the process.

As the wheel was slowly rotated, the part of the wheel that had not been visible came into view, and the holes had not been filled with stucco. The poles were inserted, and the rolling continued until only a tiny section of the wheel was visible. The workers placed a stone at the wheel's base as a chock that would stop it if it tried to roll back out.

The process was slow, but it worked. As the wheel uncovered the center of the large worked stone filling, what we knew was the opening or doorway into the next chamber became visible, and I heard Tess gasp. She and Shehata hurried forward with their flashlights, shining them on new markings carved into the stone.

"We have to move the other stone," Tess said very excitedly. I moved to where she and Shehata stood, looking at what was etched in the stone.

"What is it?" I asked.

Tess looked at me, smiling broadly, eyes wide, and said, almost as if she were out of breath, "I believe It's Cleopatra's cartouche."

Doc stepped up, added his light to the carving, and seconds later said, "I think you're right, Tess." The three of them stood there staring, not saying a word. With Joe supervising, the workers had begun moving the second wheel. As they did, the entire carving came into view.

Dr. Shehata was the first to speak. "It is her cartouche," he said as he ran his fingers over the carving, unmarred by time, looking like the stone mason had just finished it.

Below it were more hieroglyphs, obviously a text of some sort. The only things I recognized were the Ra sun symbols appearing at the beginning and end of the text. Dr. Shehata had dropped to one knee and examined it with his flashlight.

"What does it say?" I asked.

"It is saying something about where her celestial or heavenly journey begins. Finding eternal life in the house of Ra." After a pause, he looked at us and said, "That doesn't make sense; it sounds like Cleopatra was a follower of the Aten. The belief in the one sun god that Akhenaten had espoused under his reign. But that belief was outlawed immediately after his death, over a thousand years before her reign."

Tess looked at me as she said, "That is strange," with a slight smile on her face.

"I must contact Cairo immediately and inform them of our discovery of her tomb," Shehata excitedly said as he stood up.

With a worried look replacing the smile, Tess said, "I don't think that would be a good idea, Bahadur."

"Why on earth not?" he responded.

"If you made that kind of announcement without further confirmation, and you were wrong, it could be disastrous for the museum's reputation and your professional career."

He paused, eyes widening a bit as he considered what his friend and colleague had said. After a few seconds, he said, "Yes, yes, you could be right. I hadn't considered that. There was another pause, and then he continued, "But where would we find that confirmation?"

Tess smiled again as she raised her arm and pointed, "Behind that," indicating the massive stone.

The archeologist got an almost panicked look as he sputtered, "You mean, open it without the permission or approval of the ministry or museum...?"

"It's the only way," Tess answered. "If you notify them, and it is her tomb, you risk losing credit for the discovery of a lifetime. You know how the political machine can work in our world."

Now, the archaeologist was genuinely perplexed—mentally wrestling with required procedures, possible worldwide recognition, or ridicule. One of those damned if you do, damned if you don't situations. Of course, Tess's information gave us the inside track on this, but until we got behind the huge stone door blocking our way, we weren't much better off than he was.

The archaeologist finally turned to us with a look of resolution and said, "You are right; we must find a way to remove the stone."

With that comment, we all began examining the carved stone, looking for any indication of a way forward, except for Joe. He had pulled a stool in and was sitting in the middle of the passageway, staring at the stone from ten feet away and watching our search. After over an hour of scouring the surface and surrounding area, nothing had presented itself. Joe still sat staring and not saying a word.

The heat had become almost unbearable, even with the air circulation system working full blast. Our shirts sticking to our sweat-covered bodies indicated a need for hydration, and I suggested we call off the search for now. Everyone agreed, and we headed toward the exit, all of us, that is, except Joe, who stoically stayed seated, staring. I told him we needed to leave, and without looking up, he waved me off and said he would join us later. I knew there was no use in arguing with him and continued outside. The sun was setting as we exited the tomb, and the warm desert breeze actually felt cool against my face.

We went to the large canopy area and took seats around the table. Bottled water was passed out, and we gratefully began the rehydration process without speaking. In the desert twilight, our faces gave away our sense of frustration at the futility of our quest. Tess was the first to speak, "Well, anybody have any bright ideas?"

No one answered. Doc quipped, "We could use a revelation about now." Still, no comment.

The desert night had fallen. Dr. Shehata set a lit kerosene lamp in the center of the table. Its flickering flame and wisps of black smoke escaping heavenward only added to the somber feeling around the table. Its muted yellow glow lighting our faces added an ethereal sense to our gathering. I was deep in thought and chuckled out loud.

"What's so funny?" Doc asked.

"I was just thinking, here we are, an advanced civilization with numerous engineering capabilities and knowledge, and we can't figure out how to move a stone that was put in place over two thousand years ago by a supposedly primitive culture. Rather ironic," I said.

The voice from behind startled me. "Speak for yourself, Colt," Joe said, laughing. I hadn't heard him approach, and his countenance in no way resembled ours. He sat between Tess and me, picked up a bottled water, and took a long drink. His shirt was soaking wet; the rivulets of sweat running down his face created small canyons in the dust that had attached itself to him. Still smiling, he took another long drink of water and then said, "We'll open it tomorrow."

That stunning statement took us all by surprise. All eyes were on Joe as Tess said, "You found a way in?"

"Yep, I believe so," he replied.

I've known Joe for a long time. He doesn't exaggerate or jump to conclusions. They are just not part of his decision-making process. So, if he says he has found a way in, then he has.

Tess excitedly said, "Well, let's go open it."

Joe laughed and said, "While I appreciate your enthusiasm, we will need to wait until tomorrow."

"Why?" she immediately responded.

"It's going to take more manpower than we have around this table, I'm afraid. It's not going to be easy, but it will be doable with the right resources, and that's manpower." He leaned back in his chair and continued, "Besides, I'm sure you want to be rested and refreshed when we do open it." Now laughing, he added, "You know, ready for your photo op for *National G*." Tess leaned over and punched his shoulder.

Her excitement was replaced with a big grin as she said, "You're a brat, Joe Sebastiani, you know that? —A big brat and a tease."

Our mood had changed dramatically. Smiles had replaced furrowed brows, and a sense of excitement permeated the group.

"Yeah," Joe replied, "But I am extremely handsome, a great dancer, and a pretty good problem solver."

Tess punched him again and, laughing, said, "In your dreams, buddy, although, at times, your gray matter does impress."

Joe's big smile could be seen easily on his dirty face as he said, "Tomorrow, Dr. Worthington, tomorrow."

CHAPTER TWENTY-FIVE

We were standing at the entrance to the priest's tomb at daybreak, waiting for Dr. Shehata and his workers. I'm not sure how much sleep anyone got last night, as sleep was elusive for me. We didn't have to wait long. The archeologist showed up with ten men ready to work. They powered up the ventilation system and the generator for lights as we entered the tomb. When we reached the entrance to the passageway, the lights illuminating it came on.

Joe walked to the massive carved stone, once again looking at it closely as we stood back and let him work. After a complete inspection, Joe walked back to us and said to Dr. Shehata, "I need your men to thoroughly sweep this floor, starting at the stone and working this way. Every bit of sand and debris needs to be cleaned out. No question was asked as Shehata barked an order, and five of the men disappeared, returning minutes later with six brooms, shovels, and buckets. A few more commands from him and the cleaning brigade went to work.

We stepped out of the passageway as the dust got thick. Joe received questioning looks from us as we watched the cleaning from the priest's tomb. His only response was, "Just wait; you'll see." Fifteen minutes later, the crew had cleared half the passage. The floor was clean, with larger debris and piles of dust being removed by bucket. Joe stopped them and said to let the dust clear. The ventilation system did its job, and ten minutes later, the passage was clear of all the dust as Joe walked forward. Getting to the huge stone, he inspected it again, then looking down at the floor, he requested two men come back and do a little more sweeping.

Joe stood there like the head janitor, inspecting his employee's work. After resweeping the area, Joe nodded his approval and told us all to come back in. He stood with his back to the stone and addressed us as a guide would give a lecture to tourists.

"As I studied the doorway and the two wheels blocking or locking it in place, it dawned on me, blocking it as they did, there was only one way it could open." He asked for six of the men to come to the stone as he took one of the brooms and thoroughly swept the bottom edge of the stone again. He bunched the men up on the right side of the stone and gave the order to push against it. After a few seconds of the men being unsure of what he was asking, Shehata repeated the request in Arabic.

At once, the men threw their combined weight against the rock. For a few seconds, nothing happened. Joe motioned for more men to join them. It became a little crowded, but the additional force caused the stone to move inward an inch or two. Now, it was obvious to us how the stone/door opened; it rotated on a central pivot point. Joe moved to the opposite end of the block, now swinging past the wall a few inches, and examined the edge that had been revealed. Smiling, he motioned to the three men still standing with us to come to him. When they got there, he pointed at something on the edge of the stone that we could not see from our position. Immediately, the men moved in, found the handholds chiseled along its inner edge and began pulling. With the combined effort of pushing on one side and pulling on the other, the stone slowly pivoted on its center point, revealing the black chamber behind it.

Joe immediately removed the Sniffer from his vest pocket, motioned everyone away as he put a mask on, and slowly moved to the opening. A few seconds later, he abruptly turned and ran toward us, shouting, "Everybody out, now!" We didn't hesitate and bolted for the tomb's exit. Instinctively, I think we all held our breath as we ran. Once outside, we were all gasping for air. Joe was the last one out and stopped at the exhaust fan for the tomb. Sticking the Sniffer close, he turned and asked everyone to move away.

He herded the group of workers as well, periodically checking the device. Once we were about fifty feet away, he stopped, checked it once again, removed his mask, and said, "It's okay now; we're all clear."

"What the hell was that?" Doc asked.

"I got some pretty nasty readings a few seconds after we opened the door. I didn't take time to see exactly what was in there, but when this red light starts blinking and stays on," holding up the Sniffer for us to see, "you'd best get the hell out of wherever you are," Joe replied.

"Can you tell what it was picking up?" O'Reilly asked.

"I'll need to download the data into my laptop to get a detailed analysis, but whatever it was, it was bad. I'd advise everyone to stay outside until I find out what's in there," he answered, heading to our camp for his computer. Joe had created the Sniffer, which was much more than just an air quality detector. It took minute samples of the surrounding air and could detect dangerous gases and biohazardous elements. We've used it on numerous occasions, and it has saved our lives more than once.

Heeding Joe's warning, we headed for the shaded area to await his findings. The heat was already building, so this break, while unexpected, was welcomed by everyone. Dr. Shehata had gathered his workers, explained what was happening, and sent most of them on to other tasks before joining us. "It was fortuitous that your friend detected the foul air as he did," Shehata said, "and discovering how to open the door was amazing."

"That's Joe; besides being a first-class engineer and electronic wizard, his bag of tricks is quite full of other stuff. We rely on him a lot," I said. Half an hour later, Joe joined us, his laptop in hand. Sitting at the table, he said, "Well, that was very interesting."

"How so?" I asked.

"I was right; there was some nasty stuff in there, but not what I expected." He opened his laptop and popped up a data screen.

"Go on," Doc said.

"When I first stepped up to the entryway, the Sniffer started giving me the occasional blinking red light, and the meter climbed into the warning range, which I expected. But a few seconds later, it hit solid red, and the meter pegged—almost like nothing too serious was there at first, and then boom. That's when I gave the order to evacuate."

"What would cause that?" I asked.

"It was like the normal two-thousand-year-old stuff was present: ammonia, formaldehyde, and hydrogen sulfide, and then suddenly, something way more dangerous got released in the air."

"Really?" Tess said.

"Yes, and I'm inclined to believe that because when I analyzed the sample the Sniffer took, I found some weird stuff. The particulate matter included Belladonna, Castor bean, and Oleander."

"All plant derivatives!" Doc exclaimed.

"And none of those are indigenous to this area," Shehata added.

"Right, it was like someone had ground them up into a fine powder and created a way to release it into the chamber when the door was opened."

"It had to have been deliberate—a booby trap of sorts," I said. "However, it was set to give the intruder time to enter the chamber before releasing. That took some creative planning."

"And engineering," Joe added.

Doc let out a low whistle, "All of those plants have poisonous characteristics. They could induce a number of problems for a person's lungs, stomach, and heart, and depending on the dose, over time, result in death. But all mixed together in a powder form, I would say death would come quickly if breathed in through the nose or mouth."

"Then this was a trap to keep out looters," Tess said.

"Well, it was designed to keep someone out," Joe

added.

"Yes, someone wanted to protect what's in that room from any outside intrusion and came up with a creative way to do it," O'Reilly added.

"How long before we can enter?" I asked.

"That's the good news," Joe replied. "Since it was in dust form, we should be able to clear the air in an hour or so. But then someone needs to go inside with safety gear and use the forced air ventilation hose to basically blow everything off that's in there and let the venting system remove the residue. That could take some time."

Dr. Shehata, who had quietly been taking it all in, asked, "What kind of protective gear would be needed?"

"A closed hazmat suit with personal air supply would be ideal," Joe answered. "But I doubt that's available here, so one of the respirators I brought should do the trick if the time spent in the room is limited. The person should wear long sleeves, pants, gloves, and something over their head to reduce the risk of skin contact with any residual particulate matter. When the person exits, they will need to be decontaminated, washed off with water, and the clothes thoroughly cleaned or destroyed. The less time spent in there, the better, which means it could take a while to safely clean the chamber. I know this sounds extreme, but we can't take any chances with this stuff."

Without hesitation, Dr. Shehata said, "Then I suggest we get started."

CHAPTER TWENTY-SIX

Joe decided to be the one doing the cleaning. No one argued with him. He gave O'Reilly the Sniffer and a second respirator and told her to monitor the exhaust air at the outside vent. We passed out our Comms earpieces and told him to keep us posted on progress. We still hadn't gotten a look inside the new chamber, and Tess was chomping at the bit to see what was in there.

Joe wore a mini-LED headlamp and a small video camera attached to a harness on his chest. We set up a laptop to record the video just outside the entrance to the priest's tomb. Being outside kept us safe from anything he stirred up but allowed us to view the room and its contents as he cleaned it. He knew it would get hot as Hell in there, and he wouldn't be able to spend too much time inside, but he said he could probably get it cleaned quicker than anyone else.

We did a quick Comms check, and then Joe said, "I'm going in." The view on the computer went dark as he entered the chamber. As his light swept the room's interior, I think we all gasped at what lay before him. The glint of gold came from every direction he turned; it was breathtaking. Joe's voice echoed our feelings. "Holy cow, I don't think I've ever seen this much gold; it's everywhere."

None of us was prepared for what came next. The counterpoint to the opulence of the first view of the chamber became evident when Joe's light swept the floor and revealed it littered with human skeletal remains. We stood silently while Joe's light slowly danced across the floor as he carefully moved further into the room. His voice betrayed his emotional response as he quietly said, "There must be seven or eight in here."

I stopped Tess from asking questions, saying, "Let him work; we'll have time to investigate it when he's finished." Her excitement was palpable, but she nodded in agreement. As he progressed, walking through that macabre room of death, we got glimpses of some of the other objects inside—what looked like a golden throne, a gold-encrusted chariot, statues, and a beautiful sarcophagus on an ornate pedestal in the center of the room. Two more skeletal figures were seated on the floor and leaning against the pedestal, adding to the eeriness of the scene unfolding before our eyes. The richness of the tomb was breathtaking. I thought this could be right up there with Tut, but what about the human remains?

Joe kept a running dialog with O'Reilly as he cleaned, proceeding very carefully, not disturbing the remains lying on the floor and asking her to update him on the Sniffer readings every few minutes. It became evident from her readings that the further he went into the tomb, the more the readings dropped, seeming to indicate that the main concentration of poison was close to the entrance. Joe moved quickly through the tomb, and after two hours, O'Reilly told him that the levels were dropping significantly.

"Good," Joe answered, "because I've about had it in here; it's hotter than the hammered hinges of Hades. I'm going to place the hose on the floor in the middle of the room, and we'll let it keep exhausting for a while longer. I think that will be good enough. Coming out."

We had buckets of water ready to wash him off and a place for him to change out of his contaminated garments. Doc and I were masked up and dumped buckets of water on Joe once he exited, rinsing him off while everyone else kept their distance. It all went smoothly. Soon, we were gathered under the canopy, and Tess was grilling Joe on just what he had seen in the tomb as Shehata waited expectantly for his reply.

Joe explained as best he could, telling her his vision was limited by the small amount of light he had, but there was a lot of gold, the walls were covered with beautiful murals from floor to ceiling, and there were approximately eight skeletons. "I will have to say; I now think I know what it would be like walking through the bowels of Hell."

We reviewed the video that had been recorded, but, as he said, the light was feeble, and the room was quite large. Of course, Tess's excitement was off the charts as she wanted details he could not provide. She waited patiently as Joe had more water and cooled off.

Smiling, he said, "No worries, Tess, the one thing I can tell you for sure is that you won't be disappointed."

Our discussion turned to the technical aspects we had encountered. Joe said, "I'll go on record saying that the door was some piece of engineering. Moving it in there and getting the balance on the pivot point is very cool—and for it still to be functional after all these years, that's impressive."

"You figuring it out was no less impressive," I added.

"Well, the arc of the scratches I found on the stone

floor kinda gave it away. I was just concerned about whether or not we could move it. Luckily, as I said, it was good engineering."

Doc said, "Well, whoever concocted that poison dust knew what they were doing. Gathering the necessary plants didn't happen overnight, and figuring out the combination to make it quickly lethal was not the work of an amateur. And to know or guess it would retain its potency over time is very impressive."

"So, we are dealing with a highly sophisticated, well-planned trap," I said.

O'Reilly added, "This did take a level of organization and planning that surprises me and certainly took quite some time to put together. The mind behind it was nothing short of genius."

"And that's not even mentioning the reason why someone would go to these lengths. I'm getting the feeling that we don't have the whole picture yet," Tess said.

An hour and a half later, the readings were almost normal, and we all put on masks and latex gloves and, along with our two workers, entered the room. The workers moved the lights from the passageway into the tomb. As light flooded the room, it ignited a golden glow from the objects inside; it was breathtaking. We moved slowly, just in case there was residual dust on the floor, being careful not to disturb the remains lying there. Tess, Dr. Shehata, and Doc looked like kids in a candy store as they moved from object to object.

Not having any prior experience with Egyptian tombs, it was hard for me to compare the treasure we were looking at with anything other than pictures in *National G.* I went to the sarcophagus and began looking at it more closely. The amount of gold was impressive, and gems were embedded in its wooden surface. But when I looked at the burial offerings in the room and then at the sarcophagus, it didn't seem as opulent as I first thought.

Tess and Shehata joined me, and after a closer inspection, Tess said, "Colt, help me with the lid."

I was somewhat surprised, but when the archaeologist offered no objection, I said, "Okay, tell me what to do."

The lid had been sealed with some type of resin, which had deteriorated somewhat over time, and, although a little tricky, we managed to break it free. With Doc and Joe's help, we carefully removed it to reveal the mummy inside. The only problem was that there was no mummy. There was a body, but it was not what I expected. It was not wrapped in what I guess you could call mummy bandages, and certainly not what I remember from the movies. In fact, the desiccated body was only covered with what looked like a thin piece of linen.

Tess and Shehata gasped at the sight, expecting something other than what lay before us. The petite body, its bones still covered by dried, leathery-looking skin, lay there, arms folded, with empty eye sockets staring heavenward. Tess broke the silence. "This is not normal," she stated.

Shehata agreed, "No, this is not normal at all."

"What do you make of this?" Doc asked.

"I'm not sure," Tess replied, "But it doesn't look like any royal burial I've ever seen."

Other than the body, there was little else inside. I saw a few gold trinkets, but not what I would expect in a queen's sarcophagus. The lack of any covering or other valuable offerings inside was utterly incongruous with the amount of treasure in the room. Something was definitely wrong.

Dr. Shehata spent more time photographing and documenting the contents of the tomb. He indicated he would need this evidence to convince the museum he needed more help, including an artist, a conservator, a photographer, and additional workers to begin the professional documentation and cataloging of the tomb's contents.

CHAPTER TWENTY-SEVEN

We had been inside the tomb for over an hour, and Joe suggested we exit and take a break, even though the Sniffer readings were not at the dangerous level anymore—better safe than sorry. We agreed, and Dr. Shehata pulled the two workers who had entered the new tomb chamber aside and spoke with them very animatedly. When he finished, one left, and one took up a position outside the priest's tomb entrance as the rest of us convened at the shade canopy area.

After some much-needed water, sitting around the table, Dr. Shehata told us he had sworn his workers to secrecy concerning the discovery of the new tomb and the riches it held. "I am concerned that word might get out about it before we can set up proper security. I will have to return to Cairo to make those arrangements; until then, this must be kept secret. I have instructed my two men to take twelve-hour shifts guarding the entrance."

"No problem from us, Doctor," I said.

"Oh, I know," he replied. "Your people are not the issue. We still have those who would try and pillage the tomb before it can be adequately protected."

"That's a problem even with a government-sanctioned excavation?" I asked.

"Unfortunately, yes, it makes no difference to them. Word travels fast amongst the workers, and there are those who continuously keep their ears open for information of a discovery that might prove lucrative for them to plunder," the archaeologist replied. "Workers and even guards have been killed for much less than what we have discovered today. That is why I instructed my workers that they were not to speak of it."

"Can you trust them?" I asked.

He paused. "They have been with me for a while, so I hope so, but working out here, one can never be one hundred percent sure."

"How long will it take you to make the security arrangements?" Tess asked.

"Two, maybe three days," he answered. "And, Tess, I must thank you for your advice earlier. I do not believe this is Cleopatra's burial, and I was about to make a huge mistake until you warned me. Had I done that, it would have had devastating effects, as you warned."

"I'm glad it worked out," she replied. "With a potential discovery of such magnitude at stake, irrefutable evidence would be necessary before announcing it publicly."

"Yes, yes, I agree, but this discovery is still huge, even if it does present us with quite a mystery."

"True," she replied, laughing a bit. "But that's what archaeology is all about: discovery and mystery."

"Yes, it is," Shehata said, smiling. "What are your plans now?" he asked.

"With your permission, I would like to stay here and study the murals in the new tomb some more. I am still looking for any information or clues concerning Cleopatra."

"Of course," he replied, "I will make my arrangements, leave for Cairo tonight, and return in two days with the resources I need." With that, Shehata took his leave.

"So, Joe, what do you think? I'd like to get back in there and take a closer look at those murals," Tess said.

Joe got up, walked back to the tomb entrance, and checked the exhaust from the ventilation system with the Sniffer. He returned and said, "Looks good, Tess; the levels have dropped back into the safe zone, so we should be fine."

Standing up and looking at us, she said, "Shall we?"

Smiling at her, I stood and said, "Let's do it."

The worker stayed at his post outside, so we had the tomb's interior to ourselves. Tess went straight to the sarcophagus and began examining it again. As we gathered around, she asked, "What do you guys think?"

"Well, we're sure this is not Cleopatra," Doc said.

"No, it's not," she agreed.

"I think this is a key piece in the mystery. It seems someone wanted people to believe this was a royal burial, hence all the gold and exterior trappings. At least, up to a point, and I think the person there was a stand-in for Cleo."

Tess and Doc looked again at the occupant of the sarcophagus. Being very careful, Tess touched a thin silver bracelet on both of the body's crossed forearms. She moved her attention to the feet of the skeleton. Moving the cloth to examine them, she found silver ankle bracelets on both her feet.

"Doc, check those two bodies sitting down there leaning against the pedestal. Do they have silver bracelets on their forearms and ankles?"

He bent down, stood a minute later, and said, "Yes, they do."

Tess turned to me with a serious smile. "These were slaves, royal handmaidens—likely part of Cleo's entourage."

O'Reilly said, "What better way to keep your plot secret and provide some aspect of reality to anyone who would be an outside observer? Plus, ensuring the secret stays safe by killing the few participants involved in it."

"Or sentencing them to be buried alive with their surrogate queen," Joe added.

"These three seem to be the only female bodies in here. I'd postulate that the others were workers that were used to bring in objects, set the stage, and put the sarcophagus in place," Tess said with a very professorial look on her face. "Whoever executed this ploy would want to keep it a secret. We may have solved a major part of our mystery: how they orchestrated Cleo's fake death."

"We still don't know who orchestrated it or why," Doc said.

"I think we can safely say that the high priest was the person behind the whole thing or a major player in the ruse. As for the why, I'm not sure we'll ever be able to answer that," I said. We had been inside for over an hour and a half, so I suggested we exit and call it a day. The sun was going down as we left.

Leaving the tomb, Tess asked the worker on guard

duty if he needed anything, and he said no. He had built a small fire, was heating what looked like coffee in a tin cup, and had other foodstuffs wrapped in cloth sitting beside him.

We returned to our campsite, grabbed some food, and met back at the canopy cover as the sun set. We found Shehata's kerosene lamp and placed it in the middle of the table as we consumed our energy bars, Gatorade, and other goodies we had brought. As I was chewing on beef jerky, I said, "What puzzles me is how the priest knew to prepare for this event: the Roman conquest of the Egyptian army and Cleo's dethroning and capture. This whole scenario reeks of premeditation. I don't know how that could possibly be."

"It is puzzling," Tess added. "As we've said, the preparations for this charade took a lot of effort, planning, and time. Then to pull it off with such precision, I don't know, it's strange, very strange."

O'Reilly asked, "What do we know about this priest guy?"

Tess answered, "We know he had been a high priest approximately fifty years before Cleo became Pharoah, assuming that position at around the age of thirty."

"And Cleo ruled for about thirty years?" O'Reilly asked.

"Yes, that's right," Tess replied.

"So, we're saying this guy, the high priest, was able to pull off the con to beat all cons when he was over a hundred years old?"

Tess's look of surprise was stunning. She paused and then slowly said, "I hadn't done the math."

Doc said, "That seems totally impossible; who was this guy?"

Joe said, "Well, he either had one hell of a Pilates instructor, or he's not who we think he is."

"What do you mean?" Tess asked.

"Didn't you guys say this Ra emissary appeared to Cleo at night in Alexandria, stepping out of a heavenly mist that might have been the smoky mist a portal threshold creates when activated? This emissary could possibly have been from one of Jeannie's people's outposts. If that's the case, who's to say this priest guy wasn't one of them too? Maybe he had just been hanging around in Egypt, observing and influencing what was happening."

Tess, eyes wide, looked at me, then Doc, and back at me. I smiled.

"An interesting idea, Joe. At this point, I think it's a possibility," I said. "I don't think we have enough information to confirm it right now, but I don't think we can rule it out either."

"If he was, could he possibly have known what was going to happen before it happened?" Tess asked.

I answered, "With this race, our ancient ancestors, and their advanced technology, I mean thousands and thousands of years of advanced technology, it could be a possibility."

Tess put her hand to her head and mumbled, "This is starting to sound more and more like science fiction."

"Trust me, Tess," I said. "If you would have seen what we have over these past few years, that statement, I can assure you, wouldn't even cross your lips."

CHAPTER TWENTY-EIGHT

The next morning found us inside the newly discovered tomb, closely inspecting the intricate murals on the east wall. Breathtaking in their color and detail, they truly looked as if they had just been painted; they were vivid and in near-perfect condition. We had been greeted by the second worker, who had taken his guard position outside the priest's tomb entrance. He carried a large staff/walking stick and an ugly-looking curved knife in his belt as his only visible defense weapons. I hope he doesn't have to use either, I thought as we entered the tomb.

Once inside, I stood back as an observer while Doc and Tess began the verbal dissection of the murals' story. Joe and O'Reilly were involved in a closer inspection of the funerary offerings in the room. I found myself totally engaged in the story unfolding on the wall as Tess pointed out the various deities and their roles in the Egyptian afterlife journey. Osiris, the principal god of the afterlife, also known as the god of the dead, was depicted on the wall as a mummy wearing a crown and holding sceptors in both hands.

Pictured next to him was Isis, both his sister and wife, also the first to be shown to perform the mummification process on Osiris, who was killed and dismembered by his brother, Seth. Finding Osiris, she bound the pieces of his body back together with linens and then used her magic to bring him back to life in a limited capacity. She was standing next to him, wearing her signature throne emblem on her head in this depiction on the wall. The next section of the wall had a black background, indicating the body or person entering the darkness of the afterlife.

There was also Anubis, the jackal-headed god, leaning over the sarcophagus of the dead person. It was said that he was the one who had invented the embalming process and was the next stop on the journey to the afterlife.

Listening to Tess's running dialog, I felt like a student in one of her Egyptology classes. It was an enjoyable experience, except for the heat beginning to increase in the room.

The next section depicted Maat, goddess of truth, where the person's heart was placed on the scale and weighed against a feather. They were allowed to continue their journey if they balanced, showing that the person was truthful and had led a decent life. If they did not balance, the heart would be eaten by Ahemait, known as the devourer of souls. According to Tess, the picture on the wall showed the heart balancing with the feather, indicating a positive outcome for the deceased.

"You know what's interesting, Doc; see here—at the beginning of this person's journey, they seem to be depicted in a sarcophagus," Tess opined.

"Yes, I see; that is unusual since the deceased person is usually depicted standing next to Osiris as they begin their journey," he replied.

"That's true if it is a king, queen, or a personage of importance. If the deceased doesn't fall into those categories and are a commoner or slave, they are depicted in a sarcophagus, like this," Tess offered, pointing at the painting on the wall, "as they enter the afterlife."

"So that gives credence to our theory that the body in the sarcophagus is that of a slave or handmaiden to Cleo."

"I believe it confirms it," Tess said definitively.

I said, "Nicely done, you two, nicely done." My voice seemed to startle them.

Tess chuckled, "Colt, I forgot you were back there."

"Yeah, nobody really notices me; I blend in so well in the crowd," I retorted, laughing.

The laughter continued as she said, "Right, you're so easy to miss."

There was more laughter as Joe said from across the room, "What's so funny over there?"

"I think the heat may be getting to us," I answered jokingly.

"Actually, it is pretty hot in here; I suggest we all take a break," he replied. We agreed and exited the tomb, with Joe checking the air with the Sniffer on the way out.

Once outside, he said, "Good, the levels are remaining normal, so no more worries in there."

"Great," I said. "How about we break until early afternoon when it's a bit cooler, and we can work into the night, if necessary."

"I agree, Colt; no sense in killing ourselves," Tess added.

With that, we got water and some MREs that we

brought with us. The breeze was hot but not as hot as the inside of the tomb, so we sat there eating and drinking slowly, trying to recharge our bodies. The discussion revolved around the confirmation of the identity of the occupant of the sarcophagus—another piece of the puzzle put into place. In fact, I thought it was like getting the perimeter of a thousand-piece puzzle done and looking at the big empty space in the middle—progress, but still, a long way to go.

We kicked back, relaxing, rehydrating, and chatting about the discovery, what it might mean, and what our next move would be. We agreed that, without more information or clues, we may have hit a roadblock. As the sun started going down, the temperature started dropping. The desert chill began flowing in like an incoming tide, so with the drop in temperature, we decided it was time to re-enter the tomb.

We moved from the paintings on the east wall to the west. We had to move several of the tomb contents to see it clearly. That included the gold-inlaid chariot. Yes, we were very careful, but the gold statues, plates, serving and drinking vessels, and ornate boxes with gold and lapis inlays didn't make it easy. We managed to move the chariot enough for us to get up close to the wall. When we got to the west wall, the difference between it and the east wall was clearly evident. The east wall was dark, with a portion of it painted black, indicating the darkness during the journey to the afterlife. The west wall was just the opposite. The colors were bright, and the figures were presented in colorful garb. The sun symbol could be seen in numerous places.

As we all gathered around, Tess and Doc began

their dissecting discourse of the scene before us on the wall.

"Here," Tess said, pointing at the lower part of the mural. "It's obviously a royal court scene; look at the trappings." The handmaidens were bringing drink and fruit to a reclining female figure on cushions, and all were dressed very formally.

Doc said, "Look on their arms; we were right about who's in the sarcophagus." He was pointing at silver bracelets around the server's forearms and on their ankles. "That's exactly what we found on the bodies of the three females; they were servants."

The female on the cushions was draped in sheer, colorful garments with golden bracelets, arm bands, and other jewelry. Visible higher up on her arm was a golden coiled serpent wrapping around it with red eyes. The background for the court scene was a blue sky with the sun emblem featured prominently, its rays descending toward the reclining female.

"That's her; that's Cleopatra," Tess said, pointing to the sky background opposite the sun symbol. There, faintly visible, the cartouche for Cleopatra, painted in gold, with golden rays emanating from it. "It's been purposely subdued in the painting," Tess observed. "She is subtly being depicted on the same level as Ra."

"Taking her place in the celestial realm as a god," Doc said.

The paintings above it were smaller, and one had to look closely for detail. This time, the same court scene was depicted with the sky very dark blue. In the next scene, Cleo was standing, the same dark sky in the background, facing what looked like a small cloud in front of her. The next scene was the same, except there was an arm and hand extending out from the cloud in what seemed to be a beckoning motion. The next scene had half of Cleo's body engulfed by the cloud as she stepped into it. The location in the last scene was the same as the previous ones, but the cloud was gone here, replaced by the sun symbol and Cleo's cartouche.

Tess turned to Doc, eyes wide and speechless for a few seconds, then exclaimed, "She went through a portal! She went through a freaking portal."

We all gathered closer, examining the series of scenes, and sure enough, it seemed obvious that Cleo had been visited and entered a portal.

"I'll be damned; she did go through a portal, and that sun symbol at the end, I think, signifies her meeting the emissary of Ra," I said, staring intently at the wall. We were all so totally engrossed in this revelation that we didn't hear the three gunmen enter the tomb behind us.

CHAPTER TWENTY-NINE

We were startled when the loud voice shouted, "Against the wall. Now!" We turned and were staring at two AK-47s and a semi-automatic handgun pointed at us by three very unsavory-looking characters. Taken by surprise doesn't even come close to describing our reaction as we all slowly raised our hands and stepped back against the wall.

We were bunched together, and Tess quietly said to me, "What the hell...?"

I whispered, "Looks like word of the discovery got out."

The three men were joined by another, and we recognized the worker who had been part of the initial discovery.

"Well, there you have it; I guess the good doctor made a mistake hiring this one." One of the AK-47-wielding dudes took an ominous step forward and loudly said something to me in Arabic. I looked at him and said in my best Spanish, "No comprendo."

Tess quietly said, "He said if you say another word, he's going to kill you." Two more men joined the party, their eyes bugging out as they saw the riches in the tomb.

"Well, that really sucks," I whispered out of the side of my mouth.

Tess elbowed me and whispered, "No time to be a

wiseass, Colt; this is serious."

I knew she was right, so I kept quiet, glancing at Doc, Joe, and O'Reilly. Each of them gave me a slight nod, which meant they would be ready for whatever I decided to do. Now, if I only had an idea of what to do. While keeping an eye on us, the men engaged in a very animated discussion. Of course, I didn't understand a word of it, so I gave Tess a questioning look.

She whispered, "They are deciding how much they are going to try and take and when they are going to kill us."

Of all the times for us to go on a mission unarmed, it had to be this one. Of course, we had our usual arsenal on the plane, but a lot of good that did us. I didn't think we needed to be packing on this trip. I thought, note to self, Colt, always carry weapons. The one that seemed to be in charge was carrying the handgun and turned to us and said in English, "Over here, sit down." He motioned us to a somewhat clear area on the floor. Before we could voluntarily sit, he grabbed Tess by the shoulder and roughly shoved her to the ground.

I saw red and tensed. He noticed, pointing the gun at Tess's head, and with a very ugly smile, said, "Don't even think about it. Down on the floor, now." Realizing this was not the time for heroics, I slowly sat down, as did the others. He gave some orders to the men, and they all left except the AK-47 guy who didn't like me. That's okay; I didn't like him either and watched closely at how these guys carried themselves and moved. I decided they were thieves, nothing professional about them as the guard's eyes darted hungrily at the gold in the room.

I leaned over to Tess. "Are you okay?"

"Yes, I'm fine," she quietly replied, rubbing the shoulder the leader had grabbed to shove her to the ground.

"Don't worry," I said through clenched teeth. "He'll pay for that."

She leaned toward me and quietly said, "I'm worried, Colt; from what I heard, there is no way we're getting out of here alive."

I tried to give her a reassuring smile and whispered, "There's always a way." Our guard seemed less interested in our quiet communications now as he greedily scanned the wealth in the room.

"Where did they go?" I asked Tess.

"To get their vehicle and more men, the rest of their gang, I think. He told them they would shoot us in here once they got the gold loaded."

Doc understood what had been said and relayed it to Joe and O'Reilly.

"I wonder if this guy understands English," I quietly said, and then in a slightly louder voice, not looking at him, said, "Your mother's a whore who works the slum streets of Cairo." He only glanced at me and kept scanning the treasure in the room. I heard Joe chuckle, so I said slightly above a whisper, "This guy doesn't understand English. That could work to our advantage."

Joe responded with one word, "Gerber."

I smiled and nodded; he talked about the six-inch Gerber Razorback knife in his belt sheath. At least we weren't totally without weapons, but that adage came to me with mental red lights flashing. "You don't take a knife to a gunfight." Yeah, but if that's all you got, improvise, I thought. The big boss returned to the room and said something to Mr. AK-47, who abruptly left the room.

I glanced at Tess. "They're getting ready to start loading," she whispered.

Well, this is it—time to do something—what, I wasn't quite sure. That's when, in a thunderous voice, Tess said to him, "You'll never get away with this, you pig."

The man's gloating face immediately changed to one of intense hatred. "Shut your mouth," he almost shouted.

"Why should I? You're going to kill us, so to hell with you, you arrogant thieving pig," Tess roared, followed by a few choice words in Arabic. That did it; his face contorted with anger as he rushed to where she was sitting next to me and, seemingly without thinking, reached down to slap her with his left hand. That's all I needed; I grabbed his hand as it approached her face and broke three of his fingers, bending them ninety degrees in the wrong direction as I twisted his arm, pulling him screaming in pain to the floor. Tess's right hook caught him hard on the chin. Our combination attack knocked him to his back; the only problem was that he was now lying across my legs, pinning me down as I held onto his arm.

He still had the gun in his hand as O'Reilly jumped to her feet and came toward him. He got off one wild shot, which unfortunately found its mark in O'Reilly's arm.

As he swung his arm around to point the gun at

Tess and me, he paused. The screams coming down the passageway from the priest's tomb were so terror-filled that it froze the moment in time. The men's screams were the stuff of nightmares, loud and continual. I recognized them immediately, having heard similar sounds before. Two shots were fired, and then nothing. The screaming had stopped, and the tomb was silent, breaking the spell of the moment. His eyes wide, the gunman was trying to roll toward us, pointing the gun at us, when Joe grabbed him under the chin, pulled his head back, and drove the blade of the Gerber through his throat.

His final gurgling sounds ended abruptly as I got a leg free and kicked his body off my other leg. I watched as Joe retrieved his blade and said, "Thanks." He nodded in response and moved to O'Reilly, whom Doc was tending. I helped Tess to her feet and said, "That was a pretty ballsy move, lady."

She smiled, rubbing the knuckles of her right hand, "I knew I had to get him close enough for you to do something. I wasn't about to just sit there and let that low-life thief shoot us."

I said, "Well, I'm glad it worked, and by the way, nice right hook."

As we moved to O'Reilly sitting on the floor, Doc wrapping a makeshift bandage around her arm, Tess asked, "That noise from the priest's tomb, was that…?"

"I'm pretty sure it was," I replied to her unfinished sentence.

"Doc, how is she?" I asked.

"She'll be okay; the bullet went through the fleshy part of her arm, in and out. It will hurt like hell for a while, but she should be fine. Just another scar to add to her collection," he said, grinning slightly. "But we need to get her back to camp, where I can dress the wound properly."

Sitting there smiling with only a slight grimace as Doc tightened the bandage, O'Reilly said, "Doc, I love your bedside manner. You make your patients feel so special."

"Just stating the facts," he replied jovially as he and Joe helped her to her feet.

As we got to the dimly lit passageway, a large shadow flashed across its opening in the priest's tomb. As we entered, death lay before us. The gunmen and I guessed the rest of the gang that was going to rob the tomb lay scattered around the floor. Joe surveyed the scene, then looked at me and said, "I've seen this before."

"Yes, you have," I said, vividly remembering the hallway scene in Syria.

As we walked through the carnage, Doc said, "Looks like your loyal protector paid these guys a visit, Colt."

"It does, doesn't it?" I replied as we exited the tomb into the chill of the desert night. The second worker was unconscious, lying on the ground a few feet from the entrance with his hands bound.

Doc left O'Reilly and quickly checked the man for a pulse. "He's alive," he said as he untied his hands. His water jug was lying close, and a few splashes of water on his face revived him.

He tried to sit up but was obviously still dazed as he leaned back, putting his hand on the growing lump on his head. "What happened?" he groggily got out. Doc assured him things were all right and to take it easy and lay there for a little longer. His head must have cleared when he sat up and asked, "Where is Mustaf? He came by to relieve me, and then someone hit me. I don't remember anything else."

Doc told him his friend was part of a gang that had come to rob the tomb, and, during the robbery, he and others were killed.

"Killed," he repeated. Looking wide-eyed at Doc and then me, he said, "Did you kill them?"

Doc said, "No, we didn't kill anyone."

"Then, what happened?" he asked. "Who did?"

Doc looked at me, and I shook my head and mouthed, "No."

Looking back at the worker, Doc said, "We don't know. We were being held prisoner when it all happened," adding that he should come back to the camp area and let him take a closer look at his head.

CHAPTER THIRTY

Doc grabbed his med kit once we were at the camp. We lit the kerosene lamp as he began examining both of his patients in the eerie yellow glow it provided. Things were well in hand, and Joe motioned for me to join him a little distance away, out of earshot. After grabbing two bottles of water, I headed his way.

Taking the offered bottle and after a quick drink, he said, "So, what now, Colt?"

I followed his example, took a long drink, and answered, "I don't know."

"Well, we better come up with something pretty quickly. That worker is not going to keep his mouth shut for long, and we have a tomb full of mangled bodies we're going to have to explain."

I took in our serene surroundings, looked toward the tomb's entrance, and asked, "Are we?"

Looking surprised, Joe said, "Are we what?"

"Going to have to explain," I replied.

"What are you talking about? There are going to be tons of people questioning us, including the authorities. They are going to want to know what happened."

"So do we!" I said.

He stood there with a puzzled look, barely visible in the dark.

"Well, you want to try and tell them that we were held at gunpoint, and suddenly this ghost wolf appeared, killed the bad guys, and saved us?"

He paused. "I see your point. So what do you propose we say?"

"Just what happened. One of the thieves in the new tomb held us at gunpoint. Since Tess understood Arabic, we knew he had told his accomplices to kill us as soon as they returned. Next, there was some kind of loud commotion in the priest's tomb, distracting our captor. We took advantage of the distraction and neutralized him before he could kill us. Then, we warily went into the priest's tomb and saw the bodies. Nothing more. We have no idea what happened in there."

There was another pause, and then he said, "Do you think they will believe us?"

"Joe, I think they could give us a polygraph test, and we would pass! You remember the old saying truth is stranger than fiction? Well, in this case, it is."

Joe was right about being questioned by tons of people and the authorities. I told Tess to call Shehata on the SAT phone soon after coming out of the tomb. Best we get ahead of this thing, if possible, I thought. She made the call and told him we had been attacked by looters in the tomb and something terrible had happened. When asked what had happened, she replied, "I have no idea, but it is horrible. You need to get here right away and bring the authorities. There are dead people here."

He asked no more questions and said he would do as she asked and return immediately. Before hanging up, he asked if the rest of us were all okay. She assured him the whole team was, except for O'Reilly, who had gotten shot but would be "okay." He was beside himself when he heard that and assured her that he would leave immediately. The travel time from our location in Sakkara to Cairo should take no more than an hour, so we needed to be ready for the arrival of the new visitors.

When Joe and I returned to the campsite, the worker had left, so I explained our official story to everyone. I wanted to ensure we were all on the same page when the authorities arrived. It was quite easy, as I had explained to Joe. All we had to do was tell the truth. I knew convincing whatever authorities would show up that we saw nothing was going to be difficult, but the savage way in which the looters were killed was going to raise a lot of questions.

Doc asked, "I'm confused as to why this protector of yours shows up when he does. He was there at the compound battle in Syria and now here, but not when we took over the yacht. Why didn't he show up there too?"

I thought about it and finally said, "I think you answered your own question. In Syria, we were in a life-or-death situation, just as it was here. When we took the yacht, I never felt we were in that type of danger—dicey, yes, but life-or-death, no."

"Are you saying he can tell or sense when your life is in danger and only appears then to help?"

"I don't really know the answer to that, Doc, but that might be close. Remember when we first encountered the wolf out in New Mexico? He manifested himself to guide us; his protecting us came a little later. So, I guess he must know when he is needed and in what capacity and then shows up or not…. But hey, he's a spirit animal, and

I really have no idea how anything works in his world; he didn't come with an operator's manual."

"Well, he's saved our butts on numerous occasions, so I am grateful for his help."

"As am I," I replied. "But I still don't think I want to plan on him always being there for us or me. I just have a real issue accepting that as fact."

"Understandable," Doc replied. "But it's worked so far."

"That it has," I answered with a nod. "That it has...."

The entourage arrived an hour and a half after Tess placed the call. We were waiting for them, seated around the table with the lantern, our only light, in the middle. We had grabbed some food and were sipping on the single malt Scotch I had brought, trying to relax before the barrage of questioning began. Doc had done an excellent job on O'Reilly's arm, as indicated by the doctor who had accompanied the new arrivals. Shehata had arrived with a caravan of officials from the Department of Antiquities and the museum, along with some military and official-looking investigator types.

The area around the tomb took on an ominous atmosphere as the military set up a perimeter of armed guards around it, and portable lights were set up, illuminating all—a surreal daylight scene in the darkness of the desert. We were gathered up and, as a group, subjected to intense questioning. We stuck to our plan and told the truth. We didn't know what happened to those men in the priest's tomb.

As the gunman in the "new" tomb was about to kill us, we managed to overpower him, and, in the shuffle, one of our team was shot before another member was able to neutralize him. And no, we had not touched anything at the crime scene after the deaths had occurred. The main topic of discussion was how the men in the outer tomb died. The damage done to the bodies was significant and could not be attributed to being done by a person or persons. Quite bluntly, appendages had been ripped off, and deep puncture wounds were visible on the deceased. The idea of a wild animal was brought up but dismissed.

Multiple discussions were going on about the cause of the deaths as well as the discovery of the new tomb. Of course, the latter mostly involved the museum and antiquities officials. Shehata was chewed out in one breath for not following protocols and praised in the next for the amazing discovery. After listening from the periphery, I asked Tess, "Is your friend going to be all right?"

She nodded and said, "He'll be fine."

The night dragged on as more people showed up and began going about various tasks. We were instructed to stay at the table, and two of the military were posted close by. It was a long night, and by the time it was over and the sun was coming up, we were finally allowed to return to our campsite, exhaustion hammering hard on our senses, and the scotch only added to it. We left the empty bottle on the table as we turned in for some much-needed rest.

Not emerging from our tents until almost noon, we were greeted by a scene of controlled chaos. Ambulances had appeared at some point, and the last of the bodies were being removed. Most of the military had been replaced with uniformed police officers, as others seemed to be searching the entire area around the tomb entrance. When we got to the canopy and table, we found Shehata talking with the two "suits" we had talked to last night.

There was a large commercial coffee pot sitting on the table and empty cups along with some kind of biscuits. Shehata turned at our approach and said, "Good, you are awake; please, have some coffee." Filling our cups and taking a seat at the table, Shehata continued. "As you know, these gentlemen are from the Ministry of the Interior. This is Investigator Mahmoud from the Central Security Forces and Investigator Sayed from Public Security. They want to ask you a few more questions about this horrible incident."

We had spoken to them last night, so I said we would be happy to answer any additional questions they had. We ran through the whole story with them again, and when we finished, the investigator from Public Security asked if we were sure we hadn't left out anything. We assured him we had not. He continued with the strange circumstances of the men's deaths, "Mr. Burnett, you say you didn't see anything, yet the bodies of the men that died looked as if they were attacked by a wild beast—seven men killed in a room not twenty feet from you, and you saw nothing. I find that hard to believe."

"We had a man pointing a gun at our heads, about to kill us. We were focused on what was happening to us. As we fought the gunman, I heard screams and two gunshots, but by the time we had neutralized our assailant, there was no sound from the other tomb area. When we were able to get into the other room, the men were already dead, as we stated earlier."

"How long did it take you to overcome your

assailant?"

I looked at the others and said, "I would guess three or four minutes."

"And how long until you entered the room where the bodies were found?"

"Maybe another two or three minutes."

"So, you are asking me to believe that in six minutes, seven grown men were killed, some ripped apart, you overcame your assailant, entered the next room, and have no idea what killed those men?"

"Yes, I am," I replied, "because it's the truth."

"It is hard to understand, but it IS the truth," Tess added. "What possible benefit would there be for us to lie to you? You can't think we had anything to do with their deaths. You said it yourself, and we saw it with our own eyes. There is no way that three men and two women, unarmed except for one knife, could inflict that kind of damage to those armed men."

I assured him again that the only death we knew anything about was that of the person who was about to kill us, and the only thing we heard were some screams and two gunshots. I turned to the rest of the team and asked, "You guys see or hear anything that I missed?"

When they all said no, he paused, then changed his line of questioning and continued, "Who struck the killing blow to your assailant?"

Joe immediately said, "That would be me."

The investigator furrowed his brow and said, "And how did you do that?"

Joe reached behind his back to the sheath on his belt, pulled out the Razorback with its six-inch blade, and stuck it in the tabletop. "With this," he said.

The inspector paused as he looked at the knife sticking in the table and then back at Joe and said, "Do you often kill people with your blade?"

I could tell Joe was getting a little upset when he tersely said, "Only if they have a gun pointed at my friend's head."

The investigator looked closely at Joe for a few minutes, then at the knife, and said to me, "I believe your friend. I believe this was a case of self-defense. We found the weapon your assailant had and the bullet casing he shot your friend with. I saw nothing at the scene to indicate anything other than what you described occurred." He turned to the other investigator, who nodded slightly in his direction. But our investigation will continue due to the nature of the other deaths. Please do not leave Cairo until we contact you; we may have more questions."

CHAPTER THIRTY-ONE

They did ask us not to leave Cairo until the final investigation report was filed, saying it would take a week to ten days. I assured them we would stay until they notified us that we could leave and voluntarily said we would be happy to answer any further questions they might have. Satisfied, they thanked us and left.

Shehata, smiling broadly, said, "Well, I'm glad that is taken care of. I was afraid things might go much worse, especially under the strange circumstances of the looters' deaths."

Tess said, "I understand and appreciate your concern. This is a bizarre set of circumstances we find ourselves in."

"It is indeed," Shehata answered, shaking his head.

The media descended on the dig location an hour later, and the true circus began. Three TV crews were running around with their on-air talent, microphone in hand, trying to interview anyone they could who looked the least bit official. The local authorities kept them away from the tomb itself, but they prowled the area, looking for prey. Dr. Shehata tried to control them, but they descended on him like a hoard of locusts. In minutes, he was surrounded by TV crews and a bevy of print journalists.

We took that opportunity to return to our campsite a little distance away and tried to make ourselves as innocuous as possible. It didn't work. We soon heard calls from the group as some headed our way, "Dr. Worthington, Dr. Worthington, can you tell us what happened?" they shouted.

Seeing no way out, Tess looked at us rather exasperatedly and went to meet them before they got to our campsite. She spent the next hour fielding the multitude of questions flung her way, always maintaining her professional demeanor.

Tiring of the barrage and looking for a way to extricate herself, Tess spotted the worker on guard duty when the attack occurred, said something to the group, and pointed in his direction. Almost as a herd, they quickly moved to him. He was completely engulfed in minutes, and Tess returned to us. "Good Lord," she said as she returned, "that was a nightmare that I don't want to have again any time soon."

I laughed as I handed her some water. "As famous as you are, I thought you would be used to that kind of publicity."

As she sat down, taking a drink, she laughingly said, "Not hardly, and you're not going to believe the questions they were throwing at me. Get this: someone got the idea that the tomb we opened had a curse on it, and the looters were killed by some entity or force that was protecting it. They wanted to know if we found any inscriptions or magical sigils that would indicate it was true."

Doc laughed out loud and said, "You're kidding?"

She shook her head and said, "Nope, and as soon as that got asked, the whole group started following that line of questioning."

I had been sitting there, taking in all these revelations, and said, "And then you threw the poor guard under the bus? Shame on you, Dr. Worthington."

Laughing, she said, "Better him than me. I'm sure the story will only grow with his recollections."

And grow it did. Headlines in the papers the next day read, "Tomb's Curse Kills Eight Looters."

From what Shehata said the next day, the television stations were slightly more restrained in their commentary. Still, they did mention the bizarre way the men were killed, sparking another flurry of speculation and growing the curse story. Shehata bemoaned the inaccuracy of the reporting but said, "Well, there is an upside to all this nonsense. As superstitious as people are, this will probably keep them away from the site."

He was right, and on the third day after the attack, we were allowed back into the tomb and resumed our investigation of the west wall murals. A four-man security team was now assigned to the site as conservators carefully cleaned up the mess inside the priest's tomb. Removing blood splatters from ancient wall paintings was a daunting task. Other archeologists and conservators from the museum began working in the new tomb, examining and documenting its contents.

Later that day, I asked Shehata if he was in trouble over the unsanctioned entry into the new tomb. He assured me he was not. He explained my accident that opened the hidden passage and the necessity of finding out what was behind the stone doorway before alerting the museum and bringing in more staff. He also explained to the higher-ups the poison trap we had discovered and how many lives were probably saved by our quick action.

He did say things were "dicey" when he first notified them of finding and opening the tomb, but once they saw the site and its artifacts, they realized that he had made a monumental discovery, negating any anger toward him or his actions. All was well, and it looked like he, Shehata would be the head archaeologist on this project. Things were looking up.

Resuming our work where we left off at the wall, there was one more sequence of images in this row. The last image showed the same court location as the others. This time, Cleo stood in the middle of the room, arms outstretched to her sides; one of the handmaids lay before her, and two more knelt at her side. Doc said to Tess, "The three female remains we found in here?"

"Could be—in fact, I would say highly likely," she answered.

The top panel was the last on this wall and very different from the others. It was divided into two sections. The top left showed an ornate sarcophagus being carried away with a regal figure leading it and two handmaids following. The top right depicted a very large sailing ship with billowed sails on blue water. In front of it stood a male figure with the head of a peregrine falcon adorned with a sun disk with what looked like a cobra wrapped around it. Looking closely, the cartouche we had all become so familiar with could be seen on the ship's sail —Cleopatra's.

I broke the silence, "That is not a river boat, and

that doesn't look like the water in the Nile."

"You are absolutely right," Tess said. "That is a large seagoing vessel on the ocean... I think we're being shown how Cleo disappeared."

Joe had already moved into place and was taking close-up pictures of the entire wall. These murals filled the entire wall and were the focal points of this end of the tomb. Tess and Doc continued checking the murals on the side walls and determined they were just royal court scenes, not showing any references to the afterlife or its gods. After another hour, Tess finally said, "I've seen everything I need. I'm not sure how the museum archaeologists are going to interpret this wall, referring to the west end wall, but I can tell you they won't come to the same conclusion that we have."

"We do have something they don't," I said. "We have the narrative on the statues. That's what really provided us the key to the whole story."

"Absolutely," Tess replied. "Without that, I can imagine a number of directions a traditional analysis could take with this information."

Doc added, "And all of them would be wrong."

Laughing softly, Tess replied, "I believe so, but several questions remain, and I see nothing here that can help answer them."

"Well, then, I guess our work here is done," I said. "If you don't need anything else, I suggest we head back to Cairo, find a nice hotel, and review what we have so far."

"I wholeheartedly agree," O'Reilly said. "I could use a good shower and a hot meal."

"Plus," Doc added, "I need to keep an eye on that wound of yours and have access to more medications than I have in my kit."

"Well, then, it's settled. Since the authorities said we have to stay in Cairo for a few more days, we can do it in more civilized accommodations," I said. Tess found Dr. Shehata and informed him we would be leaving the site but would be in Cairo until things were cleared up with the authorities. He was sorry to see us go but could not thank us enough for our help in discovering the new tomb. He asked Tess if she had found any of the additional information she had been seeking on Cleopatra. She said she wasn't sure and that it would take some time to analyze what she had gotten and would keep him informed. He assured her he would do the same and connect with us in Cairo before we left.

Packing our gear in the rented Range Rover, we said our goodbyes and returned to the city. On the way, I got on the SAT phone and booked three suites at the St. Regis Cairo. After what we had been through, we needed a bit of a luxury respite. When we arrived, I realized camping at the site for the last week or so had left us a little rough around the edges. Entering the lobby, we drew a few stares as I went to the desk to check-in. Doc immediately went to the concierge desk to inquire about the in-house physician and the closest pharmacy and hospital in case we needed additional medical resources. He asked the concierge to let the physician know he would contact him once checked in and needed him to medically assess a guest's injury.

Walking up to the front desk, I received a rather surprised look from the desk clerk and a reserved, "May I help you, sir?"

"Checking in," I answered.

"Do you have a reservation?"

"I called an hour ago to reserve three rooms; the name is Burnett, Colten Burnett."

His fingers clicked on the keyboard of his computer, and, in a moment, he looked at me, somewhat surprised. "Sir, it says here you asked for three suites for five nights."

"That's correct."

"I'm sorry, sir, but I'm not sure of availability," he said, now with a bit of an attitude.

Realizing my week-old beard and disheveled clothes didn't present me in the best light, I dropped my AMEX Centurion card on the counter and said, "Check again, please."

CHAPTER THIRTY-TWO

We agreed to meet downstairs in the lounge in three or four hours. That would allow everyone to clean up and get a little rest. Doc and Joe shared a suite, O'Reilly had her own, and Tess and I had the third one. In the elevator, Doc said he would stay with O'Reilly until the doctor came by. He wanted to hear what he had to say.

O'Reilly protested, "Doc, I'm a big girl; I can take care of myself. I know how to talk to doctors, and I've been shot before and recovered."

"I know you do, but as long as Colt gives me the responsibility of taking care of this team medically, I plan on doing just that. Hearing what this guy has to say will help me ensure you get the best treatment possible."

"Come on, Doc; it's no big deal...."

Doc gave her one of his famous "withering" looks—the one that says, "Discussion over!"

She finally acquiesced and begrudgingly said with an eye roll, "Fine, just to keep you happy, my dear colleague."

Dr. Ryan Greene was not a medical doctor, having multiple doctorates in linguistics and ancient languages, but he was one hell of an emergency medic, having received his paramedic and advanced medical training in the Coast Guard as a Rescue Swimmer. I will say that as a member of the Risky Business team, our adventures have given him ample opportunity to keep his medical skills honed.

Our suite was on the top floor with a beautiful view of the Nile and the surrounding area. Throwing our bags on the floor, Tess flopped on the king-size bed and was elated at its comfort. I said I would call the investigator who had questioned us at the site, let him know we were in Cairo, and give him our contact information.

"All right, while you do that, I'm going to take a nice relaxing hot shower," she said, getting up and heading for the bathroom. Standing in the huge shower and letting the multiple jets of water hit her body underscored how sore she was. It was glorious. Standing there basking in the warmth of the water pelting her, she was not really surprised when the two strong arms wrapped around her from behind and held her tightly.

Colt kissed her neck, and as he pressed his body against hers, she exclaimed, "My God, Colt!" He turned her around, smiling, and kissed her firmly and passionately as she felt those strong arms tighten around her. He lifted her and pressed her back against the shower wall, never removing his lips from hers. Moments later, she broke the kiss with a gasp. Looking into his sparkling green eyes, she smiled, pulling her body even harder against his. She bit his lower lip as she kissed him long and hard. She lost herself in that moment of bliss, never wanting it to end; it didn't. Later, he carried her to the king-size bed, both still dripping wet, and the moment arrived again.

Three hours later, she awoke with her head on his shoulder and her body nestled against his. A damp sheet covered them, and she put her arm around his chest and pulled him closer.

"You're awake," I said as I leaned over and kissed her on the forehead.

"I am," Tess murmured.

We lay there luxuriously savoring the moment, holding each other close. I could hear her deep, rhythmic breathing and feel her heartbeat as she lay pressed against me. You are one lucky man, Colt, I thought. I'm happy and satisfied, and I'm pretty sure I'm in love with this lady.

As if reading my mind, Tess softly said, "You know I'm in love with you, Colt. I have been for a long time." She continued before I could say anything, "But I also know our worlds are so far apart sometimes. Like two planets orbiting around the sun, they constantly move, and sometimes their orbits bring them close before sending them off again in different directions. You have your life, and I have mine, and we both are always looking for the next challenge and adventure, but wow, it is amazing when our worlds collide."

I didn't know what to say. After a few minutes, she said, "You know I will always be there for you, and I know you will be for me. I never doubted that for a minute, and maybe someday, our orbits will become one, someday.... As much as it hurts me to say it, it's not time yet." I couldn't see her face, but I felt the warm teardrops fall on my bare chest and knew she was crying.

I felt a wave of emotion growing inside, and as I stared at the ceiling, my vision became blurry. I pulled her closer, took a deep breath, and softly said, "I love you, Tess Worthington... and I understand. When the time does come, and I know it will, I will be there waiting for you."

I turned until we were face-to-face and saw the tears. I softly wiped them away. She took her fingers and softly brushed my cheek, smiling now.

Though the tears still flowed, she said, "I know you will be... and I know you do." She pressed her warm lips against mine in a soft, loving kiss that became more fervent as I pulled her tighter.

I don't know how long we lay there, but neither one of us moved until the phone next to the bed began ringing. I looked at her questioningly. She smiled broadly and said, "You better answer that, you big Palooka, or they'll wonder what we're up to." I returned her smile, rolled over, and picked up the phone.

It was Doc. "Hey, Colt, we're down in the lounge waiting for you guys." As I listened, I watched Tess get out of bed and walk to the bathroom. Her naked body glowed in the afternoon sunlight coming through the windows.

"Yeah, Doc, we'll be down in a few minutes," I said as I hung up quickly, got out of bed, and followed her to the bathroom.

Everyone looked rested and refreshed when we joined them in the lounge. O'Reilly's arm was in a sling, and her wound had a fresh bandage. Everybody had clean clothes, and the men were freshly shaven. On our way into Cairo, I called Max, our pilot, and had him bring over our additional bags from the plane. They were waiting for us when we checked in. He usually stays on the plane when we arrive at our destination since we wouldn't want anyone nosing around and finding our cache of weapons and explosives that travel with us. He didn't mind having the luxury of the jet to himself.

Tess and I ordered drinks, kicked back, and relaxed—no talking business, at least for now. I knew the diversion wouldn't last long, and it didn't.

After two rounds of drinks and some appetizers, O'Reilly asked the first question. "So, where do you think Cleo went?"

Tess took a sip of her Bloody Mary and said, "That's the million-dollar question, and right now, I have no idea. But I can tell you this—she went to sea. That was a seagoing vessel depicted on the wall."

"I didn't know they had seagoing vessels back then," Joe said.

"They didn't until about fifteen hundred BC. That's when they learned how to make boats with a keel and internally reinforced hulls. After that, their seafaring took a major leap forward. They were no longer stuck with just riverboats and vessels that could only safely operate close to shore."

"She could have gone anywhere," I said.

"Well, yes and no. She couldn't have gone anywhere that she would be recognized. Word could get out, and that could alert the Romans. I'm sure Octavian would have loved to find out she was alive and get his hands on her," Tess said.

"So, her options would have been pretty limited," Doc added.

"Yes, they would, but my instincts tell me Cleo was a very resourceful person," Tess answered.

We finished our drinks, lingering for a while and thinking about recent events, when my SAT phone chimed. The caller ID showed Tony in our Comms center.

I answered, "Hey, Tony, what's up?"

"That's the question we have for you. Reggie and Dimitri are here, and you're on speaker."

"Hey, guys," I replied jovially.

Dimitri's voice came through loud and clear, "Colt, we don't go on one trip, and all hell breaks loose? How's O'Reilly?"

Before I could ask how they knew, I heard Reggie say, "You guys have been all over the news here. Discovery of a mysterious tomb, attacked by looters, multiple mysterious deaths, and O'Reilly getting shot. I mean, come on. If we knew you would have that much fun, we wouldn't have let you go without us," she said in a cheerfully chastising way.

I said, "Hang on," and told the crew what was happening and what was being said. That brought a chorus of smiles, and some chuckles. "It's all good over here; O'Reilly's fine and the situation seems to be well in hand," I added.

Dimitri's voice came on. "Tell O'Reilly I'm jealous; I think that puts her one scar ahead of me." Laughing, he said, "Guess I've got some catching up to do."

"I don't think this is the type of competition I want my team to be involved in," I said harshly in a good-humored way. "Everything okay at the ranch?"

Tony returned and said, "Yeah, we're all good here. Nothing major to report, so you guys take care and stay in touch."

"And no more shenanigans without me and Reggie;

she's starting to feel left out.... Ow, stop hitting me!" Dimitri exclaimed.

"Shut up, you caveman!" I heard Reggie exclaim.

"All right, you two, settle down," Tony laughed. "You better get home soon, Dad; the kids are getting restless."

Now, I was laughing and answered, "Hope to be back within five days or so. Tony, try and keep those kids under control."

"Boy, that's asking an awful lot, but I'll try," he replied.

"All right, I'll keep you posted."

"Do that, and you guys be safe," I heard Dimitri reply with an assent from Tony and Reggie.

"Roger that, catch you later," and they hung up. I had to spend the next ten minutes filling everybody in. The Dimitri and Reggie antics were met with peals of laughter. We adjourned to the hotel dining room and had an enjoyable and relaxed dinner. It beat the heck out of MREs, power bars, and jerky. After finishing dinner, I suggested we head back to our suite, hit the mini-bar, and discuss our next move.

CHAPTER THIRTY-THREE

We sat around in the parlor part of our suite for the better part of an hour, not really making much progress. The mini-bar had been attacked, and everybody was kicked back and relaxed; ideas were flowing freely, just none that we could wrap our heads around.

Sipping his Jack and Coke, Doc said thoughtfully, "Do we really think Cleo met one of Jeannie's people?"

"It looks that way," Tess said.

"But to what end? How did they choose her to visit and why?" Joe asked.

O'Reilly, sipping her cold beer, said, "You know, I really think we need to find out more about this priest. He sure seems to be a major player in all this, and I'll bet he oversaw the painting of the murals in that tomb."

"If that's so, then it would mean he's familiar with portals... but how?" Joe added.

"Didn't you say you thought he was over one hundred years old, O'Reilly?" I asked.

"That was a guesstimate based on the information Tess had on him. I think that needs to be investigated more closely. I've got a feeling there is more there than we think."

"I can do that," Tess answered. "The museum has pretty good documentation on the priests of that period, but it will take some digging."

"Okay, so we look into this priest. Just what are we looking for?" I asked.

"I'm not sure," O'Reilly said, "but I would start with where he came from. And when did he become an influential high priest? We know when he died, but our only other information comes from the wall murals in his tomb. Tess, I think you may have to bring your friend, Dr. Shehata, into the research end of things. He's been working in his tomb for what, five years or so?" O'Reilly said.

"Yeah, he took over just after I left following the robbery. I'm sure he would be willing to help us."

"What are you getting at, O'Reilly?" Doc asked.

"I'm wondering if the priest might have been one of Jeannie's people," she answered.

"Hang on, so it seems like you and Colt always go back to the idea that this whole thing might have been planned and executed by Jeannie's people. Why?" Joe asked.

"I never left that idea, but we needed more proof, and it's starting to look like some of the pieces might be falling into place," I answered.

"Before we go jumping the gun here, we need to see what Tess finds out. That could make or break that theory," O'Reilly added quickly.

"I agree," I said. "It's just speculation at this point, but the sooner we can get that information on the priest from Tess, the better."

"And like Joe said, why would they want to help?"

O'Reilly asked.

"I don't know; that's the big question. I've been trying to think of why an emissary of Jeannie's people would contact her."

"And very possibly have taken part in facilitating her fake death," Doc added.

"That too," I agreed, "and we still have no idea where she would have headed."

Our discussion had been running in circles for a few hours now with no conclusion. It was frustrating, and with no answer in sight, and since we didn't seem to be getting anywhere, I suggested we call it a night. Tess said she would contact the museum and Shehata in the morning and start looking into the priest. With that, everyone said their goodnights and headed to their rooms.

I mentally ran through the litany of questions that needed answers. Getting more and more frustrated, I wasn't ready for sleep. I kissed Tess quickly and told her I would join her in a bit. I walked out on the balcony, whose vista of the Nile was now bathed in darkness, and the city's lights below glowed in the haze of the evening. As I stared into the darkness, my mind kept swirling. For some reason, the tentacles of the mystery we found ourselves wrapped up in would not turn me loose.

Leaning against the railing, trying to clear my head, a cool night breeze picked up, carrying a faint sound that I knew all too well—like a crystal chandelier tinkling in the wind. As the city sounds below grew silent, I quickly looked around, expecting to see the form of our extraterrestrial benefactor, Jeannie. She was nowhere to be seen. However, her soft voice came to me clearly. "You are troubled, Colt," it said.

Now, returning my gaze to the night sky over Cairo, I answered skyward, "Yes, I am, but it's more frustrating than troubling."

Her soft, mirthful laugh filled the air around me as she said, "You have yourself wrapped up in too many questions when the answer to one will provide all the answers you seek."

"So, you know what's got me going in circles? Well, I'm trying to determine the answer to any of them."

"I do," she replied.

There was a pause before I said, "So, are you going to help…?"

I heard that soft, mirthful laugh again. "And what would you have me do?" she asked.

"Give me some answers, for crying out loud," I said tersely, my frustration coming out. "I'm pretty sure some of your people were involved in the disappearance of Cleopatra. We have found some pretty specific clues for that hypothesis, but why? To keep her from being captured or killed by the Romans?"

The disembodied voice took on a more serious tone, "You are still not asking the right question…."

"Then tell me what the right question is," I shot back at the night sky, spreading my arms wide in frustration.

"Think, Colt. You have the capacity to see the broader scope of this enigma, yet you stumble and are blind to the one thread that will lead you."

I paused, getting my emotions under control, and started mentally running through the questions we had. Where did Cleo go, and who was the emissary she met using a portal? Why did whoever it was help her? Why would she fake her own death? Who was the priest, and why did he help her? With that final thought, the breeze picked up, and the chill of the night warmed dramatically.

Jeannie's voice filled the night, "I will only say this: a parent always protects the child." With that, the chilling breeze returned, and the sounds of the city below intruded. I stood there feeling thunderstruck at another of her mysteriously cryptic responses to a simple question. What the heck was she talking about? Had I heard her correctly, or did I miss something? I shook my head, trying to clear my thoughts.

I had hoped she would be more helpful, but I felt no closer to solving this mystery than before speaking with her.

I returned to the bedroom, closing the balcony doors and shutting out the night noises from the city below. Tess was asleep, and I quietly went into the bathroom. I looked at my reflection in the mirror as I turned on the cold water, wondering if that face staring back at me had completely lost it and was tumbling down a rabbit hole.

No, I thought, this mystery had stood the test of time and still confounded historians, archaeologists, and academics. I looked at the face again, smiling grimly back at me, and felt a new sense of commitment. No rabbit hole here, just the mother of all mysteries, and, by God, we were going to solve it.

CHAPTER THIRTY-FOUR

The ringing phone woke me up at eight-fifteen. It was the inspector asking if we would all come by his office on Friday for an official deposition/statement. He assured me that would be all they needed, and afterward, we would be free to go. I told him we would be there, and we set the meeting for ten on Friday morning.

Tess rolled over and sleepily asked who was on the phone. As I lay back down and pulled her close, I whispered in her ear, "I'll tell you later."

At nine-fifteen, the phone rang again. This time, it was Doc. "Hey, Colt, we're meeting for breakfast in about thirty minutes if you guys want to join us?"

"You bet," I replied, "we'll see you downstairs," and hung up the phone. I playfully smacked a "strategic" lump under the sheets with my hand, jumped out of bed, and mockingly hollered on the way to the shower, "Time to get up, Sleeping Beauty; we're burning daylight."

I dodged the pillow flying in my direction as her voice followed me into the bathroom, "You Barbaric Cretin," she called out, smiling broadly while getting out of bed and following me.

I didn't mention my exchange with Jeannie the night before as I continued mulling over her comments. They still were not making sense. Tess had contacted the museum and was heading there after breakfast to start digging into the priest's background; Shehata would be there in the afternoon and had agreed to help. O'Reilly's arm seemed to be doing okay, sore, but being the trooper she was, she could handle it. After breakfast, we decided to play tourist a bit and took a cruise on the Nile. Instead of one of the tour boats, we rented a smaller private boat, kicked back, relaxed, and enjoyed the amazing sights. The sun, the breeze, and the unique smell of the Nile, along with the ancient structures along its banks, seemed to transport us to another time.

Four hours later found us back at the hotel, relaxing by the pool, continuing our "tourist" break. The discussion had returned to the questions we had all been wrestling with, with lots of speculation and little progress. The dearth of solid facts kept us swirling in that "what if, would it be possible, and maybe" arena. While it made for lively conversation, in the end, we were right back where we started; we just didn't know.

The rest of the week flew by, and we made our appearance at the investigator's office on Friday, gave our sworn statements, and were told we were free to go. The death of our assailant was ruled self-defense, and Joe was cleared of any wrongdoing; the other deaths, however, were still a mystery. Tess had spent all her time at the museum, delving into the archives and searching for information on the priest.

We decided to leave Saturday morning for our return to the States, but Tess would stay behind to continue her research. Our final dinner in Cairo on Friday night was somewhat subdued. I think we all felt a sense of—not failure, but a troubling lack of closure to the mystery—a sense of a task left uncompleted. It was not something we were used to, plus I was not thrilled at the idea of Tess staying behind. Deep down, I knew she wouldn't leave until she had found the information she was looking for, but that didn't make the goodbyes any easier. I was going to miss her—so much.

Later that night, as she lay in my arms, I told her how I was feeling. She smiled sweetly and said, "I feel the same way, Colt, but I will see you soon. I know what we are looking for is here, and I am determined to find it, so you know I have to keep searching until I do."

I knew that feeling well, having experienced it many times over these past years as I searched for my own answers to the mysterious questions I had encountered. I understood how that burning desire could drive you and control your actions until that questioning fire inside was finally quenched. I kissed her softly and told her I understood completely, but that wouldn't make our parting any easier.

"No, it won't," she replied, "but it sure will make for one hell of a reunion," she said with an impish grin. I knew she was right, so we reveled in our last night together, and as the jet took off the next morning, I smiled as I looked forward to that reunion.

Our return to the "Lair," as Dimitri called it, was an enthusiastic one met with welcome homes, and what the heck happened over there? Everyone had met in the conference room, where Tony put up the news reports about us that he had recorded on the video screen. Dr. Tessa Worthington and Dr. Shehata were frequently mentioned along with Joe and O'Reilly. Doc and I were identified as associates, which was fine with me.

Most news outlets had reported on the possibility of a curse unleashed when we opened the tomb. Dimitri was beside himself like a kid on Christmas morning, "Wow, a lost tomb, a mummy's curse, and a bunch of looters with guns; you guys had all the fun," he gleefully stated. After rounds of laughter, we set the record straight, and a few hours later, the true story had been told. The stay at homes, Dimitri, Reggie, and Tony, had expressed their great displeasure at missing all the excitement but were engrossed in the intricate story that had been woven by our discoveries. We were pelted with questions like ice chunks in a hailstorm and did our best to respond with the little information we had.

"Well, that's a real head-scratcher," Tony said when we had finished.

"It is that," Doc replied, "and will remain so until we are able to gather more information."

"We're hoping Tess's archive search at the museum will provide us with some clues or information so we can make heads or tails out of this mystery," I added.

"This has been a tough one," Dimitri said.

"Yes, it has," I answered, "and I'm afraid it's going to get tougher before we get an answer... that is if we do!"

The next three days turned out to be busier than I expected. Nils and Gus on the *Falcon* had made an interesting discovery off Amelia Island. It was a 1634 French cargo vessel that had sunk and had a substantial amount of treasure. Since it was within the three-mile limit, it was in Florida waters, and therefore, they had been under intense scrutiny by state officials during the operation. We had a lease, were working legally, following state rules, and were entitled to a significant share of the find. Nonetheless, our past run-in with the state a couple of years ago on our discovery of the Spanish galleon off Cape Canaveral has kept us glowing brightly on their radar. Their new claim against the vessel we had found, stating its unique historical significance, led them to believe it should become the sole property of the State of Florida, and any treasure returned to France didn't hold much credence with us. I felt it necessary to contact our legal eagle and wine expert, Lawrence. Since we beat them in court before, I think they have removed us from their Christmas card list, if you know what I mean.

I got on the SAT phone and contacted him. He was still in Ecuador overseeing our vineyards and wine-making company, something we had acquired after another of our adventures a couple of years ago, but that's another story. I asked Lawrence to return to Florida ASAP, given that we may need his legal skills in the not-too-distant future. Dr. Lawrence Goodson had a Ph.D. in microbiology but had made a rather drastic mid-life career change and graduated from Harvard Law School with his JD. His love for law drove his unusual decision, and his rationale could not be argued with: "If not now, when?" Thus, he had become another unique member of the Risky Business Team. He would arrive in two days.

Another thing ticked off my list that seemed to grow longer daily. I had requisitions to sign, correspondence, and other mundane tasks that had to be dealt with. I will admit it did take my mind off our mystery that continued to hang over my head like a dark raincloud but allowed me to channel my energies in other productive ways, running our large company.

The team had dropped into their regular routines while still pursuing information that might benefit us in the Cleopatra conundrum. We had been back seven days before I got a notification on my computer of a video call coming in from Tess. I eagerly made the connection, and her lovely face appeared on the screen. I immediately noticed she looked tired, very tired, but excited. "Hey, Tess, what's up?" I asked.

She smiled and said, "I'm beat; I've been at this day and night since you guys left, but I finally found what I was looking for."

"Fantastic," I replied, "fill me in."

"Too much info and way too involved to do now. I just sent Tony a massive digital file with everything I discovered, and boy, do we need to talk. But it needs to be in person."

"All right, do you want me to arrange a flight?"

"No need; I'll be leaving in four hours, so I'll see you tomorrow."

"Got it," I answered. "Send me your flight info, and I'll have someone waiting for you when you arrive."

"Fantastic," she replied, "and Colt, get the whole team together. This is big."

CHAPTER THIRTY-FIVE

As soon as we broke the connection, I sent the word to the team, putting everybody on standby. I contacted Tony to inform him of the incoming file from Tess. "It's here," he replied, "and it's big. I'll send it to your computer now. Let me know if you want a hard copy." I told him I did and waited to see what she had sent.

I opened the file and found it contained a partial chronological list of rulers in Egypt, along with familial connections, spouses, and siblings. There was dynastic information and much more. While I could figure out a lot of it, I knew it would be best to wait and have Tess walk us through it when she arrived. My phone rang, and it was Doc. "So, Tess found something?" he asked quickly.

"Yes, she said she found what she was looking for."

"And?" he asked.

"And she will be here tomorrow; she'll brief us then."

"So, no hint as to what she found?" he continued.

"None," I replied, "but she did say it was big!"

"Till tomorrow, then."

It was mid-afternoon when she arrived. I had gotten wrapped up in the legal hassles over the Amelia Island wreck and couldn't break away to pick her up, so I had to send one of my security people. I was in a three-way conversation with Lawrence, who was in the air on a flight from Ecuador, and Nils on the wreck site off Amelia Island aboard the *Falcon* when she strode into my office, briefcase in hand.

Without hesitation, dropping the case to the floor, she came around my desk, took my face in her hands, and kissed me firmly. I had been on speaker with the guys, and after a minute or so, they asked if I was still there. Before I could answer, she laughingly said, "He's still here; he was just momentarily indisposed."

Almost simultaneously, they said, "Oh, hey, Tess."

She went back around the desk to the wet bar, pulled out a cold beer, popped the top off, came back, pulled up a chair, kicked off her shoes, leaned back, and put her feet up on my desk as she took a long drink. I sat there smiling and staring, not saying a word. She took her bent hand and began flipping it toward me like she was telling someone to go away or get back to work. Duh, she was signaling me to hurry up and finish my conversation.

I took the hint and immediately told the guys I would get back to them later. They laughed as they said, "No problem, we'll wait to hear from you, " and then added, "Bye, Tess," before hanging up.

"Well, Dr. Worthington, nice to see you too. I hope you had a good flight."

"Oh, it was just fine, Dr. Burnett," she said as she took another long drink from the beer. "Man, I've been thirsty for the last three hours." She raised the bottle in salute, "Thanks for your generous hospitality."

Now, I laughed and said, "Okay, now that we have the congenial salutations out of the way... what the heck did you find?"

Without changing her relaxed position or demeanor, she said, "I suggest you get your team assembled because I am about to knock your socks off!"

Ten minutes later, everyone was gathered in the conference room with Tess and Tony at the head of the table. She was talking quietly to him as his fingers flew over the keys of his laptop, and the rest of us sat there staring at each other.

Tess finally looked at our expectant faces and said, "The short of it is this: the high priest, whose name was Atum, was, as close as I can figure it, at least three hundred years old."

While surprised... we were all smiling except for Tony, Reggie, and Dimitri, whose surprised faces were counterpoints to ours.

O'Reilly said, "I thought so."

"Yep, you were right," Tess said, "but here's the deal: this guy drops in and out of the limelight all during that time."

"What do you mean?" I asked.

"He shows up in the courts of several rulers, usually as a person of influence. He's very careful and has changed or used a variant of his name over the years. That was what made him so hard to track down."

"Like what?" Doc asked.

"Once I figured out what he was doing with the name change and identified the variations, I was able to track down the role he played within the pharaohs' courts. He would drop in and out but was never out of the pharaoh's inner circle. For instance, in Ptolemy I

Soter's court, he was an advisor; that was in 304 BC. He carried that position through part of the Ptolemy II reign and disappeared around 273 BC. We don't see him again until 220 BC when he showed up as a physician in the court of Ptolemy IV and his wife Arsinoe III. He stayed in court through the first part of Ptolemy V's reign, then disappeared again and didn't show up again until 121 BC, when he worked his way into the court of Ptolemy IX around 118 BC as a priest/physician."

"Should we be taking notes?" Dimitri asked with a dazed look on his face.

"No, no, sorry," Tess said. "I know this is all confusing, but I need to put this into a chronological context for you, and I'm almost done."

Reggie leaned to Dimitri and said in a not-so-quiet whisper, "Don't worry, big boy, if it's on the test, you can copy from mine," and laughed.

Tess continued, "So, Atun stayed in the royal court when Ptolemy XII and Cleopatra V came into power. That's our Cleo's mom and dad. He is elevated to high priest and physician to the king and queen. Not long after coming into power, some of the texts state Cleo V seemed to be having some questionable recurring health issues, and Atun became her personal doctor, spending a lot of time with her. The pharaoh had to make a diplomatic trip to Nubia and was gone for almost three months. Upon his return, he learns that Cleo V is pregnant, and he is delighted."

Tess chuckled, "Only problem is, he didn't do the math."

It hit me like a lightning bolt as I sat straight up

in my chair, looking at Tess. It all made perfect sense—Jeannie's cryptic message, Atun's special interest in Cleo, and his involvement in helping her fake her own death and escape. "A parent always protects the child," Jeannie's words came roaring back to me.

"Holy crap," I said, "he was Cleo's father."

Tess, smiling broadly, said, "I believe you are correct, Dr. Burnett."

Tony had been placing Tess's timeline info on the big monitor, and looking at it helped show how this guy was covering his tracks and keeping people from noticing he wasn't aging. With his name adjustments and the skill sets he possessed, it would make him valuable to any royal court.

"So, this guy was hiding in plain sight for three hundred years... genius," Doc said.

"It could have been longer," Tess added. "I only went back around three hundred years and thoroughly checked. I remember seeing a reference to a very talented engineer in one of the earlier pharaoh's courts with a derivative of his name. I would bet it was him, remembering what you told me, Colt, about Jeannie's people's longevity technology."

"So, he was virtually ageless like that priest in Ecuador," Dimitri said.

"Sounds like it," O'Reilly added.

"That would mean she, Cleo, may have the same genetic makeup as her father, possibly the built-in longevity that her people are born with," I said.

"So, does that mean she was in on this escape plan

the whole time and knew who her father was—or did he just tell her he put it together to save her life, providing her with minimal information about who he was and who she was?" Doc asked.

"That's an excellent question," O'Reilly said, "and now the bigger question is, where did she go?"

"It seems like the more we find out, the more questions we are confronted with," Tess said, leaning back in her chair.

There was silence in the room as I again thought, "Curiouser and curiouser."

CHAPTER THIRTY-SIX

The following two days were pretty crazy. We met in the conference room most of the time. The air was filled with, "Where did they go...? Who was he really...? How did he know when to leave...? Why...? How did he manage it...?" and a million other questions. After the initial shock of the family revelation, we began trying to attack the multitude of questions one at a time, logically. Since the escape required a fair amount of advanced planning, Atun must have used the wealth of knowledge he gained over his extended life span and information gleaned during his disappearing acts to understand what was going on politically in the world around him, prompting him to start preparations for Cleo's escape. We guessed that he somehow took over an existing tomb excavation and prepared it for his use.

For a person of power, that shouldn't have been too difficult. The why was obvious: protecting his daughter, which brought up another thought. He must have really cared for Cleopatra V, and very probably, they had fallen in love. She would have known the child was his and so kept the secret. His staying close during the pregnancy and remaining a member of the royal court was part of their plan to protect her.

We agreed that the "where" would have been Atilia, or as we know it, Atlantis. Her ship would have had to traverse the Mediterranean and exit through the Pillars of Hercules, i.e., the Straits of Gibraltar. The world map Jeannie had shown us in Ecuador clearly had an island continent in the Atlantic beyond Gibraltar; she called it Atilia, an outpost settled by her people.

It made sense that Cleo would have been told to head there for safety by her father, Atun. We felt like we were making progress until Tess got her phone call. She answered and, after a few acknowledgments, was silent. Then, there was a "You're kidding," a pause, then "Are you sure?" Her eyes had grown wide, and her mouth hung slightly open; then she said, "All right, keep checking and keep me posted." She put her phone on the table, both hands resting palms down, staring at it like she was waiting for it to do something. She finally looked up and said to the group, "That was Dr. Shehata; he has just confirmed that the mummy he and his team found in the priest's tomb was not Atun."

"What?" Doc and I both said simultaneously.

"He has been continuing his research on Atun, and the written accounts he uncovered from 31 BC indicate Atun was a man of good health, possibly in his late thirties. That was two years or so before he was supposed to have died. The mummy that Shehata took from the priest's tomb has been tested, x-rayed, and scanned. They determined the remains were of a short man in his eighties with a terrible leg deformity. Atun was described as being tall, so it couldn't be Atun," she said.

"Are you serious? Is he sure?" O'Reilly asked.

"Yes, I am, and yes, he is. He had never considered any age difference until we started researching him, tracking him through time, and finding some physical descriptions of him. I had no idea about the mummy's age in the tomb and had never heard any reference to it since

I walked away from the project five years ago," Tess said.

"Well, that throws another wrinkle into this mystery, a big wrinkle," O'Reilly said.

"So, now, we have to figure out what happened to him and where he went," Doc added.

I sat there thinking, letting the new information sink into our existing framework of thought. After a few minutes, I looked at everyone and said, "What if he went with her?"

"Went with her?" Doc asked.

"Yes, what if that was his plan all along? He never intended to leave his daughter, and he put together this elaborate ruse to ensure her safety and give him a way to get away from the Roman occupation of Egypt and be with her."

"Wow... that really kind of makes sense," O'Reilly said.

"And he would know the location of Atilia, what it would take to get there safely, and what would be waiting for them," Joe added.

"That's brilliant," Doc interjected and, after a pause, said, "Do you really think that's what happened?"

"I think it's a real possibility," I said. "What better way to ensure the continued safety of your daughter than to accompany her? I think any father would want that assurance of security, especially in those tumultuous times."

Tess turned to Colt with a questioning look on her face. "I didn't know you had that kind of paternal instinct, Colt."

He smiled and said, "There are still a few things you don't know about me, Tess."

Smiling back, she said, "I suppose there are."

Joe jumped in and said, "So, we agree that the father went with her?"

Everyone agreed. "Until we develop an alternative plausible explanation, I think that should be our working hypothesis."

Tony joined the conversation, "So, that begs the question: Was this Atilia their final destination, or was it just a transit point?"

"Well, I'm not sure where else they could go. Africa doesn't sound like an option, and certainly no place where Rome would have influence," Tess said.

"What if they continued toward her initial destination, the Temple of Ra?"

"You mean further west, Colt?" Tess asked.

"Yeah, toward the setting sun, the home of Ra."

"But there's nothing out there," she said.

"Isn't there?" I asked.

"Well, there's only the Americas," she answered.

I turned my hands palms up and said, "So?"

She paused before speaking, "Are you saying they came to the Americas?"

I looked around the table, then at her. "I'm just suggesting it's a possibility we might want to consider."

There was a lot to process; it turns out Atun wasn't who was in his tomb. Atun was Cleo's father, and he possibly accompanied her on her escape, presumably to Atlantis. Yeah, I'd say that was a bit much to wrap your head around in one sitting. And don't even begin thinking about how this would change world history as we know it if we could prove it and word got out.

We had been at it all day, and I figured this was as good a time as any to adjourn, so I called it. We all needed some rest and time to wrap our heads around the possibilities presented. I realized I was starving and thirsty. Another noteworthy fact about today's meeting is that none of the team had hit the wet bar in the conference room, as usually happens during our marathon meetings. Now, that's what I call some task-focused people.

Everyone else had left. Tess and I were still sitting at the conference table.

"This is unbelievable," she said, "absolutely unbelievable."

I looked at her furrowed brow and scrunched up eyes and said, "Which part?"

Laughing, she said, "The whole damn thing—that's what part." She got out of her chair and said, "Come on, Bubba; I'm hungry and need a drink... in fact, I think I need a few drinks."

I stood and said, "As you wish."

CHAPTER THIRTY-SEVEN

Archeologist Dr. Timothy Cunningham loved his work. It was dirty, tiring, sometimes dangerous, didn't pay well, and certainly wasn't nearly as glamorous as it was made out to be in the movies. But there was something exhilarating about uncovering man's history one small piece at a time. That, to him, was very rewarding and gave him a profound sense of purpose. So, he kept moving the dirt, one trowel-full at a time, occasionally even whistling a little tune while he worked, which greatly amused the two workers assigned to him. They could tell he loved his work, and he treated them with respect, always telling them he would not ask them to do anything he would not do himself, and on many occasions, he had lived up to that motto.

However, today was especially tiring, and a sense of gloom hung over his work site. There were three days left on the grant, and in three days, the entire dig would be shut down until the next season, provided they got funded again. His site was about one hundred yards from the main structure, which had been garnering the lion's share of workers and resources since they had found the tunnels running underneath it.

He understood and accepted it. It's just how things worked—you make a discovery, and the limited funds the grants provide and its resources shift to you from other parts of the project. His discoveries in no way rivaled those, so he was left with only Santiago and Muncho, which he didn't mind. They were hardworking and had a lot of experience in archaeological digs. They both spoke passable English and had great dispositions. They were actually fun to work with, so it made the reduction of his workforce a little easier to swallow.

While the rest of the team was breaking down camp, packing equipment, and closing/protecting their dig area, he continued his work, noting he had not uncovered anything of any significance that would require such attention. He was notified that a team meeting had been called for right after the evening meal.

The head of the project, Dr. Rogers, stood up and announced that even though their permit lasted another twenty days, they would be shutting down and returning to the States the day after tomorrow. Other team members asked a couple of questions about funding. He informed the group that there was enough money in the grant to pay the workers what they were owed and get everyone back to the States, but nothing more.

Cunningham returned to the little campsite in the center or courtyard of the four platforms where he was working. Santiago and Muncho were there waiting. After finishing their evening meal, they sat around the small fire, talking when he walked up.

Santiago, probably five years older than Muncho, spoke to him first. "Jefe, we have some tortillas and beans left if you are hungry."

"No, thanks; I'm not really hungry," he replied. "I'm afraid I've got some bad news. The project has run out of money, so they are shutting down everything at the site and letting everyone go." I saw the concern on their faces and quickly tried to reassure them, "But don't worry;

you will be paid for the work you have done through tomorrow."

The concern was still there. "So, does that mean you will be leaving, Jefe?" Muncho asked.

"I suppose so. We still have time on our permit, but it doesn't make any difference without funding. I had really hoped we would be able to look at the west platform before we closed down, but that's not going to happen now," he said.

Santiago got up from his seat, walked to his sleeping area, reached into one of his bags, and pulled out a bottle of clear liquid with no label on it. Cunningham recognized it immediately as the local homebrew tequila that was so prevalent amongst the workers.

"Jefe, I think maybe it's time for this," he said as he sat down, pulled out the cork, and handed the bottle to Cunningham. He thanked him as he took it and drank a swallow from it, feeling the liquid fire running down his throat and making his eyes water. He handed the bottle back as he tried to catch his breath. He took a drink and passed it to Muncho, who did the same. They laughed slightly at Cunningham's facial expression as they sat there unfazed by the fiery liquid they had just consumed.

Santiago said jovially, "Senor Tim, I'm afraid, even after all this time, you still need practice learning to enjoy our drink." That brought peals of laughter from both of them.

As Tim grimaced, he said, "I do believe you're right, but I will continue to try," as he took the proffered bottle again and took another hit. He thought this one didn't seem as bad as the first one. The second one never does, nor does the third or the fourth, and that's how the trouble begins. They talked and drank for another hour or so before calling it a night. Sleep came easily, but morning sucked.

The guys had the fire going and coffee ready while they cooked up some black beans and rice with chopped ham and fresh tortillas. The breakfast of champions, Tim thought as he devoured the burrito and chased it with a hot cup of coffee. Did it rejuvenate him? Not a chance, but at least it didn't feel like he was going to puke his guts out. Note to self, he thought, don't try to keep up with the locals when doing shots of homemade tequila. Gee, that's the same thing he thought the other time he did that and the time before. Scratch note to self, he decided as he got ready for his last day's work.

It was early afternoon when Santiago called Tim to the area of the temple he was excavating, where an old looters' trench had been started years ago. When Tim got to him, he was on his knees, picking away at something lodged in the side wall of the trench, sweeping away the loose dirt with a paintbrush as he cleared it. Tim looked down as he got closer and saw a small figurine protruding from the wall. When Santiago uncovered it completely, Tim was amazed at what he saw. While having the attributes of other figurines found at the site, this one had strange headgear, with crossed arms holding a rod in one hand that had something dangling from one end. Tim stared, trying to understand what he was seeing. It was definitely a pre-Columbian personage. He had seen similar ones found at the site, but this one was slightly different. It was unusual, an artifact that the looters of old had missed, luckily for this group.

"What is it, Jefe?" Santiago asked.

"I'm not sure," Tim replied. "I've never seen anything like it found around here." He grabbed his digital camera and documented the figurine, its surroundings, and then a full shot of the platform where it was found. The surrounding platforms or small stepped pyramidal structures, including this one, were around twenty feet tall.

Tim was sitting, reviewing his digital photos, when Dr. Rogers strode into camp. "Dr. Cunningham, you're not packed. We leave first thing in the morning."

"Yes, I know you are, but I think I would like to stay a little longer."

"Longer?" he asked. "We're done, and there's no funding to extend our time here."

"I understand, but I have a couple of small things I need to wrap up, and since our permit doesn't expire for another twenty days, I thought I might use that time to finish."

Dr. Rogers looked around, and seeing nothing of significance, he said, "Well, there's no money to pay you or your workers, so if you want to stay, you're on your own. But when our permit expires, I expect you to be gone, or the Mexican government will evict you, and I do not want that blemish on our research record here. It would not bode well for your future employment on this project and may jeopardize future university permits."

"I understand completely, and I assure you I will be gone, no problem."

"In that case, I don't have a problem with you

staying. I will inform the local site manager that you will be here for possibly twenty more days." He turned to leave and said, "Don't forget to check in with me when you return to the States," and was gone.

Tim had just bought himself twenty more days to work on the platform where the figurine was found. He had no idea what he might get done in that short period by himself, but he had to try.

Santiago and Muncho had heard the verbal exchange and walked up. "So, does this mean you are not leaving tomorrow, Jefe?" Santiago asked.

"No, it looks like I will be here for a couple more weeks."

"Good, then we can get more work done over there," he said, pointing to the looters' trench in the platform where he had found the figurine.

"No, I'm afraid not; I have no money to pay either of you," he said.

They looked at each other and smiled, "No problemo. We have enough tortillas and beans to last for that long; we have nowhere to go, and we have another bottle of tequila," he said, smiling from ear to ear.

Tim grinned at the logic he had applied to the situation and was buoyed by his sincerity and enthusiasm. He laughed and replied, "Well, as long as we have tequila, I guess we should be all right. Let's get to work."

CHAPTER THIRTY-EIGHT

The next three days were grueling as they worked in the narrow trench, moving ever closer to the end of the tunnel. They found nothing more than some pot shards for their efforts. The platform was about forty feet square, and the looters had dug in about eight feet or so, removing the larger outer stones and uncovering the fill layer behind them. That put them about twelve feet from its center. Tim decided to continue digging the trench, a dangerous proposition with the potential of the overhead collapsing on them at any time.

The trench was about five feet wide. As the two workers carefully examined the side walls, Tim continued removing the dirt and fill at the end of the tunnel, passing it back in plastic buckets to one of the men, who would then dump it onto a pile they had started outside the structure. Tim planned to sift it later for any artifacts it might hold. It was slow, tiring, and hot. Day four saw them returning to their established routine: dig, fill bucket, pass back, empty, start again.

The trench, which had now become a tunnel, had a ceiling height of a little less than six feet, so at six feet tall, Tim was always bent over or on his hands and knees working. He used his small hand-pick to carefully break up the dirt in front of him, starting at the top and working his way down to the floor. He was standing, more or less, and struck the dirt packed in front of him when it suddenly began peeling off in a layer and dropping to the floor. He gasped at what had been revealed: a stone wall with an intricate fresco stood before him. He took a half-step back and could tell the fresco continued to the left and right of the tunnel, disappearing into the dirt and fill of the tunnel walls. It was beautiful. There were two large fresco faces adorned with the traditional ear flares. Encircling them, he recognized a partial image of Quetzalcoatl, the feathered serpent, the mysterious deity credited with bringing civilization to many early cultures of central Mexico. The work was exquisite and beautifully preserved. It was obviously part of a wall fresco on a structure that had been built over, as was often done by the Maya, Aztec, and other pre-Columbian cultures, using the old structure as fill and constructing a new grander structure on top of it.

They had been careful not to widen the trench/tunnel for fear of causing a roof collapse, but now Tim gently cleared away some small sections of the fill dirt covering the frescos on both sides of the tunnel. Sure enough, they continued to either side, confirming his guess. Santiago and Muncho had squeezed in beside him and looked wide-eyed at the wall.

Santiago said in a hushed voice, "Jefe, you have discovered something truly remarkable."

Clearing away more dirt from the sides, Tim started finding rows of hieroglyphs, none of which he recognized. He had been on digs in Egypt and had worked there his last semester as a doctoral student. So, he knew what their hieroglyphs looked like, and it wasn't like this. It was getting dark, and he only had a small flashlight with him in the tunnel, not enough to light up a work area. Moving back out to the little campsite, they discussed the discovery. Neither of the workers had ever been directly involved in a discovery of this significance and were very excited.

Tim was still puzzled by the hieroglyphs; he didn't remember seeing anything like them in or around the other structures at the site. He realized that he needed help but didn't think anyone at the university would be helpful and really didn't want to reveal his discovery to anyone else at the moment—not until he knew more about what he had found.

Santiago broke out his stash of tequila, and he and Muncho started celebrating. Tim had one small drink but knew he needed a clear head to determine his next move. He stared into the fire, racking his brain… what to do? He only had sixteen days left, and the clock was ticking.

It came to him the next morning; Tim's good friend Duane had been a fellow doctoral student in his semester in Egypt. He remembered him as being very adept at reading the Egyptian hieroglyphs, and Duane had espoused an interest in specializing in that area. After graduation, they parted ways, Duane returning to Egypt and the Middle East. They had stayed somewhat in touch via email, but he hadn't heard from him in a while. Well, at least that might be a place to start. He got his laptop and established an internet connection, sending Duane an email with a picture of some of the hieroglyphs from the wall. It was a couple of hours later that he got a response. The email was short.

"Glad to hear from you, Tim. It sounds like you're into something cool. Sorry, I can't help you. I have never seen anything like the photo you sent me. I understand your time crunch and suggest you try for a big gun.

Remember our prof during our semester in Egypt? I know she has become a real hotshot expert in the field and is an international superstar when it comes to stuff like that. I would try her; maybe she can help or suggest someone who can. I'm sure you remember her; she was a hottie. Worthington was her last name, I believe. Good luck, buddy. Stay in touch, Duane."

Strike one. After trying to come up with other possibilities, he had none. What the heck, he thought; there was little to no chance she would even remember him or respond to an email. However, during that semester, he recalled that Worthington treated the doctoral students a whole lot better than other professors he had, and he did remember her saying that if they ever needed help, contact her. Why not? It was worth a try. The internet search took him ten minutes to find an email address for her. He identified himself and sent her the same digital image he had sent Duane, asking if she could shed any light on the strange glyphs. Thanking her in advance but not holding out much hope for a response, he started trying to figure out other options he might have.

Twenty minutes later, while mentally wrapped up in his dilemma, Tim was surprised by the alert chime on his computer, notifying him of an incoming email. He grabbed it and saw that the email was from Dr. Worthington. He couldn't believe his eyes as he opened the document.

Dr. Cunningham, I received your email. Can you please send me additional information on these glyphs, such as where you found them, how long ago, and the circumstances surrounding your discovery? Please respond promptly. I believe I might be able to help you.

Best Regards, Dr. T. Worthington

Amazed at her response, he quickly composed an extensive description of his current situation, providing the details she requested, and hit send. An hour passed as he held the computer in his lap, watching the screen.

Suddenly, the chime went off again with another email. This one was even more exciting than the last.

Dr. Cunningham, please be advised that I will arrive at your location tomorrow at noon. Do not publicize your find in any way. Keep people away from your site and tell no one about it. I will explain when I get there. Thank you for reaching out to me. I look forward to seeing you tomorrow, Timothy.

"Timothy," he read again. I wonder if she does remember me, he thought. Now, he was doubly excited at her interest in his find and her using his first name. As he sat thinking of his time in Egypt in her graduate seminar, he recalled her effect on all the male students and his confession to Duane about being enamored. He then remembered their ensuing conversation very clearly.

"Forget it, Tim. Number one, she's way out of your league, and number two, I hear she is seeing someone, and you wouldn't want to mess with that guy." When Tim had asked him why, did he think he was some kind of badass? Duane had laughed loud and long.

When he could finally speak, he slapped Tim on the shoulder and said, "No, not some kind of badass, but from what I hear, the badasses don't mess with him." Tim remembered his testosterone-driven machismo got knocked down multiple pegs at that comment.

After a somewhat sleepless night, Tim saw the

SUV kicking up a trail of dust, arriving at noon as Dr. Worthington had promised. Vehicles were not allowed within the tourist part of the site, but a dirt road had been created for the archaeologists to come and go, bringing in supplies and equipment. As it pulled to a dusty stop, Tim went out to meet her and was greeted by a tall blonde in khaki trousers, a long-sleeved Columbia shirt, sunglasses, and boots. Wow, he thought, she was more beautiful than he remembered.

She smiled as she strode toward him, stuck out her hand, and, with a brilliant smile, said, "Timothy, so good to see you again."

He was startled and said, "You remember me, Dr. Worthington?"

"Of course, you and your friend Duane were two of my best students, and I always remember my best students. Now, where's this find of yours?"

CHAPTER THIRTY-NINE

Tess was working to keep her excitement under control as she followed her former student to the four large platforms. Walking between them into the small central courtyard they formed, she saw the looters' trench dug into the side of the western platform. She loved Teotihuacan, its majesty, beauty, and mystery instantly coming back to her, having spent a short time working the site several years ago.

While brief, her time here had left a lasting impression. Not knowing exactly when it was constructed, somewhere around 100 BC has been hypothesized, or who built its soaring structures imbued the site with a sense of mystery. Adding to the mythos of the ruin was its discovery by the Aztecs sometime in the 1500s, finding it completely abandoned as it had been for centuries, its monumental structures still intact. The Aztecs, not knowing who its inhabitants had been and in awe of its majesty, named the city Teohuacan, which translated means "Place where the gods were created." More recently, it is believed by some that the Spanish may have changed it in the 1600s from Teohuacan, "City of the Sun," to its current spelling and interpretation. "City of the Gods." The possible significance of this did not escape Tess.[JP2]

Still, the mystery is pervasive as one walks its streets and sees the spectacular murals, mosaics, and mysterious mica-lined room, the walls, ceiling, and floors completely covered with the same material NASA uses on its spacecraft to dissipate heat and protect them from burning upon reentry. Why build a room like that, and what was its purpose? It was similar to the conundrum raised by the recent discovery at the site of various-sized golden balls or globes found in tunnels under the pyramid of the sun and the presence of liquid mercury—all thousands of years old and placed in a sacred space—but why?

The mysteries abound in that glorious citadel, and a new one may have just presented itself. Tess realized that Dr. Cunningham had been speaking to her while she was lost in her nostalgic reverie. "I'm sorry; you were saying, Timothy?" she said.

"I was just saying, if you follow me, I'll show you the wall."

"Please, lead the way."

She ducked her head and followed him into the tunnel to the fresco wall. His lantern, lighting the area, revealed the beauty of the workmanship in great detail. The rows of glyphs were clearly visible. Her breath caught in her throat as she realized she was looking at hybrid Egyptian/"Jeannie" text, much like they had found on the golden statues and in the murals in Cleo's supposed tomb.

She photographed the entire wall, close up, with her small digital camera, then said to Cunningham, "That's all for now; I have to make a call," as they exited the tunnel.

Outside, she took a couple of minutes to compose herself. Her excitement had her pulse racing. She pulled the SAT phone from her pocket, flipped up its antenna, and hit the speed dial. Moments later, a male voice cheerfully said, "Hello, Tess."

Without responding to the salutation, she said, "Colt, you and the team need to get to Mexico as soon as possible."

There was only a slight pause, then, "Got your location; we're on our way."

"Oh, and Colt, tell Joe to bring his toys," Tess added as she broke the connection.

Cunningham was staring at her, wondering what had just happened.

She looked at him, smiling slightly, and said, "We've got some time, Timothy; let's sit down. I've got a story to tell you."

Two hours later, he sat there with a dazed look. He had asked numerous questions during their discussion. Tess had the answers, backed up with physical proof most of the time. Cunningham had sent his workers home hours ago with a hefty salary bonus out of his own pocket, telling them things may be changing, and he might be leaving sooner than he had planned but would let them know. They asked no questions but thanked him profusely for his generosity, shook hands with Tess, and left.

"Can you trust them?" Tess asked as their old pickup truck headed down the dirt road.

"Yes, I believe I can," Cunningham replied. "They have worked for me for two seasons and have been dependable and trustworthy."

"Good," Tess replied, "because we may need them

to forget everything they have seen here." Tess had been taking measure of her former student since she arrived, some of her questions more probing than others, were meant to give her a true sense of who this man was. She knew he was an excellent archaeologist; his credentials were impressive. However, he had only been doing seasonal contract work with various universities, not having a full-time position at any of them.

She had asked him about this, and he replied that he didn't like being tied down. The money would have been marginal, and the academic bullshit would be more than he could bear for an extended period. Five and a half hours after her arrival, they heard the sound of a helicopter and saw a speck growing larger and larger in the distance until it was hovering in the area next to Tess's SUV and slowly settled to the ground.

"Ah, good, they're here," Tess said as Cunningham watched the doors open and figures pile out in tactical gear, heading in their direction. Cunningham looked at Tess, then at the approaching group. He noticed that the pilot had exited the aircraft after shutdown, her bright red ponytail topping off an ensemble consisting of a baseball cap, aviator sunglasses, a faded Pink Floyd *Dark Side of the Moon* T-shirt, a handgun in a shoulder holster, six-pocket BDU pants, and desert combat boots… and she was gorgeous.

When the group got to them, Cunningham thought, as he looked at the array of characters before him, holy crap, they look like part of that group from *The Expendables* movie. Now that they were close, he could see they all were armed. The obvious leader walked to Tess, spread his arms with his palms up, and said, "You said to bring the whole team... well, here we are," before giving her a somewhat collegial embrace.

Tess, smiling, said, "And I see you're taking your new rule seriously."

The leader laughed and said, "Damn straight, not going on another mission unarmed," patting his holstered sidearm.

Tess turned to Cunningham and said, "Timothy, let me introduce Dr. Colten Burnett, CEO of Risky Business Ltd. and leader of this band of rouges."

He stepped forward and held out his hand as the rest of the team exhibited various degrees of mirth at Tess's remark, acknowledging her with, "Hey, Tess, Good to see you, Tess, and Aw, Tess, that's not nice...."

I accepted the big man's hand and felt a borderline crushing pressure in his grip. This guy was at least six-foot-five and easily three hundred pounds of suntanned muscle; his salt-and-pepper hair added to his aura of experience and authority. I gulped as I wondered if this was the guy Duane had told me about all those years ago, and in a split-second thought, yeah, that's him.

"Pleasure, Dr. Cunningham," he said, releasing his steel grip as he turned to Tess.

"So, what have you got us into now, Tess?"

She said, "Follow me," as she pulled a flashlight from her bag and walked to the trench/tunnel in the platform. Her friend had to really duck going into the tunnel part and stopped when Tess lit the stucco frescos.

Burnett moved closer and said, "I'll be damned." He produced a light of his own and examined the glyphs more closely. It was tight in the tunnel, but he turned to Tess and said, "You think this might be it."

"That's why you're here, to help me find out," she said, heading back outside.

CHAPTER FOURTY

The team had gathered at the campfire area, sitting on the ground, on rocks, or standing. As we walked up, Doc asked, "Well?"

I nodded my head and answered, "I believe so."

He then said, "So, what now?"

I shot Tess a questioning look and waited.

"I've told Timothy our story and how this might fit into it, depending on what's behind that wall, if anything."

I looked at the young archaeologist and said, "Well, Dr. Cunningham."

He stopped me and said, "Please, just Tim."

I nodded and said, "Well, Tim, what do you think?"

"I believe you have been meticulous in your research. As bizarre as some of your methodologies and situations have been, I think you may have discovered a history-changing event and the answer to a two-thousand-year-old question. Dr. Burnett, you have one hell of an organization, and you are doing amazing things, not only in archaeology but the hard sciences as well."

As I quizzically looked at Tess again, she said, "I pretty much told him everything."

"Everything?" I asked, both surprised and

incredulous.

"Well, there's no way we could proceed with him only knowing part of the story. And besides, Timothy was an excellent student and has become a first-class archaeologist."

"So, you told him everything?" I asked again. She nodded. "Even about Jeannie?" She nodded. "What about the...?" she stopped me before I could say more.

"Yes, even about the wolf," she said.

I looked at Cunningham again, and he was grinning like the cat that got the canary and excitedly said, "That is some of the craziest, cool freaking stuff I have ever heard."

Dimitri had been standing quietly next to him. He looked at me and said, in his "Boris speak" voice (channeling the old *Rocky and Bullwinkle* cartoon TV show's bad guy, Boris Badenov), "I should kill him now, Boss. He know too much, Da?" puffing out his chest and reaching for the ugly-looking eight-inch blade strapped to his tactical vest. Cunningham's eyes widened as he took a small step away from this now-menacing figure. Let me stop here for a moment and put this interaction into context. Dimitri was born in the States, served as an officer in the Army, and spoke fluent Russian and German. His parents were German immigrants who fled Germany to Russia when Hitler took power and later came to the U.S., where he was born. So, he's an American through and through. Amusingly, he had developed a habit of launching into a fake, heavy Russian accent and making jokes at the most inappropriate times. This was one of those times.

The look of terror on Cunningham's face and the evil

smile on Dimitri's were priceless. I said, "No, Dimitri, not this time."

He got that forlorn puppy dog look on his face as he took his hand away from the knife and said, "You no fun, Colt. You never let me kill anyone." That did it; everyone burst out laughing, excluding Cunningham, who took a minute to realize he had just been pranked.

Tess, still laughing, said, "I'm sorry, Timothy, but this is kind of an inside joke with this crew."

Dimitri was laughing as he slapped Cunningham on the back and said, "Just kidding, man," then immediately stopped laughing and got that look back on his face, gripping his shoulder tightly and said, "…until I'm not." I swear, Cunningham blanched. Seconds later, laughter broke out again as Dimitri gave his shoulder a playful shove.

"Enough levity," I said, chuckling as I looked at the archaeologist. "It seems Tess thinks you can be trusted. Can you?" I asked.

"Yes, definitely yes." (Really, could he have said anything else after Dimitri's show?) I would never repeat anything Dr. Worthington has told me or anything I learn from what happens here. I understand the need for secrecy concerning the resources and knowledge you have entrusted me with. I will never betray that trust."

I believed the kid… what am I saying? He's no kid; he had to be in his late twenties. Perspective, Colt, perspective. I only had a couple of decades on him, I thought.

"Okay, people, it's time to go to work and find out what's behind door number one. Joe, break out your toys."

Joe removed the drilling/x-ray device from his bag and walked to the entrance of the trench. He fiddled with the controls and pointed it at the fresco wall at the end of the tunnel. Thirty seconds later, he said, "Well, the wall is a couple of feet thick, but there is a chamber behind it. There's nothing large in it, but it's not empty."

Tess said, "We need to get inside."

"You know the only way will be to destroy the wall."

She paused, then said, "I know, Colt, but we've come too far to stop now."

I turned to Cunningham and said, "You heard the lady, but it's your discovery...."

Without hesitation, he said, "Do what you have to do. What you are onto is more important than a fresco wall."

I considered his statement and said, "Joe, make a hole."

"Roger that, Colt." He turned back to the trench, touched the top of the device again, pointed, and activated it. There was no real noise, just a bit of falling debris. Pulling out his flashlight and the Sniffer, he walked into the tunnel. Coming back out, he said, "Let's give it a couple of minutes and let some fresh air in, just to be sure, but I detected nothing dangerous inside."

A few minutes later, we entered, Tess leading the way. The hole into the chamber was not large, so we all had to stoop, and only three of us could fit in the room that was maybe seven feet square. I followed Tess with Cunningham close behind as the others waited outside. Our flashlights showed a beautiful interior; all the walls were covered with colorful murals, but the focal point was the three niches on the wall, each containing what is known as a "cylindrical tripod" vessel, a common piece of ceremonial pottery in Meso-American cultures.

They were about six inches in diameter and seventeen inches tall, including the three two-inch-high feet or legs. They all had lids on them that were sealed. As Joe had indicated, there was nothing else in the room. After surveying it one more time, we each took a vessel and exited. I told Joe to document the chamber with our digital equipment photographically.

We set the vases on a makeshift table as everyone gathered around. The seal on the lid seemed to be some kind of resin. I took my knife and carefully began running it around the edge, on each revolution applying a bit more pressure until the lid separated from the jar. Lifting it off, I looked inside and saw a rolled paper. I gently reached in and removed it. I feared it might disintegrate in my hand, but it didn't. In fact, the material was not paper, papyrus, or cloth. I couldn't tell what it was, but it was supple and unrolled easily.

The document was about fifteen inches wide and at least seventeen inches long. The text on it started with a row of Egyptian hieroglyphs, and then the rest of the page was covered with the ancient hieroglyphs of Jeannie's people. Elation and disappointment hit us. Disappointment because we couldn't read it and elation because we held in our hands a document written in an ancient extraterrestrial language, thousands of years old. We replaced it in the vase and opened the others, finding similar documents in them.

Cunningham sat there, looking perplexed. Tess

asked, "What's wrong, Timothy?"

"Well, I was hoping we would be able to learn something from what was inside."

I said, "Don't worry, Tim; I've got this covered."

I told Doc, "Secure these and get them to the chopper."

I looked at Tess and Tim, then at the looters' trench. "What are we going to do about that?" I asked.

"We can't leave it. Timothy, you were the last one here, and there would certainly be questions if that chamber were found open. I'm sure looting would come up, and you would be suspect number one."

"You're right; we have to fill it in or something." He was nervous.

I looked around the area littered with building debris and random stones the size of basketballs and larger. Joe had finished and was putting the gear away when I called him.

He came over and said, "Yeah, Colt?"

"Can you close that up?" I said, pointing to the trench area.

He looked at it and said, "How closed do you want it to be?"

"Closed enough so no one can access it for a long time."

Joe said, "I think I can do that."

"But it needs to look natural."

"Then I would suggest we fill the opening we

created with rocks. I can fuse them together into a solid mass. Remember how we repaired that thing for Jeannie in Ecuador? Once that's done, I can cause a cave-in to cover it all up, and if you want, we can toss a few more rocks on it to make it look more like a natural cave-in."

"Good; get the team to help and make it happen."

"Roger that, Colt."

The jars were being secured, and the hole was going to be taken care of; now, for the last big problem. Tess, Tim, and I were sitting alone, and I said to Tim, "So, what's next for you?"

He got a surprised look on his face, looked around, and said, "I don't know. I don't think I want another contract with the university for next season, not after what I know now."

"You ever do any diving?" I asked.

"Yeah, I've been certified since I was eighteen, and I did some undergraduate work at Texas A&M in their underwater archaeology program. Why?"

I saw Tess smiling at me out of the corner of my eye. "You have a wife or girlfriend or any other serious commitments?"

"No, neither; I did have a goldfish, but he died," he replied seriously.

"What do you do for work in the off-season?"

"I usually try and scrounge up some research work at the university."

"The university?"

"Well, actually, any university that might have grant

money and needs some research done."

I paused and glanced at Tess, who nodded her head slightly. "Where do you live now?"

"I had an apartment off-campus that I let go when I came down here. So, I will have to find a new place when I get back to the States."

"Tim, you have been made privy to some very sensitive and potentially dangerous information about my company and our activities."

"I swear, I would never say a word about anything concerning you or your company."

"Well, I'm not sure I believe you just yet." I saw the panicked look on his face. "You are going to have to do three things to convince me."

He actually gulped and said, "Dr. Burnett, what do you have in mind?"

"Good," I said. "First, I want you to move close to my headquarters in Cocoa, Florida; second, I'd like you to come to work for my company, Risky Business, Ltd., as our in-house archaeologist; and third, your assignment will be to assist Dr. Worthington in her continuing research until I need your services elsewhere."

He was wide-eyed when I said, "Your salary will be one hundred and twenty-five thousand dollars a year, and you start today." I put out my hand and said, "Agreed?"

He paused momentarily, his disbelief slowly fading as he took my hand and said, "Agreed," smiling broadly.

I told him to arrange a substantial payment for his two workers, whatever he thought reasonable, and inform them that a tunnel collapse had occurred. He should tell them he wouldn't be returning to the site and suggest they forget about the fresco wall since it was destroyed in the cave-in.

Tess would arrange for his flight to Florida once his tasks were complete and accompany him. I said I would have them picked up at the airport. I received a vigorous handshake from Tim and a nice kiss from Tess. I told them I would see them in Florida and boarded the chopper with the rest of the team.

EPILOGUE

It had been three weeks since our return from Mexico. Tess and Cunningham had arrived, and he was settling into his new apartment. Reggie and Dimitri had helped him find a place and gave him the orientation tour of our facilities, and I also gave him a small office on the second floor. Tony set him up with the latest and greatest computer system that we all used, a new laptop, and one of our worldwide GPS locators that Joe had developed for us, explaining the switch for the red and green transmission lights. Dimitri explained it in his Boris speak, "Green light, pick me up this location, need ride. Red light, pick me up this location, need ride, bring cavalry." Cunningham got the message.

I had been wondering what to do about translating or deciphering the three documents we had recovered in Mexico as they lay open on my desk. It was late afternoon, just at dusk, when the faint tinkling crystal chandelier sound alerted me to Jeannie's presence. She appeared as she usually did, a misty cloud coalescing into her glowing blue human form in front of my desk.

"It seems you are in need of my help once again, Colten."

I smiled broadly at her glowing, ethereal presence and said, "It's nice to see you too, Jeannie," chiding her slightly on her lack of salutation and said, "And, yes, I do," while pointing to the documents on my desk. She moved to look down at them. Jeannie's form is close to seven feet tall and beautifully proportioned. She always appeared in a semi-transparent blue diaphanous gown, looking like a Greek goddess. Knowing she could read a person's thoughts kept me on my best behavior, sorta.

"Now, Colten, you were saying," she said, smiling that lovely angelic smile.

"Yes, I'm sure you already know we found these documents in Mexico at the site of Teotihuacan, and the text is obviously in your language. Can you help translate it for us?"

"Of course, the first is a record of a sea voyage from Atilia to the continent you call South America. The second is an accounting of meeting the indigenous inhabitants and creating an alliance: sharing information and technology and building a new civilization. The third is a history of that civilization's development, accomplishments, and final end."

I sat there, speechless. This is precisely what we had been looking for. Excitedly, I asked, "Can you somehow record what is there for us in detail? This is the information we have been searching for."

She laughed softly as my laser printer came to life and began printing page after page; neither it nor my computer had been turned on. As it was printing, she said, "Colten, I do expect a visit from you soon. It has been too long since your last," then she disappeared in a blue mist as my printer continued to print page after page. Fifty pages later, it stopped. Three pages of her text were fifty pages in our language, unbelievable.

I had my administrative assistant scan them and send digital copies to Doc and Tess. I kept the last page to review out of curiosity. The final couple of sentences blew me away. "The inhabitants have all left and will be safe from the plague that will soon be brought upon us by the new visitors to our lands, as our seers have warned us. Our group, however, chose not to accompany them. Instead, we will continue to the temple of the setting sun. A new journey begins." I thought, a new journey, more questions... again.

So, Cleo and her father took a group and continued west. To where? How many were there? How did they travel? I had so many questions and so few answers. The continuing gift of this mystery keeps on giving.

The evening air was cool as Tess and I walked hand-in-hand, chatting about nothing in particular. We turned the corner onto the Boulevard du Montparnasse, and it took her a few minutes to notice. Ahead was the little café where Tess had presented me with her idea about recovering Cleopatra's golden statues. We took seats at the table, and I ordered a bottle of wine, cheese, and, of course, bread.

She looked into my eyes and said, "Why, Dr. Burnett, I didn't know you were a romantic at heart," as the wine was delivered.

I poured our two glasses and said, "Just don't tell anyone. It will ruin my reputation as a barbaric cretin," I said as our glasses clinked.

She laughed and said, "Your secret is safe with me. I can't believe you brought me back to the place where I initiated so much trouble."

"Just another adventure to be had, another challenge to be met. No doubt, there are still many adventures in our future," I said as I poured more wine.

"I'm sure there are," she replied, touching my glass again to hers and lightly brushing her fingertips against my other hand.

"Besides, it's our last night in Paris, and I plan on being the one causing the trouble tonight!"

She smiled broadly, took my hand in hers, and said, "I would expect nothing less."

ABOUT THE AUTHOR

Hep Aldridge

Hep Aldridge is a certified scuba diver, cave diver amateur archaeologist, and retired college administrator whose main area of interest in Pre-Columbian cultures of the Americas has expanded to mysteries of ancient civilizations worldwide. He has led or been part of archaeological expeditions to Mexico and Honduras, making discoveries that have been reported in National Geographic Magazine. Hep's related interest in space and "things unknown" was fueled by his time living in New Mexico as a teenager when he began to question the many strange and unexplained things he saw in the the night sky in the mid 60's. Some years later, chance meetings in Florida with well-known treasure hunters, Art McKee and Kip Wagner developed his interest in salvage operations for lost undersea treasure. The combination of these interests led to the genesis of the Risky Business Chronicles, a series of books which now spans five distinct sagas with a recurring memorable cast of characters. Hep is an Air Force veteran and resides on Florida's Space Coast.

To be the first to hear about news, new book releases and

bargains from Hep Aldridge

GO HERE TO SIGN UP TO BE ON THE VIP LIST
http//mailchi.mp/b0c291dd854f/hep-aldridge

Learn more about Hep and his background on his webpage
http//hepaldridge.com

You can write directly to Hep and connect with him online.
EMAIL: cxburnett@gmail.com
FACEBOOK: https//www.facebook.com/hep.aldridge7
X: https//x.com/AldridgeHep
INSTAGRAM: https://www.instagram.com/hepaldridge/

BOOKS BY THIS AUTHOR

Sunken Treasure Lost Worlds-Book 1

From the depths of the Atlantic off Cape Canaveral Florida, searching for sunken Spanish treasure, to the Andes mountains of Ecuador chasing the legend of a lost golden library, Dr. Colten X. Burnett and the Risky Business team are on a quixotic adventure.

While trying to make an honest, well sort of honest living, searching for remnants of the lost 1715 fleet, Risky Business Ltd. becomes entangled in a mystery that covers two continents and may rewrite history.

The lure of uncovering a lost civilization, as well as the secrets it holds, motivates the team on their dangerous journey into a cosmological unknown.

Revelations: Sunken Treasure Lost Worlds-Book 2

As the mystery deepens from the peaks of the Andes to the ocean floor off Florida's Space Coast, Colten X. Burnett, and the Risky Business team are confronted by new perils and discoveries in their extraordinary quest for both treasures and what might be explosive, historical findings.

New friends and new adversaries make their quest a suspense-filled thrill ride.

Will they find the elusive treasure galleon, is the legendary golden library in Ecuador real?

Encounter: Sunken Treasure Lost Worlds-Book 3

This final installment of the #1 bestselling Risky Business Trilogy finds Colten Burnett and his intrepid team of adventurers in the jungles of Ecuador in search of the elusive Golden Library.

Pursued by multiple enemies, the team uncovers jaw-dropping otherworldly treasures linked to a mysterious lost civilization that has the potential not only to enrich them but to save the planet Earth from self-destruction.

Buried Treasure : Lost Worlds, A Search For Aztec Treasure-Book 4

In 1521, the Aztec empire fell to Spanish Conquistadors in bloody genocide. The Aztec ruler, Montezuma, was murdered, and his treasure… disappeared.
Legend says the treasure was spirited away by Montezuma's elite Eagle warriors, headed for an unknown desert location in the southwest of what is now the United States. It has never been found.

Dr. Colten X. Burnett and the Risky Business team have a lead. Will the unexpected map they now have in their possession guide them to the long-lost treasure in the land of the Mescalero Apache?

Printed in Great Britain
by Amazon